When Ailsa stumbled, he was quick to reach out and steady her. Something ignited within him, a sudden rush that heightened his senses.

Only by a supreme effort of will did Logan resist the temptation to kiss her. She was an innocent. She had put herself under his protection and he must not abuse that trust!

"Careful now. I know you would dearly like to tell me to go to the devil, madam."

"I should not be so uncivil," she retorted. "It is merely that I hardly know you."

"How so?" he teased her. "Have you forgotten we danced together on the night of the ceilidh?"

Was it his imagination or did her hand tremble on his arm? What might she have thought if he had told her how much he had enjoyed that dance in the moonlight? What hopes might he have raised? Hopes that he could not fulfill because he had left his heart in England.

To mislead her in such a way would not be the action of an honorable man. It would be the action of a scoundrel.

Author Note

Since I moved to the remote Highlands of Scotland eighteen months ago, it was inevitable that the wild beauty of this remote and magical place would inspire me to write a book set here. *Forbidden to the Highland Laird* is the result.

Logan and Ailsa's story is set in the early days of the eighteenth century, when life in the rugged Highlands was harsh. Most people were farmers or fishermen, there were few roads and only the rich owned horses. Allegiance was to the clan rather than to the government in far-off Edinburgh, and clan chiefs took their responsibilities seriously.

For someone more accustomed to writing about the English Regency, I have had to do a lot of research, and I am still learning! My Scottish friends have been extremely generous with sharing their knowledge and I am especially grateful to my fellow author Mairibeth MacMillan; I owe her a huge debt for checking over the Gaelic words I have sprinkled throughout the story. Any errors I have made with this ancient and fascinating language and also any mistakes in the interpretation of Scottish history are entirely my own.

Writing this book has been such a joy. I hope you will love Ailsa and Logan as much as I do.

Happy reading, as ever.

SARAH MALLORY

———

Forbidden to the Highland Laird

ISBN-13: 978-1-335-50588-0

Forbidden to the Highland Laird

Recycling programs
for this product may
not exist in your area.

This edition published by arrangement with Harlequin Books S.A.

For questions and comments about the quality of this book, please contact us at CustomerService@Harlequin.com.

Harlequin Enterprises ULC
22 Adelaide St. West, 40th Floor
Toronto, Ontario M5H 4E3, Canada
www.Harlequin.com

Printed in U.S.A.

Sarah Mallory grew up in the West Country, England, telling stories. She moved to Yorkshire with her young family, but after nearly thirty years living in a farmhouse on the Pennines, she has now moved to live by the sea in Scotland. Sarah is an award-winning novelist with more than twenty books published by Harlequin Historical. She loves to hear from readers; you can reach her via her website at sarahmallory.com.

Books by Sarah Mallory

Harlequin Historical

The Scarlet Gown
Never Trust a Rebel
The Duke's Secret Heir
Pursued for the Viscount's Vengeance
His Countess for a Week
The Mysterious Miss Fairchild

Saved from Disgrace

The Ton's Most Notorious Rake
Beauty and the Brooding Lord
The Highborn Housekeeper

The Infamous Arrandales

The Chaperon's Seduction
Temptation of a Governess
Return of the Runaway
The Outcast's Redemption

Brides of Waterloo

A Lady for Lord Randall

Lairds of Ardvarrick

Forbidden to the Highland Laird

Visit the Author Profile page
at Harlequin.com for more titles.

To the Romantic Novelists' Association,
celebrating sixty wonderful years of romance.

Chapter One

The Highlands of Scotland—1720

There was a small stone chapel at the centre of the burial ground. It had sheltered the remains of the Rathmore clan chiefs for generations and had been freshly turfed before the latest interment, which had taken place a month ago. A month before Logan Grant Rathmore's arrival. Now, he stood alone in the chapel, silently regarding the stone slab that recorded the name of his father as well as that of his mother, who had died three years earlier. United at last in the grave.

It grieved him that he had not been present for the passing of either of his parents. The letter warning Logan of his father's illness had reached Hampshire only a day before the express telling him of the old Laird's decease. He thought bitterly that the adage of bad news travelling fast obviously did not apply to letters penned more than six hundred miles away in the Highlands of Scotland.

After a tortuous journey north, Logan had arrived last night to find his father buried and Ardvarrick in mourning. However bitter his regrets at not being able to speak one last time with his father, there was nothing Logan could do to change that.

With a final nod of reverence towards the tomb, he left the chapel and stopped for a moment at the entrance to button his coat. He had forgotten how the cold could cut through to the bone here, even in early September. Frowning, he stared around the burial ground, then he looked out over the low stone wall to the sea loch beyond, where the grey waters tossed restlessly beneath a lowering sky. This was his inheritance, this bleak, harsh land of mountains, streams and lochs on the western edge of the Highlands. He had known he would have to return one day and take up his duties, but not yet. Not at six-and-twenty.

Turning quickly, Logan strode out of the burial ground to join his cousin, who was waiting at the roadside with the horses.

'Are ye done, master?'

Logan frowned as he took the reins of his horse. 'You have no need to call me master, Tamhas.'

'But you are clan chief and Laird of Ardvarrick now, and I am to look after you, since you've no servants with ye. 'Tis not seemly that I should call you anything else.'

'Then call me master in company, if you must, but in private you will use my name, do you understand?' Logan climbed into the saddle and turned his horse. 'Come on. I want to go home.'

'Back to England?'

Logan threw him an impatient glance. 'I meant Ardvarrick. This must be my home now.'

He kicked his horse on, leading the way along the

well-worn track that ran between the meadows to the house, a recent and substantial building on two storeys, built in the French style. When Logan had left the Highlands ten years ago to finish his education in England and abroad, his father had been drawing up plans for a new house, a building he considered more appropriate for the Lairds of Ardvarrick. His mother had included sketches and a description of the proposed dwelling in her letters. It was a far cry from the blackhouse, the low, thatched building that had been the home of his youth.

Sadly, his mother had never lived to see the new house completed. Logan had been undertaking a tour of Europe when she died and by the time the news reached him it was too late to return for her burial. Logan had chosen to remain in England with his maternal family, rather than travel back to the land of his birth.

Until now.

'Ye really mean to live here, then?' Tamhas pressed him.

'I have no choice. I am the Laird.'

'If you are that set against it, an agent could collect the rents for ye.'

'I've not yet been home a day, Tamhas, are ye so eager to be rid o' me?'

Logan heard himself slipping back into the familiar brogue of his early years as he teased his old playmate. Tamhas had remained at Ardvarrick when Logan went south, but they had fallen into their old, easy ways within hours of his return.

'Nay, man, I'm fair pleased to see you back, but you

always spoke so well o' Hampshire in your letters. I thought you was settled there.'

Logan's heart contracted. He had thought so, too, but that was only ever a dream. A dream that had been shattered when his proposal to Lady Mary Wendlebury had been so brutally rejected.

It was not only her father's scathing refusal to allow him to offer for her, but her own laughter when he had dared to declare himself.

'La, how droll you are, Mr Rathmore, to think I could ever love a man who is so, so Scotch!'

He had been a callow youth, just one-and-twenty, when he had laid his heart before Lady Mary Wendlebury. Five years on, her words still cut into him like a knife. He had embarked upon the Grand Tour, hoping to eradicate his Scottishness and try his luck again, but when he returned it was to the news that Lady Mary had married the aged, but very rich, Earl of Fritchley.

He said now, 'No, Tamhas. I am my father's heir and I mean to do my duty as the new Laird of Ardvarrick.'

Shaking off the memories, Logan touched his heels against the horse's flanks and cantered on to the stables.

Two weeks later, Logan set off from Ardvarrick to pay a call upon his neighbour, Fingal Contullach. He was accompanied by Tamhas and two of his men, not that he feared for his safety, but he knew Fingal Contullach would expect him to arrive with an escort, as befitted the new Laird.

It was a clear, calm day. The trees were a glowing mix of green, gold and russet in the bright sunshine and there was as yet no sign of snow on the distant mountains. In Hampshire, on such a day as this, his aunt would be planning an outing of pleasure. A carriage drive or a picnic, perhaps, with their friends, the Stewkeleys at Hinton Ampner. If Logan had still been there, he would be going with them. He would be anticipating a day of pleasure, not a difficult meeting with a curmudgeonly neighbour.

They had left Ardvarrick land and were travelling through thick woods when he heard it, a bright tinkling sound that at first he thought was water in the burn, but as they moved on the sounds grew louder. He recognised a melody. Someone was playing a harp, the sweet, clear notes carrying to him on the slight breeze. The path continued through the woods, but to one side the pines thinned out and the ground fell away to the edge of a loch whose waters reflected the clear blue of the sky. And sitting on the rocks at the side of the loch was a young woman.

Logan silently waved to his men to stop. From the shelter of the trees he watched her playing the harp, the sun glinting off the silver strings as they moved beneath her fingers. It was a very agreeable picture and her appearance was much in keeping with the surroundings. Her kirtle and cape echoed the varied greens of the lush grass while her long hair was reddish brown and gold, like the autumn moors and the bracken that covered the hill slopes on the far side of the loch.

'Wait here,' Logan ordered, keeping his voice low. 'The sight of all of us might frighten the lady.'

He dismounted and made his way forward alone. The harpist was intent on her music and did not hear him approach. It was only when the little pony grazing nearby raised its head that the woman realised she was not alone. Her hands flattened on the strings, killing the bell-like sounds as she turned her head to look at him.

He said quickly, 'Forgive me. I did not mean to startle you.' With a smile that he hoped would reassure her, he swept off his hat and made a flourishing bow. 'Allow me to introduce myself. I am Rathmore of Ardvarrick.'

'The new Laird?'

He found himself being appraised by a pair of violet eyes fringed by thick, dark lashes.

'The very same. I had not expected to hear such beautiful music this morning. I pray you will not stop on my account. And if you do not object, I should like to rest here a while.' He sat down on a stone, keeping a good distance between them, but when she remained silent, he said gently, 'Pray continue with your music, ma'am. I should very much like to hear more of it.'

He could not detect any fear in her eyes and she continued to regard him in an unselfconscious way. After a slight hesitation she began to play again, this time a merry reel that plucked at his memory. He sat forward, listening intently.

'I recall that piece,' he said, when the music stopped and she muted the strings. 'My grandmother was wont to play it. I remember her telling me her father had been a fine harper and highly regarded. He played for some of the most powerful families in the land. My English mother preferred the spinet, but I grew up with Grandmama's jigs and reels, which I especially enjoyed. I cannot recall hearing the *clàrsach* for many years. I have been in England, you see.'

Her eyes widened. 'And they do not have music?'

Her voice was soft and lilting, with a melodic quality all of its own.

'They have a great deal of it,' he assured her, smiling. 'Alas, on the rare occasion I heard the harp, it was played by young ladies of much fashion, but little musical ability. Nothing as good as this.'

He saw a blush paint her cheeks before she turned her face away. She picked up a silver tuning key and began to adjust the strings, the movements of her slender fingers deft and assured. She appeared to have forgotten him and he thought with some surprise that she was not overly discomposed by his presence.

'Is this a favourite spot for you to practise?'

'Contullach harpers have come here to play for generations,' she told him, waving a hand at her makeshift seat. 'These are the harp stones, perfectly proportioned for the harper to sit on one and rest the foot of the *clàrsach* on the other. Even the loch is called Loch nan Clàrsairean—the Loch of the Harpers.'

'I did not know that.'

'How should you?' Her unselfconscious gaze swept over him again. 'You are a stranger to Contullach.'

He laughed at that. 'I am no stranger. I lived at Ardvarrick or at school in Edinburgh for the first sixteen years of my life, before being sent off to England.'

'But this is Contullach land,' she pointed out. 'You have no authority over it and the people of Ardvarrick keep away. I doubt you ever ventured here.'

'Not often, I admit,' he conceded. 'I am sorry to say our families were never on good terms.' Raids between the neighbours were not unheard of, even now. Logan looked around the deserted glen and thought of his men concealed in the woods behind him. 'Are you not afraid to be here, alone?'

She looked at him in surprise. 'Why should I be? I am Contullach's kinswoman.'

'But this is rough country. Wild and savage. I am surprised he allows you to come here without an escort.'

'I can look after myself. The people know me.' Her head came up and she gave him a challenging look. 'It would be a foolish man who incurred the wrath of Fingal Contullach by attacking his harper.'

Logan grinned. 'Foolish, perhaps, but a man might risk much to steal a kiss from a pretty woman.'

Her eyes darkened angrily and he put up his hands. 'Be assured I would not attempt such an outrage, mistress, but there are many who might.' He rose. 'I am on my way to Contullach Castle now. Will you not allow me to escort you back?'

She shook her head. 'Thank you, but I have not yet finished my practice. It is a rare fine day and there will not be too many more before winter.'

'Aye, the winters here can be damnable, as I recall.' He grimaced at the thought. 'Very well, I will leave you, but I beg you will take care. I wish you good day, mistress.'

With another bow he turned and walked back towards the trees. It went against his instinct to leave her there alone, but, as she had reminded him, this was not his land. Yet however much he told himself that she was not his responsibility, it was an effort not to turn back and look at her, especially when she began to play again, the notes falling on his ears like a siren song.

Ailsa concentrated on the music, keeping her fingers moving, plucking the strings of another familiar piece. She really needed to practise the tune she had composed for the forthcoming gathering at Contullach, but she could not do that until the new Laird of Ardvarrick had gone on his way. His presence disturbed her. It had been as much as she could do to play anything, with him sitting so close.

It was his strange style of dress, she told herself. The coat, top boots and doeskin breeches were much finer than anything she had seen before and so very different from the tartan trews or the belted plaid worn by her kinsmen. She had heard talk at Contullach Castle about the new Laird. They said his years in England had made him soft, a weak Sassenach, unfit to take charge of Ardvarrick, but having seen him, Ailsa was not so sure. His shoulders filled the fine wool riding jacket perfectly and he moved with the lithe grace of a wild animal. Strong, healthy. Leader of his pack.

She gave a tut of frustration and tore her eyes away from his retreating form. She could only be thankful that he had not looked back and found her watching him. He had said he was on his way to the castle and it was possible she would meet him on the road when she eventually made her way back. Unless Fingal persuaded the new Laird of Ardvarrick to accept his hospitality and stay the night.

Contullach Castle was a square stone edifice, tall and forbidding, its stables and outhouses built around a yard and set within a curtain wall. Huddled around the outside of the wall were the black houses that comprised the township. Compared to Ardvarrick, the land looked in poor heart, and Logan thought the same of the villagers, who watched them with unsmiling, sullen faces.

He shook his head and looked across at his cousin, his mouth twisting downwards. 'Nothing much has changed since I was here as a boy.'

Tamhas shrugged. 'Contullach supported the Stuart cause in the Fifteen and only kept his lands by the skin of his teeth. Your father was a canny man and more cautious. He wanted no part of it. That's why he was happy for your mother to send ye to England.'

'I thought as much.' Logan nodded. 'He was afraid I'd have some romantic notion of running off to fight for the Jacobites.'

'And if you had, Ardvarrick would most likely have lost his land *and* his heir.'

A sobering thought that kept Logan silent as he and his entourage rode between the dwellings and through the gates to the castle yard. Inside the walls there was more sign of affluence, although nothing to rival Ardvarrick. In the cobbled yard, servants came running to take their horses and Logan waited to assure himself his men would be given refreshments before he and Tamhas followed a servant into the castle.

They were shown into the main hall, a large chamber whose stone walls were clothed in colourful tapestries depicting hunting scenes that Logan thought more suited to a medieval court than a great house under the reign of the new King George. It was a mild day, but a fire roared in the huge stone hearth and there was a fine selection of flasks, goblets and glasses arranged on a side table. Fingal Contullach wanted to impress him.

Logan stopped some distance from the small dais at the far end of the room where his host was waiting for him. He had not seen Fingal Contullach for more than ten years, but he would have known the man anywhere. His squat, powerful frame was a little stockier and the untidy mop of hair was now iron grey rather than reddish brown, but the eyes set beneath their bushy brows were as sharp as ever. He responded to Logan's greeting with an unsmiling nod and waved his guest towards one of the two chairs on the dais.

'So, you've returned to Ardvarrick,' said Fingal, resuming his own seat.

It was a signal that the other men in the room could sit down at the long table that filled the centre of the room. Logan noted that Tamhas had chosen a stool at one end, free to move swiftly, if need be. Did he expect trouble?

Contullach spoke again. 'I was sorry to hear of the old Laird's passing. We had our differences, but Grant Rathmore was a just man and a fair neighbour.'

Logan inclined his head. 'I am only sorry I could not get here in time to speak with him again before the end.'

'Will ye stay?'

Logan's brows went up and he felt a mild irritation. Did everyone expect him to shirk his responsibilities?

'I am Laird. It is my duty to stay.'

'You've been away in England for some time. You are more of a Sassenach now. You'll have forgotten how things are done here.'

Contullach was regarding him with ill-disguised contempt, but Logan held his eyes steadily.

'I know fine well how things are done,' he retorted. 'That is what I am here to discuss with you.'

The older man shrugged. 'Aye, well, before we get down to business, you'll drink with me, Ardvarrick. What will ye have?' He waved towards the side table. 'There's heather ale and cordial. Or I have French wine, if your palate is grown too fine for our Highland brews.'

There was a challenge in the tone. Logan smiled.

'I'll take a tankard of heather ale and I'll thank you for it.'

The drinks were duly poured and distributed. Tamhas was talking with his companions at the table, all of them feigning indifference to what was going on between the two men on the dais. Logan sipped at his ale and waited. It was going to be a difficult conversation and he was not going to rush into speech. His host eyed him over the rim of his tankard.

'Well, Logan Rathmore, what is it you want of me?'

'Cattle are being stolen from my land,' Logan told him, choosing his words with care.

'Are they now?' Contullach shook his head. 'These are terrible lawless times we live in, Ardvarrick. I could help ye, for a price. I could have my men look out for your cattle.' He threw a sly look at Logan. 'Protect them.'

Logan said, without heat, 'We both know that game, Contullach. Lifting cattle is a common practice here and has been for generations, whenever the owner will not pay the blackmail.'

A sudden silence fell over the long table, but

Logan ignored it and fixed his eyes on the man sitting opposite.

He said, 'There has been bad feeling and worse between our people for years because my father refused to pay for your *protection*.' With an oath Contullach sat up in his chair, but Logan continued calmly. 'I want you to know that neither have I any intention of paying you.'

'By God, sir, is that what you've learned in England, to insult a man's hospitality? How dare ye come in here and accuse me of stealing your beasts!'

'I have been very careful not to accuse you of anything,' Logan replied. 'Come, sir, I do not want to live at odds with my neighbours. You know as well as I that raiding cattle prompts others to retaliate. Protecting livestock takes men who could be better employed elsewhere. There is another way. One that would benefit both of us.'

He kept his voice calm and his eyes on his host. This was a battle of wills and one he could not afford to lose. After a moment, Fingal sat back in his chair.

'And what is it you are suggesting?'

So, the man was prepared to listen. Logan held back a sigh of relief.

He said, 'Because of the…er…differences between our families, my father would never allow Contullach cattle to cross Ardvarrick land to reach the markets in the south.'

'Aye,' growled Contullach. 'When the drovers come to collect the beasts, they have to take them around the long way, through Gleann an Lòin.'

Logan nodded. 'The aptly named Valley of the Bog. That way is slow and arduous. Dangerous, too, I hear, if the season has been particularly wet. It is hard on man and beast alike.'

He stopped and took a long draught of ale, allowing his host to think about his words. The old man was watching him intently.

'Go on.'

'If I could be sure there would be no more raids on my land, Contullach, I would allow your beasts to join with those from Ardvarrick. They would all be driven across the Bealach na Damh—the Pass of the Stags. If the drovers can move the cattle together it will save them time and save your beasts travelling an extra two dozen or so miles.'

'And they could pay more per head,' muttered Fingal, tapping his fingers on the arm of his chair.

'Yes, I believe they would do that,' Logan agreed. 'We should both gain from it. Well, sir, what do you say, are we in accord on this?'

'I say no!' There was the sudden scrape of wood on stone as one of the men at the table jumped to his feet. 'Ye cannot trust the Rathmores to keep to a bargain. 'Tis a trick, Fingal.'

Logan regarded the stocky, red-haired figure glaring at him across the room. It was Ewan Cowie, a kinsman of Fingal Contullach's wife. As children they had met on occasion and disliked each other cordially. By the look of hatred in the man's face, Logan guessed that had not changed, at least on Cowie's part.

'The new Laird has learned English tricks,' the man went on. 'When the time comes, he will refuse to honour any agreement we make now.'

'I could hardly do that, when there are so many witnesses.'

Logan's cool response only angered Ewan Cowie even more. He took a few steps forward, his hands clenching and unclenching at his side.

'Let us settle this the old way,' he declared. 'I will fight you, Ardvarrick, for the right to take our beasts across your lands.'

Contullach waved his hand. 'Away wi' ye, man. What do you know about it? You are too hot headed by half, Ewan. Go and sit ye down!' He turned his fierce eyes back to Logan. 'A truce between our people? I admit it's a tempting thought, Logan Rathmore, but I cannot make the decision alone. I will talk to my kinsmen when they come here for the ceilidh at the full moon. If they are minded to agree, then we could try the plan for next season.'

'Very well, I will wait to hear from you.'

'If we decide to go ahead, there must be a legal agreement between us,' said Fingal. 'It must be clear, and in writing, that Contullach beasts can be driven across your land.'

'I shall ensure it is. I will have the agreement drawn up myself. But first *I* need proof that you are as good as your word, Fingal Contullach. A winter of peace, with no raids on Ardvarrick.'

The old man hesitated. 'I cannot be responsible for what others might take it into their heads to do…'

'No raids, Contullach. If you can assure me of that, I'll have the agreement ready to sign in the spring.'

Logan waited, watching the old man as he deliberated.

'Agreed,' Contullach said at last. 'As far as it is in my power, there will be no attacks on your land.'

Logan took his time, as if considering the matter before he nodded. Fingal sat back, satisfied.

'You'll sup with us, Ardvarrick. And bide here 'til morning? 'Tis a long ride back and you'll not make it before nightfall. Your men can sleep above the stables and there's a room here in the castle for you and your cousin.'

'Thank you, we will stay.' There was a vicious hiss of disapproval from Ewan Cowie, who was still looking furious. Logan shot him a glance and added, 'That is, Contullach, if you can assure me we'll not be murdered in our beds.'

'Damn your eyes, man, honour demands I keep ye safe while you are under my roof!'

'Of course. I beg your pardon.' Logan gave a little bow. He had offended his host, but he could not let Cowie's behaviour go unmarked.

'A satisfactory meeting,' murmured Tamhas, as they were escorted out of the hall a short time later. 'The old man was more amenable than I thought he would be, although you strained his hospitality when you mentioned his stealing your cattle!'

'There was no other way to broach the subject. It was a risk, but it worked.'

'And in the end Contullach was minded to invite you to the ceilidh.' Tamhas chuckled. 'That fair put Ewan Cowie's nose out of joint and no mistake. His face was like a thundercloud until you declined the invitation.'

Logan shrugged. 'It was never my intention to make an enemy of Cowie. Or to make a good friend of Contullach, for that matter.'

They were shown to a small but comfortable chamber and Tamhas sat down on the bed, nodding approvingly at the thick mattress.

'I had a busy morning even before we set out to ride here, so I am going to take a rest while I can. I vow I could sleep for a week, could not you, Cousin?'

Logan grinned. 'You are growing old, Tamhas Rathmore. I'll not lie down yet, but you go on and rest your aged bones!'

Taking him at his word, Tamhas stretched himself out on the bed and by the time Logan had made use of the water provided to wash off the dust from his long journey, his cousin was fast asleep.

Chapter Two

It was not unusual for Ailsa to practise until darkness was falling over the land, but today she finished early. Nothing to do with her encounter with the Laird of Ardvarrick, she told herself as she strapped the *clàrsach* to the pony, yet she could not deny that thoughts of him had distracted her. When she reached Contullach it was evident that the Laird and his party were still there, for their horses were in the fold beside the stables.

Simple Rab was in the yard and she asked him to carry the harp into the house for her while she stabled the pony. Only when she had rubbed down the animal and seen him comfortably stalled did she make her way into the house and up to her room. She changed her gown and made her way to the family parlour, where her cousins Màiri and Kirstin and their mother were sitting before the fire, busy with their embroidery.

'Ah, here she is, the little harper,' Màiri greeted her with a smirk. 'I hope you are well practised, Ailsa, for we have guests and Father will want you to play for us after dinner.'

'Ardvarrick is here,' Morag Contullach explained. 'When they finished their business, Fingal persuaded him to stay and we must entertain him.'

'Not that you will be playing all evening,' put in Kirstin. 'Màiri wants to sing for him. She has a mind to be Lady Ardvarrick, even though we have not seen him since he was a wee boy.'

'And why not?' Màiri retorted. '*You* cannot have him, you are betrothed to our cousin Ewan. Remember that tonight, Sister, and do not be making sheep's eyes at the Laird!'

'I would not stoop so low!' Kirstin tossed her head. 'And why should I want to make eyes at Logan Rathmore? Ewan tells me he has become an English fop.'

'Nothing of the sort. I was watching from the high window as he rode in and I thought him very handsome,' declared Màiri. 'Ewan is jealous. As are you, Kirstin, because you are not free to throw your cap at the Laird!'

Morag put up her hand and said sharply, 'Girls, enough of this foolishness. Logan Rathmore has come here to talk business with your father and you will behave yourselves when he sits down to dinner with us tonight. I will not have either of you putting yourselves forward. For one thing, Màiri, I'll not have a daughter of mine married at fifteen. And, Kirstin, neither do I want to see you sitting in Ewan's lap, as if the two of you cannot keep your hands off each other until your wedding day.'

Both daughters cried out at this and, as their protests looked as if they would rage for some time, Ailsa quietly left the room before she could be drawn into the argument. She was very likely to lose her temper and, if she did that, Aunt Morag might banish her to her bedchamber for the evening.

If she could not sit in the parlour with its warm fire, then the next best place was the small solar on the top floor of the tower. It had once been the domain of the ladies of Contullach, but had long ago been abandoned for the larger and more comfortable rooms below. However, its southerly window made a cheerful place to sit and when the sun was shining, as it was today, it stayed comfortably warm into the evening.

Ailsa ran up the stairs and entered the solar, stopping when she saw there was someone already sitting on the stone window seat. The new Laird of Ardvarrick.

Logan heard the click of the latch and jumped to his feet as the young woman came into the room. He recognised her immediately, but before he could speak she stopped and began to back out of the door.

'Oh. I beg your pardon, I did not think—excuse me!'

'No, do not go,' he said quickly. 'We met at the loch side today. I am Ardvarrick.'

'I remember.' She flushed. 'That is, I was told you were staying here as my uncle's guest.'

'That is correct. Perhaps you will tell me your name, now we have met again.'

She eyed him, far more wary here at the castle than she had been at the loch, but at last she seemed to make up her mind.

'I am Ailsa McInnis.'

Ailsa. Not a local name, but it suited her. He sketched a bow.

'Then I bid you good day, Mistress McInnis. Is this your room? I will remove—'

She disclaimed and after a heartbeat's hesitation came a little further into the room.

'No, no, I use it sometimes.' A tiny smile tugged at her mouth. 'When the family are in the parlour.'

'For a little peace?' He grinned. 'My cousin is snoring heartily in our chamber and I was looking for somewhere quiet to read.'

'To *read*?'

Logan bit back a laugh. She sounded quite incredulous. Perhaps Contullach and his family were not great readers.

'Aye.' He held up the small book. 'Poetry. Lovelace.'

'Oh, I see.'

He held it out. 'Would you like to look at it?' When she backed away he said, 'You *can* read, can you not?'

Her head went up. 'Of course I can read. And write, too, but mostly letters.' Her spurt of indignation faded and she gave a little sigh. 'There are no printed books at Contullach, save for the Bible.'

'Are all your songs and your music learned by rote, then? They are passed down to you?'

She nodded. 'Aye. Poems and stories, too, are told around the fire, over and over until one knows them by heart.'

He smiled and glanced at the book in his hands. 'It is the same for me with these poems. Would you like me to read one to you?'

She nodded and he stood aside, gesturing that she should sit in the window seat. As she made herself comfortable, he thumbed through the pages, looking for a poem she might enjoy. At last he found what he was looking for.

He looked up, smiling. 'Richard Lovelace was a soldier and a loyal courtier of King Charles I. He died more than fifty years ago, but his poetry might have been written yesterday. This one he wrote after he had fallen foul of Parliament. It is called, "To Althea, from Prison".'

He knew it so well he did not need to look at the lines. Instead he watched Ailsa. She was gazing out of the window, but he could tell she was concentrating on the poem. He regretted that she had not fixed those deep violet eyes upon him, but at least that left him free to observe her. He liked the way the sun glinted sparks of fire in her red hair. It also highlighted the delightful sprinkling of freckles across her dainty nose.

He finished the poem and for a moment there was silence, then Ailsa sighed.

'Poor man. I hope he did not die in prison. How dreadful, to be locked up, unable to walk free in the air. Not to feel the wind on your face, or even the rain.'

'He was freed soon after writing that poem, I think.' Logan knew he should leave. There was no furniture in this little room and it would not be proper to sit in the window so close to the lady. Then she turned to smile at him and thoughts of withdrawing faded. He said impulsively, 'Would you like to hear another poem?'

The Laird of Ardvarrick had a smooth, rich voice and Ailsa listened, enraptured, as he read to her. She dare not watch him, because he often looked up from the page and, for some reason, when she met his eyes she could not prevent a blush from heating her cheeks. So instead she gazed out across the glen while in her head she conjured music to accompany the poem. Soft, wistful tunes, but not melancholy. She stored them in her memory to be revived later, perhaps the next time she was at the loch, where she could compose and re-fine her music.

Time flew on wings. The Laird had just finished reading a sonnet when they heard voices calling from below.

Ailsa scrambled to her feet. 'It is late, they will be serving dinner. I must go.' She paused at the door and glanced back. 'Thank you, sir, for reading to me. I have rarely heard anything so beautiful.'

She spoke on impulse and immediately the fiery blush ignited again. Without another word she turned and fled, her cheeks burning.

Food was served in the hall with the Laird of Ard-varrick sitting with his host and the immediate fam-ily on the dais. Ailsa was amused to see how Kirstin and Màiri vied for the Laird's attention, but she was glad to be eating at the big table in the centre of the room. There was a melody running through her head, distracting her, and her fingers moved restlessly. She was impatient to try out the new tune on the *clàrsach*, but that could not be until she was alone. Perhaps later, in the privacy of her chamber. It was inspired by the poetry she had heard earlier, but dare she acknowl-edge that?

She glanced again towards the dais. Ardvarrick was listening to something Fingal was saying and she stud-ied his profile, the smooth, lean cheek, the strong chin and the faint smile playing on his lips. She could not see his eyes, but she guessed they would be smiling, too, as they had earlier, when he had been reading to her. The memory of it sent a little thrill of pleasure skittering through her.

'So our harper has fallen under the fop's spell, too.'

Startled, Ailsa looked up, Ewan was sneering at her across the table, 'Ardvarrick is a charmer, that's for sure. He has all the lassies at his feet.'

'He has good manners, Ewan Cowie,' she flashed back at him. 'Something you could do well to study!'

Her retort brought laughter from those close enough to hear, but it caused Ewan's face to darken with rage. Ailsa knew he was smarting because Fingal had not invited him to join the family at the top table and she had no wish to make matters worse, so she turned to speak with her neighbour and left her cousin to mutter angrily into his soup. Kirstin's coquettish behaviour with the new Laird was making him jealous, but he himself flirted outrageously with every pretty woman he encountered, so she thought it might do him good to be treated to a little of his own medicine.

She fell into a reverie again, working on the melody in her head and by the time the meal was over it was fairly well established. But as for a title? She glanced back at the dark-haired man sitting on the dais. Given the bad feeling between the two families she dare not call it Ardvarrick's song, but she was sorry for it.

Logan and Tamhas went to the hall to break their fast the next morning and Logan was aware of a momentary relief when he realised Ailsa was not there. He had shown her rather too much attention yesterday and it had not gone unnoticed. After dinner, Fingal had ordered Ailsa to play for them. The tables had been cleared away and the *clàrsach* brought in. Logan tried to concentrate on the conversation, but he could not prevent his attention wandering back to the dais and Ailsa, watching her slim fingers dance over the strings.

'Taken a liking to our harper, have you, Rathmore?'

Logan had turned to find Ewan Cowie at his shoulder.

'She is very proficient,' he replied cautiously.

'She is Contullach's kinswoman,' Cowie told him. 'And not to be trifled with, if you value your life.'

Logan stiffened at the other man's aggressive tone. 'I am not in the habit of *trifling* with young ladies.'

'Just as well. As the clan chief's harper she is held in special regard. Contullach would not take kindly to losing her.' Cowie glowered at him. 'You'd do well to remember that, Ardvarrick, and keep away from the lady.'

Logan had watched him walk away, thinking it a strong warning and for little reason. Why should that be? He had already learned that Cowie was engaged to Contullach's daughter Kirstin, so he had no right to be jealous.

Logan glanced now across the table to where Ewan Cowie had taken a seat for breakfast. The fellow had objected violently to the suggestion of an agreement and it was clear he did not want to be on better terms with his neighbour. Logan shrugged. Old enmities ran deep, but he could not help that. His time in Edinburgh and England had shown him the prosperity that peace could bring. Prosperity that he wanted for Ardvarrick.

As Laird it was his responsibility to do what he could to bring that about.

With peace in mind, when he and Tamhas rose from the table and he had bid farewell to his host, Logan made a point of taking a polite leave of Ewan Cowie.

'So, you are going.' The man glowered at him. 'And when shall we see ye back at Contullach?'

'That depends. If there are no raids on my lands, I shall return in the spring with the document for signature.'

Cowie scowled as if even that was too soon for him. He said, 'You'll not be at the gathering, then?'

'I have already said I will not.' He hung on to his temper in the face of the other man's open hostility. 'I see no point in returning until Contullach is ready to sign an agreement and for that there needs to be accord between your uncle and his kinsmen.'

'If it was up to me, that would never happen!'

'It is as well, then, that the decision is not yours to make.' Logan gave him a curt nod and went out, joining his cousin on the stairs.

'The men are all ready to leave, Tamhas?'

'Aye, they are, Cousin. They should be waiting for us in the yard.'

'Good. Let us collect our things and get back to Ardvarrick.'

'Back to a comfortable house,' murmured Tamhas, flicking him a grin.

'Back to a friendly one,' he responded. 'If Cowie and his friends have their way, there will be no accord between Contullach's people and our own.'

'And is that likely, Logan?'

'That depends on Fingal Contullach. He must overcome old prejudices and persuade his people that co-operation is more profitable. Once they have tried it and can see that it is, I have no doubt they will want to continue.'

It did not take long to pack up their saddlebags and make their way out to the stables, where the Ardvarrick men were already bringing out their horses. Logan climbed into the saddle and as he waited for the others to mount, he noticed two women hurrying across the yard to the house. One of them was Ailsa McInnis.

Her auburn hair was loose and it bounced over the green mantle that covered her shoulders. His spirits lifted at the sight of her. Wherever she had been this morning, the exercise had done her good, for she was positively glowing as she chattered away in an animated fashion to her companion.

Of everyone at Contullach, the only person he would regret not seeing again was the little harper. She had enchanted him with her playing, but he had also found great pleasure in reading to her, sharing with her the poems he loved and relishing her enjoyment of them. It would be a sadness not to see her again.

Logan turned to his cousin, 'Tamhas, before you get too comfortable in that saddle, will you be so good as to jump down and carry a message for me to Fingal Contullach?'

Ailsa struggled to keep her eyes from the Laird of Ardvarrick as she walked towards the house with Jeanie Barr. She tried to concentrate on what Jeanie was saying, but she heard the footsteps running behind her and for one frightening, exhilarating moment she thought it was the Laird. Her heart leapt alarmingly, as if it was trying to batter a way out of her chest. But it was only his kinsman, dashing past her to go back into the house.

Pride was a sin, she reminded herself. The disappointment she felt that Logan Rathmore had not come running to bid her goodbye was just punishment for such vanity. She must pray for forgiveness and the strength to keep her mind on her music. To keep her thoughts away from the Laird of Ardvarrick.

'I think I'll go to the loch today,' she said to Jeanie. 'I shall ask Simple Rab to carry the harp out and fasten it to the pony.'

'You should take him with you, too,' Jeanie advised her. 'I know you like being on your own, but the lad won't be in your way, and you should have someone with you when you are out of doors. You are grown too pretty to be out alone, Ailsa.'

She tossed her head and was about to object when she remembered her meeting at the loch yesterday with Logan Rathmore. She had felt no danger when he was near; no physical danger, that is. But she could not deny that he had had a strange and unsettling affect upon her. A feeling that had not yet passed.

'Very well,' she said meekly, 'I will take Rab with me.'

'What?' Jeanie stopped and looked at her in mock amazement. 'Well, now, that is a surprise! I thought you'd tear up at me for even suggesting such a thing.'

'No, why should I do that?' Ailsa flushed. 'I am not so unreasonable.'

Her companion laughed. 'That red hair of yours tells a different story, lass. When you believe you have been wronged you have the very devil of a temper!'

* * *

That evening Fingal summoned Ailsa to play for him in his private chamber. The days were growing shorter and candlelight already glowed around the room. Her uncle was engaged in writing letters at his table and Ailsa played the soft, soothing tunes that she knew he liked. He said they helped him concentrate on his business. She had been playing thus, and her aunt and mother before her, for so many years that none of the servants or family who came and went paid any heed to the harper in the corner. They spoke freely and Ailsa was accustomed to ignoring their chatter, but tonight her attention was caught when Ewan Cowie came in. He had clearly been drinking, his eyes were bloodshot and the parts of his face not covered by his beard were unnaturally red and his breathing noisy.

'Uncle, I heard at dinner that Logan Rathmore had changed his mind. He is coming to the ceilidh.'

'Aye. His man came back to tell me. What of it?'

'I don't want him here. The man's a damned Sassenach. Once he has put his plans in place he'll be off, back to England. He will leave his factor to bleed the tenants dry and your lands will be tied into it by that damned agreement.'

'You are talking nonsense, Ewan. I'll not sign anything that isn't in my interest.' Fingal shrugged. 'It may well be that Rathmore has grown soft with his years in the south, but he is our neighbour and the Laird of Ardvarrick.'

Ewan gave a snort of derision. 'He's a fraud!'

Fingal chuckled. 'I knew him as a boy, Ewan, as did you. I grant you Logan Rathmore speaks and dresses differently now, but he has not changed sufficiently for me to doubt his birth.'

Ewan ignored his uncle's attempt at humour. He waved a dismissive hand.

'I am not disputing he is his father's son, but I cannot like the man. I don't trust him.'

'Och, 'tis more that you are jealous of him, I'm thinking.'

A shrewd guess on Fingal's part, thought Ailsa. Ewan Cowie was not ill looking, but he rarely trimmed his red hair or his thick beard and his face grew blotched when he was angry, which happened frequently. She recalled Logan Rathmore's countenance, lean and clean-shaven. True, he wore no powdered wig, which she had learned was the fashion among gentlemen, but his long dark hair was brushed until it gleamed and tied back neatly with a ribbon. There was no doubt in her mind which man was the more handsome.

'Jealous, of that weakling?' Ewan gave a bark of laughter. 'You should have let me fight him, one to one. We would then see who is the best man.'

Without breaking the rhythm of her play, Ailsa stole an anxious glance across the room. Ewan was half a head shorter than Logan Rathmore, but his stocky build looked far more powerful. Even so, she thought Ewan underestimated the new Laird of Ardvarrick. He might be lean, but he was no weakling. She had sensed strength and power in the man.

She wondered what he could have done to enrage Ewan so. Perhaps he had shown an interest in Kirstin. Ailsa had not noticed him paying any especial attention to either of her cousins, but as Fingal's eldest daughter, Kirstin would inherit her father's estate and Ewan's hopes of becoming clan chief could be dashed if she broke off her engagement to him in favour of Ardvarrick. It was possible Ewan was worried that Fingal would look favourably upon a match that joined together not only the two families, but the neighbouring lands.

The thought of Kirstin marrying Logan Rathmore did not please Ailsa and she was relieved to hear her uncle give another reason for Ewan's hatred of the Laird.

'You never liked each other as children, but it is time to put that behind you, man. Ardvarrick's plan to combine our cattle for the drive to the southern markets makes some sense. We would all gain more. And my tenants farming the lands bordering Ardvarrick could rest easier in their beds if they were not forever fearing reprisals. Maybe 'tis time we lived peaceably with our neighbour.'

'And maybe 'tis you are growing soft, Fingal Contullach!'

Ailsa kept playing, her eyes fixed on the *clàrsach*. Ewan had gone too far and she did not need to look up to know Fingal was angry. She heard his chair scrape back as he jumped to his feet.

'I'll not take that from anyone, Ewan Cowie,' he bellowed. 'And especially not from a young whelp like you!'

'I beg your pardon, Uncle. Forgive me. I forgot myself. But all the same—'

'Enough!' Fingal interrupted him. 'We will discuss this with the rest of the clan, when they arrive. Ardvarrick will not be privy to that meeting, I will make sure of that, but he will be welcome at the gathering and to sleep here the night. No harm will come to him while he is under my roof. You understand me, Ewan? I'll not be shamed by such an abuse of my hospitality.'

There was no doubting the menace in Fingal's voice. Ailsa had come to the end of her piece and as the final notes died away an awkward silence filled the room. Finally, Ewan gave a reluctant growl of assent before flinging himself out of the room. Fingal sank back on to his chair with a heavy sigh and a muttered curse.

'Shall I leave you, Uncle?'

'What?' For a moment he frowned at Ailsa, as if he had forgotten her presence. Then he shook his head. 'Nay, lassie, play on. Play that new piece I heard earlier. God knows I need your soothing music to calm me after that. What am I going to do about that damn fool boy, eh?'

She kept silent and began to play again, the new lyrical melody she privately called 'Ardvarrick's Air'. Fingal was leaning back in his chair, eyes closed. He clearly did not want or expect an answer to his question, especially from a woman.

Chapter Three

The gathering at Contullach Castle was timed to co-incide with the full moon, giving the clansmen the advantage of moonlight to travel, providing there was no heavy cloud. They began arriving days before, the favoured ones putting up at the castle itself, others filling the local inn, staying with family or bedding down wherever they could. Ailsa had been very busy, helping out in the kitchens as well as practising her new pieces in readiness for the festivities.

On the night of the ceilidh she asked Simple Rab to carry her harp to the great hall and place it on one corner of the dais, the chairs reserved for Fingal and his most honoured guests taking up the rest of the space. The room was filling up, voices rising as the guests greeted one another with boisterous good humour, and Ailsa had to lean close to fine tune the strings. She enjoyed these evenings; they gave her an opportunity to play jigs and reels for dancing rather than the slow and often melancholy airs that Fingal preferred.

A sudden hush fell over the room and Ailsa glanced up in time to see the Laird of Ardvarrick walk in, his

kinsman at his side. Tamhas Rathmore had honoured
the occasion by wearing tartan trews and jacket, but
Logan Rathmore was resplendent in a blue velvet coat,
heavily laced with silver, and white knee breeches.
Ailsa had never seen any man dressed in such a sumptuous manner before and guessed it was the English
fashion. She could not deny he looked very handsome,
so much so that the breath caught in her throat just to
look at him.

'Whisht now, Ailsa McInnis, this will never do,'
she told herself crossly. 'Get on with tuning the *clàrsach* and let the man be.'

She managed to adjust the strings to the correct
pitch, but it was a struggle. Unusually, she could not
drag her attention away from what was going on in the
hall. Her uncle was in the best of moods and greeted
Ardvarrick cheerfully.

'Logan Rathmore, welcome to you. I hope you have
come prepared to dance, sir.'

'I have indeed.'

Ewan was standing close by and gave a snort of
derision.

'*Can* you do so, in those heels?' He pointed to the
Laird's blue leather shoes with their red heels and silver buckles.

Ardvarrick glanced down at his feet.

'Oh, I think I shall manage. They are very *low*
heels, after all.' There was a definite drawl to his voice
and Ailsa thought he was teasing, although his face
was perfectly serious. 'The ladies will have to forgive me if I am a little out of practice when I stand
up with them.'

He looked up as he spoke and caught Ailsa's eyes,

a gleam of amusement in his own. Now she knew he was teasing! She quickly averted her gaze and bent her head over her harp as a hot blush mounted her cheeks and her heart pattered unsteadily in her chest. It was as if he had been inviting her to share the joke.

Fingal was laughing. 'Och, I am sure they will do that! And talking of the ladies, you will remember my daughters, Màiri and Kirstin, but there are others here you may not know…'

More guests were arriving and everyone was beginning to chatter. Gradually Ailsa relaxed. Her uncle had not noticed the look Ardvarrick had given her and now the Laird's attention had moved on to the other ladies, those who were free to dance. Which was as it should be.

She placed her fingers on the strings and began to play softly, waiting for Fingal to give the word for dancing to commence. It would not be long now, most of the guests had arrived and servants were refilling glasses and tankards. Suddenly she realised Ardvarrick was approaching her, the skirts of his blue frock coat swinging gently against his long legs.

'I have not yet bid you a good day, Mistress McInnis. A thousand pardons, it was very remiss of me.'

Ailsa swallowed and looked up, murmuring a reply. She could not ignore him when he was addressing her as if she was a fine lady. He was smiling at her and it was impossible not to smile back, to feel the tug of attraction. How she managed to keep her fingers moving and playing the right notes she could never afterwards understand.

'Come, Ailsa, time to play the first reel of the evening!'

Fingal's impatient bark brought the tell-tale flush to her cheeks and she bent her head closer to the strings.

'And I am engaged to dance the first with your charming lady, Contullach, so lead me to her!'

She heard the Laird's cheerful words, glimpsed him walking away with her uncle and turned her attention back to her music. Good heavens, what was wrong with her, that she should turn into a simpering miss because he had deigned to greet her? Foolish, she berated herself. Foolish and dangerous.

Ailsa watched the company as her fingers drew one lively tune after another from the strings. It was easy to spot Logan Rathmore in his velvet coat, the silver lace gleaming in the candlelight. He joined in every jig and reel, dancing with grace and agility. His heeled shoes were no impediment and although he went the wrong way occasionally, it was no more than many others on the dance floor. It amused her to see how Màiri and Kirstin were falling over themselves to catch the attention of the new Laird and how Ewan, who rarely danced, claimed Kirstin for his partner as soon as she had finished reeling with Logan.

And so it went on. Ardvarrick showed no preference for any lady, partnering old and young alike with equal delight. The perfect guest, thought Ailsa, and for the first time in years she wished that she might dance. That was impossible, alas, her uncle would not allow it.

When the initial round of dancing had ended, Logan escorted his partner back to her seat and went off to the table to collect his glass. Ailsa McInnis was still at her harp, busy adjusting the pegs with her silver tuning key. Her burnished curls fell over her shoulders and along with the tartan gown of green and purple, the colours reminded him of the varied hues of the moors and glens. She was definitely a lady of the Highlands, he thought, enjoying the pleasing picture she made.

'You are smiling, Logan Rathmore.' Morag Contullach came up to him. 'I hope that means you are enjoying yourself.'

'Aye, madam, I thank you. 'Tis a while since I attended a gathering such as this.' He glanced towards the dais. 'I am particularly liking the music.'

'Ailsa is a good harper, better even than her mother now, I think.'

'Music is a gift that runs in the family, then?'

'Aye, and a much valued one. Contullach women are generally fine musicians, although sadly, my own girls take after me and do not have a musical ear. But Ailsa's mother, and then her aunt—both Fingal's sisters, you know—were harpers here for many years.'

'And does Mistress McInnis dance as well as she plays?'

He knew as soon as the question left his lips that he had made a mistake. The lady's response was undoubtedly cool.

'My niece's role at Contullach is to play the harp. It is an important post and Fingal values her highly. I am aware that many now prefer pipes or fiddles to be played at gatherings, but my husband's family have always had harpers.' She looked him in the eye and added, 'Ailsa never dances, so it will do you no good to ask her, Logan Rathmore.'

He inclined his head in acknowledgement and thought ruefully that he was again being warned off. Odd, but of no matter, since he would be leaving Contullach in the morning and would not return for months.

Fingal was calling for another reel and Morag turned to him.

'If you are free, sir, I will find you another partner.'

Logan would have liked to remain at the side of the room, listening to the music, but he knew his duty. With a smile and nod of acceptance, he drained his glass and followed his hostess.

Another hour of dancing and the room had become very warm. More refreshments were brought in, including pastries, and the assembly fell upon them, eager for their share. Logan was not hungry, but he was hot and in the crowded confusion it was easy for him to slip away. From the window he had noticed a small paved area below, edged with a stone balustrade. It had presumably been built by some earlier Contullach in an attempt to soften the austere appearance of the old castle and it would be the perfect place to cool off.

He quickly left the house and made his way around the building to the small terrace. The moon was sailing high, painting the landscape in blues and greys, and Logan perched himself on the balustrade, twisting to look out across the glen to the rising hills beyond. It was a calm night without a breath of wind. After the heat and noise of the hall it was a relief to sit quietly, away from the curious glances and speculation of so many strangers.

He wished he had not come. He scowled down at the ground, kicking at one of the weeds sprouting between the stone flags. What had possessed him to change his mind about Fingal Contullach's invitation? He could not deny he knew the answer to that. He had walked out of the castle in a buoyant mood, his spirits lifted by the successful meeting with Contullach and the exceptionally fine weather, so that when he had seen the pretty harper tripping across the yard he had yielded to the temptation and sent Tamhas back to say he would return for the gathering, after all.

He should have realised the Contullach ceilidh would be a far cry from the elegant parties he had attended in Hampshire. Not that he was so grown in conceit he could not enjoy dancing the jigs and reels he had learned as a boy, but he did not like being the object of speculation, the women eyeing him as a potential husband for themselves or their daughters and as for the menfolk—

Logan sighed. The men regarded him as an outsider and some, especially Ewan Cowie and his cronies, looked at him with barely concealed hostility. Not that it surprised him. There had been no love lost between their families for generations and that would not change overnight. Perhaps he had been away too long, perhaps he had grown soft. He did not relish battling his neighbours and the elements to make a life for himself here.

He heard a faint rustle and looked up as a figure appeared. Even in the moonlight he recognised the dainty outline immediately. Ailsa McInnis. When she saw him, she stopped and began to turn back.

He rose. 'No, don't run away, mistress. I pray you, stay.' He added coaxingly, 'There is sufficient room out here for both of us.' She had not moved, but at least she was still on the terrace. 'I promise you I am perfectly harmless.'

She shifted from foot to foot, clearly nervous. 'I came out for a little air.'

'Yes, I did the same. We are fortunate, fine evenings such as this are rare. The weather in this damned place is something savage.'

'It cannot be so different from Ardvarrick.'

She sounded offended and he immediately begged pardon.

'You are right, although my home benefits from being nearer the coast.'

'No doubt you are missing your English weather.'

'I am. I am missing England a great deal.' He shook off the thought and gave a rueful laugh, 'I beg your pardon, I am being very ungracious and without cause, too, for the night air is balmy and, even in the moonlight, the view from this terrace is pleasing.' A noise from above made him glance up. 'Although they have now opened the window so it is not quite as *peaceful* here as it was.'

Ailsa moved silently towards the balustrade and looked out across the valley.

'On a clear day one can see the full length of the glen,' she told him. 'It changes with the seasons, but is always beautiful.'

'I am sure it is.'

She was quick to discern that he was being polite rather than sincere and turned to look at him. 'You do not agree?'

'On the contrary, the mountains and glens of the Highlands are magnificent, as fine as anything I saw on the grand tour.'

'But you do not love it.'

'I was very fond of it, once.' Logan hesitated. 'No doubt I shall be so again. In time.'

They stood in silence, each lost in their own thoughts while chatter and laughter floated down from the hall.

At last, Logan said, 'Do you play again tonight?'

She nodded. 'Later. First there will be poetry and song, even stories. Do you not wish to go back and listen to them?'

'When I am a little cooler, perhaps. You play very well.'

'Thank you. You dance very well.'

Her polite response made him smile. 'You flatter me. I am out of practice, but I am surprised how quickly the steps came back to me. How long have you been Contullach's *clàrsair*?'

'More than four years now.'

'Truly?' He was surprised. 'You must have been full young when you took up the post.'

Her head went up, as if he had insulted her. 'I was fifteen. Many girls are married by that age.'

'True.' He made a slight bow. 'I beg your pardon, mistress.'

She frowned at him. 'Now you are mocking me.'

'No, no, I assure you I am not! I would never mock you.'

She looked unsure and for a moment he thought she might run away. He wanted to keep her with him and sought quickly for something to say.

'Do you not wish to listen to the poems?' Logan cursed himself silently for his folly. He was giving her the opportunity to leave him! To his relief she shook her head.

'I have heard them many times before and I know them by heart. 'Tis the same with the songs. But perhaps *you* should listen to them, Master Rathmore. They are entertaining.'

'I am sure they are, but I will no doubt be expected to dance again later.' He sat back down on the balustrade. 'I need to rest.'

He was relieved that she recognised he was teasing and did not look at him with disdain. Instead she laughed, a rich, merry sound that was very pleasant on the ear.

'And I can hear the poems from here,' he continued. 'I should miss too much if I left the terrace now.'

She rested against the balustrade and they listened in companionable silence while from the window above the calm night air carried a loud, stentorian voice, rising and falling with the cadences of an epic poem. Another followed, then someone began to sing. It was a woman's voice, loud and not particularly tuneful. Logan glanced at Ailsa and saw her wince.

'That is Kirstin,' she told him.

'Ah, yes. She is betrothed to Ewan Cowie. Is it a love match?'

She hesitated. 'Kirstin certainly loves him.'

'But it is not reciprocated?'

'He professes to love her, but one cannot deny it will be a providential union for him. Ewan is my aunt's nephew and my uncle's nearest male relative. By marrying Kirstin, it secures his claim to Contullach lands.'

'There is a lot to be said for putting such matters beyond doubt.'

In the moonlight he saw her lips tighten, as if she had decided to withhold a response. Was she not happy with the betrothal, was she perhaps a little in love with Cowie herself? He was surprised at how much the idea irked him.

She looked up at the window as a new sound issued forth, the scrape of a fiddle. 'Ah, now old Iain is playing. That is much better.'

Soon the notes of a familiar tune floated down from the window.

He said, 'Perhaps you would like to return to the hall and dance.'

'I was never taught the steps.'

'I thought all young ladies learned to dance.'

Her hand fluttered. 'I spent all my time with the harp.'

'That surprises me.'

'It was not considered necessary for me to dance, only to play.'

He heard the wistful note in her voice and said upon an impulse, 'Then dance with me now. I think I can remember the steps.' She looked up, startled, and he held out his hand. 'You must have seen it performed often enough and will soon pick it up.'

Cautiously she took his fingers and he helped her through the moves. She was light on her feet and quick to learn. Logan guided her around, giving the occasional word of instruction. As her confidence grew, so did her smile and with the music drifting down from the open window, they danced on in the moonlight, laughing when they made a mistake.

All too soon for Logan, the dance ended. When they stopped, he bowed low over her hand.

'Excellently done,' he praised her. 'You learn very quickly.'

'Thank you, Laird.' She dropped him an equally low curtsy. 'I should hesitate to try it in company, but I did enjoy it.'

When she raised her head, he could see she was laughing. The moonlight sparkled in her eyes and he felt suddenly winded. By heaven, she was beautiful!

His hand tightened on her fingers as he felt a sudden desire to kiss her, but when he would have pulled her closer, she resisted him, the laughter dying from her face.

'Sir—'

'My name is Logan,' he interrupted her softly. 'I would be honoured if you would call me by my name.'

'I cannot,' she cried. 'I should not be here. Oh, pray you, let me go. I should never have come outside!'

She was genuinely distressed and he released her immediately.

'You have done nothing wrong, mistress. I assure you.'

She shook her head. The moonlight glinted on the tears trembling on her lashes and his hands went out again.

'Ailsa, believe me—!'

But she was already hurrying away from him.

Logan watched her disappear around the corner of the house but he made no attempt to follow her. He rubbed his chin. It had been nothing more than a dance, a shared moment of innocent pleasure. He had acted purely out of a wish to amuse her, to entertain her. What was there in that to distress her so? He remembered his sudden flare of desire. Perhaps she had seen that in his eyes, perhaps she had guessed how much he wanted to kiss her. If that was the case, then he was sorry for it. He meant her no insult and he would tell her so. He *must* do so, if he had the opportunity, before the evening was out.

He sat down again on the balustrade, a rueful smile twisting his lips. He could not deny the encounter had entertained *him*, too. He felt a little jolt of surprise when he realised it was the first time since Lady Mary had so cruelly rejected him that he had felt a spark of interest in any woman. Not that Ailsa could be likened to Lady Mary Wendlebury, whose fair beauty had been considered by everyone to be incomparable.

How could one favour wild red hair and violet eyes over golden curls and eyes like the loch under summer skies? So blue that a man could drown in them. Who could prefer a slender sylph-like figure to Lady Mary's luscious curves? She danced like an angel, too. He remembered watching her dance the courtly sarabande, her dainty foot peeping out beneath the brocade skirts, a froth of lace at her elbows enhancing the elegant lines of her arms. All London society worshipped her.

His English friends had given up on him, labelled him a lost cause where love was concerned and they were right. Until he met Lady Mary's equal, he would not lose his heart again. Certainly not to the Contullach harper, it was inconceivable.

He was roused from his reverie by the sounds of the *clàrsach* cascading down to him from the open window. Ailsa had resumed her playing, this time a merry reel. It reminded him of his duty. Logan pushed himself to his feet. He should return to the hall if he did not wish to offend his host.

He brushed his hands over the skirts of his frock coat and began to walk back, but when he reached the corner of the house he stopped and looked back at the now empty terrace. What in heaven's name had possessed him to try to flirt with Ailsa? For that was all it could have been, a sudden desire to enjoy a little dalliance with a pretty woman. It had meant nothing, that dance in the moonlight, the touch of hands. The exchange of glances.

Nothing.

Ailsa hurried back into the hall. The fiddlers were playing their final jig and she stood quietly at the side of the room to listen. Her heart was thudding quite painfully in her chest, but that was the exertion of running up the stairs, wasn't it? Nothing to do with recognising the look in Logan Rathmore's eyes. A look that both frightened and excited her, arousing unfamiliar feelings that must be suppressed. She knew all about the temptations of the flesh. The minister preached of it constantly, but until tonight she had not understood how powerful a feeling it could be. To want a man to hold you, to kiss you. She closed her eyes. To do more that she could not even imagine!

A voice hissed in her ear. 'I saw you, flirting with the new Laird of Ardvarrick.'

'Ewan!' Her eyes flew open and she stared into his blotched and angry face. 'I was not flirting, I would never do that!'

'You know what will happen if Fingal finds out you were alone with him.'

She put up her chin. 'I came upon Logan Rathmore by chance and he—he showed me how to dance.'

Ewan's lip curled. 'Is that what it was? I was watching you from the window and I would call it damn close to fornication!'

She flushed and swelled with anger at the injustice of his accusation.

'How dare you! It was nothing of the kind!'

'Fingal will not see it that way.'

Alarm fluttered in her breast. 'You will not tell our uncle!'

'Not if you do as I say.' He picked up a lock of her hair and curled it about his finger. 'You've grown into a fine woman, Ailsa McInnis. I had not seen it until now.'

'Stop that.' She slapped his hand away. 'You are betrothed to Kirstin!'

'That is a different matter.' He leaned closer. 'Leave your door unlocked tonight.'

'I will not!' She heard her name from across the room. 'Fingal is calling for me to play. I must go.'

As she stepped away from Ewan, he caught her arm. 'Let me into your chamber tonight, or I shall tell our uncle what I saw.'

Ailsa shook off his hand. She said scornfully, 'Do so and *I* will tell him of your threats!'

With a toss of her head she returned to the dais, her hands clenched so tight the nails dug into her palms as she tried to calm her rage. How dare Ewan talk to her in that way? There were rumours that he flirted with the women in the village and she had once caught him kissing Peggy, the kitchen maid, but he had never before shown an interest in her. Why should he do so now? Perhaps he thought that because she had been out of doors and alone with Logan Rathmore, she would welcome any man's attentions. The very idea of it made her shudder.

She was a harper. It was what she was born to be. Music was her calling and to allow herself to become attracted to any man would be disastrous. Dancing on the terrace with Logan Rathmore, her pulse racing when he smiled at her, she had come close to forgetting that. She must never do so again.

Taking a few steadying breaths, Ailsa sat down at the harp and ran her fingers over the strings. She longed to play something slow and soothing, but her guests had eaten and drunk well and were in a lively mood. They cried out for more reels and jigs and she must oblige them.

Gradually, as her fingers plucked out the familiar tunes, the music worked its magic, driving away her cares. She was no longer anxious about Logan Rathmore. Why should he notice her when almost every woman in the room was sighing after him? It was only kindness on his part that led him to indulge her in a dance. Most likely he had forgotten all about it now and that was what she must do. He would be returning to Ardvarrick tomorrow and it was unlikely they would meet again for a long time, if ever.

Perhaps Ewan was right and the new Laird would soon return to England. Glancing up, her eyes immediately locked on to Logan Rathmore as he partnered a pretty young woman around the floor. One thing was certain: whether he stayed or not, it would not be long before such a handsome laird would find himself a wife and then he would have no time for being kind to Contullach's harper.

As for Ewan, she would lock her door securely tonight and, if he carried out his threat to tell their uncle, she would deal with that when it happened.

All signs of the night's revelries had been removed when Logan and Tamhas entered the hall the next morning, but few of their fellow guests were present.

'I am not surprised,' muttered Logan, when his cousin remarked upon it. 'The wine and ale flowed freely last night. I wager there will be any number of sore heads today.'

Fingal Contullach was at the head of the table and he invited Logan to sit beside him, that they might break their fast together. Conversation was stilted, but food was plentiful, fresh bannocks served with ham, eggs and cheese, and Logan was content to enjoy his meal in near silence. However, when he would have taken his leave, Fingal invited him to go to his chamber where they might talk in private.

'I have spoken with my kinsmen and tenants regarding the moving of our cattle,' said Fingal, when they were alone.

'Have you now? I thought that meeting would take place after the gathering.'

'Aye, I had planned it that way, but those who mattered arrived early and we were able to discuss your proposal yesterday. We have come to a decision.'

Logan waited. He knew this would not come easy to Fingal Contullach, who was more used to resolving his arguments with violence than compromise.

'We are minded to try your way, for next year,' the older man said at last. 'There are one or two more who need to be consulted, but I am sure they will fall in with our plans.'

Logan nodded. 'Very well. I will get the papers drawn up and when the drovers arrive at the end of the summer they can be instructed to move your beasts with mine through the Bealach na Damh. But I give you fair warning, Contullach. This deal depends upon nothing breaking the peace between our people in the meantime.'

Fingal's fierce eyes met his steadily. 'There'll be no more lifting of cattle if I can help it, Ardvarrick. You have my word on that.'

'That is good enough for me.'

'And you plan to bring the documents for signature in the spring?' Fingal frowned. 'You'll not be thinking to travel here for the Candlemas Quarter Day.'

'February?' Logan shook his head. 'Short days and foul weather make that impractical. However, Beltane should be time enough to have everything signed and sealed before the drovers arrive.' He rose. 'If the weather holds, though, I should like to call at Contullach again before—'

'That you will not!'

The swift rebuttal of his suggestion caused Logan to raise his brows in surprise.

'Oh? I had hoped we might put an end to this eternal feuding between our people.'

Contullach flushed and his chin jutted pugnaciously.

'I am one for plain speaking, Logan Rathmore, and

I tell you the ladies here are inclined to look favourably upon you. Too favourably!'

Logan felt self-conscious colour staining his own cheeks. 'That may be so, but I assure you it was never my intention—'

'It ain't what you *intend*, man, it's the ideas the women get into their foolish heads that is the worry! Ye're a handsome dog, I'll admit it, and your fancy English ways might well turn an innocent lassie's head.'

Logan felt his irritation growing. He had spent the evening dancing and making polite conversation, as any guest should, and this was the thanks he received!

'You may be assured I would not encourage any one of them to lose their heart over me,' he retorted. 'I am not in the market for a wife and so you may tell them. But I take your point, Contullach, and I will stay away until the spring. Then, if all goes well and your people keep to the bargain, I shall return with the agreement drawn up for our signatures.'

Logan left Fingal Contullach and set off to find Tamhas, who had gone on ahead to the stables to make ready the horses. When he reached the outer door, Ewan Cowie was waiting for him.

'A word before ye go, Ardvarrick.' The man stepped in front of him, blocking his way. 'I saw you, last night. On the terrace.'

The tone was belligerent and Logan stiffened, sensing danger.

He said coolly, 'What of it?'

Cowie moved closer. 'I wanted to give you a friendly warning. Do not trifle with Ailsa McInnis.'

'Unnecessary!' Logan's hand went to the hilt of his sword. It was one thing for his host to voice his worries about the women under his protection, but he would not suffer an insult from Ewan Cowie! 'I have already told you it is not my habit to trifle with young ladies.'

Something of his anger must have shown in his eyes, for after a moment Cowie stepped aside.

'I am glad to hear that. Fingal is very fond of his music. It calms him. Soothes his temper. He would not take it at all kindly if he was to lose his harper.'

With no more than a contemptuous look Logan went out, but his thoughts were racing. Everyone was warning him away from Ailsa McInnis and now Cowie hinted at severe reprisals for anyone seducing her. Was the lady so special, or was he merely looking for an excuse to quarrel? Logan could not decide.

'Well?' Tamhas asked him as they rode away from Contullach. 'What did the old man say?'

'Contullach has agreed to sign. Not that I doubted he would. He knows that moving his cattle with ours can only be of benefit to all his people. I have made it conditional upon matters going well between us through the winter. If there are no serious breaches of the peace, then I shall return at the Beltane Quarter Day to sign the agreement with Contullach.'

'Good work, Cousin. This should bring a lasting accord between the clans, because 'tis in all our interests to make this work, is it not?' When Logan did not reply immediately, Tamhas turned to look across at him. 'You are silent, man. What is troubling you?'

'Ewan Cowie.' Logan frowned. 'I cannot be easy about the fellow. I fear he will cause trouble if he can.'

'Nay, Cowie is a hothead, but he is to marry Contullach's daughter next summer. He will not risk the old man's displeasure, at least until the knot is tied.'

'I wish I might share your confidence, Tamhas, but something tells me Ewan Cowie would risk a great deal to do me an ill turn.'

Tamhas laughed and shook his head and Logan said no more. Perhaps he was being fanciful, but he decided he would maintain the patrols watching over the cattle on his land and advise his tenants to remain vigilant. Just in case.

Ailsa kept out of the way until she was sure the Laird of Ardvarrick had left the castle. She had no idea if Ewan had carried out his threat to tell their uncle, but she would not risk encountering Logan Rathmore. Even a look might be misconstrued and bring Fingal's wrath down upon her. She busied herself in the kitchens, then returned to her room where she lost herself in her music and did not emerge again until it was time for dinner.

With most of the guests departed, Fingal and his family were seated at the long table with those that remained and the rest of his household. Ailsa hurried in and slipped into her place, murmuring an apology for keeping everyone waiting. Across the table, Ewan Cowie gave her a bland smile. Hope began to rise. Perhaps he had not said anything after all.

By the time the meal was over Ailsa was feeling much more confident. Talk at dinner had been all about the ceilidh and she held her breath when Ardvarrick's presence was mentioned. Kirstin and Màiri declared that he was indeed a fine dancer, but no mention was made of his absence during the interval and she began to relax.

After dinner Fingal called for the harp to be brought in.

'You will play for us, Ailsa.'

'If you wish, Uncle.'

Màiri giggled. 'If she *can* play!' When Ailsa looked up, she added spitefully, 'We have heard all about you slipping away with the new Laird last night.'

Ailsa looked at Ewan. His smirk told her all she needed to know and her anger rose.

'I did not *slip away* with anyone!' She turned to Fingal. 'I went outside for a little air and Ardvarrick was already there. It was nothing more than a coincidence, Uncle, I swear it.'

'That is not what Ewan told me.'

'Then he lies!' She glared at Ewan, who raised his brows at her.

'Do you deny you were alone out there with Logan Rathmore, flirting with the man?'

'I was not flirting! It was a chance meeting. He showed me how to dance a few steps and then I left him.' Ewan's sneering laugh enraged her still further. 'How dare you accuse *me* of dishonourable behaviour, Ewan Cowie, when you wanted me to buy your silence.' She turned again to address Fingal. 'He said I should leave my door unlocked last night, Uncle. He promised if I allowed him into my room, he would say nothing!'

Kirstin gave a little scream. 'Is that true, Ewan?'

He was quick to deny it. 'She lies, sweeting. She is

trying to shift the blame from herself on to me.' He took Kirstin's hand and went on, his tone as sweet as honey, 'She is jealous of you, Kirstin. She knows I am in love with you and will not even glance at her.'

His earnest manner and soft looks convinced his betrothed. She cast an angry glare at Ailsa, who tried to protest.

'Kirstin, I have never—'

'Enough!' roared Fingal. He waved towards the dais, where Simple Rab had placed the *clàrsach*. 'Play me one of your airs, lassie, and we shall soon see how innocent ye are.'

With a defiant toss of her head Ailsa sat down at the *clàrsach*, but as she ran her fingers over the strings she was assailed by doubts. She might argue that it was nothing more than an innocent encounter with Logan Rathmore, but she could not forget the exhilaration she had felt dancing with him, the little shiver of pleasure that had run up her arm when he had taken her hand, or the way her insides had twisted when he smiled down at her. She had relived the moment over and over again. It was burned into her memory, but was that enough to destroy her gift for music? She knew she was about to find out.

Ailsa took a deep breath, clearing her mind and giving her attention to her fingers as they began to pluck a tune from the silver strings. She relaxed as the familiar music filled the room. As she played, her aunt and Màiri busied themselves with their embroidery, and her uncle leaned back in his chair, listening with his eyes closed. Only Ewan and Kirstin paid no heed to the music. They were sitting together in the corner, whispering and giggling. Ailsa lowered her head again. Far from being jealous, she pitied Kirstin. Ewan might have reassured her this time that he was faithful, but sooner or later his future bride would discover the truth.

Ailsa played on until Ewan took his leave and Màiri and Kirstin drifted away. Only her aunt and uncle remained. She finished her piece and rested her hands against the strings to silence them. Fingal was asleep in his chair and snoring gently.

'I hope, Aunt, that you and my uncle believe now that I have done nothing wrong.'

'Aye, we believe you,' replied Morag, packing away her tambour frame. 'But you must take care, Ailsa. You must always be on your guard. You know the consequences of becoming too friendly with any man, do you not?

'I do, Aunt, and I have no intention of losing my gift for music. It is my life and I want no other.'

Fingal stirred in his chair. 'Aye, well, don't you forget that, lassie.'

'I am not likely to do so, Uncle. It is Ewan Cowie who wants to make mischief.'

'He was trying to protect you, girl. You should be grateful!'

'Grateful!' She gave a gasp of indignation and was about to make an angry retort when she saw Aunt Morag shaking her head at her, warning her to hold her peace.

'Perhaps, Husband, you should drop a hint to Ewan,' Morag murmured with a quick, sympathetic glance towards Ailsa. 'He would do well to remember that he is engaged to our daughter and he will answer to you if he hurts her!'

Chapter Four

Ailsa had no idea what her uncle said to Ewan, but he had clearly said *something*, because for the next few days he was unusually attentive to Kirstin, while pointedly ignoring Ailsa. She was relieved, but still she did not trust him and made sure she was never alone with him.

A week of rain and wind had lashed Contullach, confining everyone to the castle, but at last the storms abated and the sky cleared, promising a few days of dry weather. Ailsa decided to take her harp to the loch, knowing it might be her last opportunity before winter took its grip of the land, so when she heard Fingal making plans with Ewan to ride out the following day, she made up her mind.

She rose early and asked Simple Rab to carry her *clàrsach* out to the stables.

'D'ye want me to come with you, mistress?' he asked as he helped her secure the harp's oilskin case on to the pony.

Ailsa preferred to be alone and, since Ewan would

be safely out of the way, she decided she could manage without the boy's escort.

'Thank you, Rab, but I think not.' She saw his shoulders slump with disappointment and patted his shoulder. 'You will be needed to help in the fields while the fine weather holds,' she told him. 'They cannot do it without you, Rab. You know Mrs Barr depends on you to make sure the vegetables are harvested and stored correctly.'

His round, kindly face lit up with pleasure at her praise and he went off back to the house, a definite swagger in his stride.

Smiling, Ailsa spent a few moments checking the pony's halter and testing the straps that held the harp in place. She was about to lead the pony from the stable when she heard Ewan's voice. She froze, but her panic subsided when she realised he was not entering the stable. The sound of more than one voice was coming in through a narrow slit in the stone wall at the back of the building.

She exhaled with relief. Ewan was talking with his cronies and would not trouble her. He would not even see her leave, as she would be going in the opposite direction. She was about to lead the pony out of the stable when she heard a name that caused her to stop. Instead of leaving, she moved quietly towards the small opening, straining her ears to hear what was being said.

She recognised a voice. It was Donal, a loutish, shambling dolt who was often seen in Ewan's company.

'When do you plan to lift them?'

'It must be soon. 'Tis a pity it cannot be tonight.'

She winced as Ewan cursed. 'Fingal wants me to go with him to visit our kinsman and we'll not be back until the morning. But if we wait much longer there will be no moonlight to aid us. No, if this weather holds, then we must do it tomorrow night, or the next.'

'But why Ardvarrick's own fold?' objected another guttural voice. 'It would be easier to take the cattle from one of his tenants, nearer our own lands.'

'That's where Rathmore will be expecting trouble. If he still has men on watch, that is where he will put them. What he won't anticipate is a raid on his own beasts.'

Ailsa pressed one hand to her mouth. She had not been mistaken. They were talking about Ardvarrick.

'And it will hurt him more,' Ewan went on, his voice dripping with scorn. 'A raid so far inside his lands will show how unfit he is to be Laird. But we go armed and ready for trouble, you understand? Now, I must get back, before Fingal comes looking for me. Remember, he must know nothing of this...'

The voices were fading. She risked peeping out through the opening and saw Ewan and his cronies moving away. She should tell her uncle, but Ewan would only deny it and it would once again be her word against her cousin's. He might also persuade his friends to continue with the raid. Ailsa went back to the pony and stood for a moment, thoughtfully rubbing its nose and trying to decide the best way to foil Ewan's plans. Finally, she untied the reins and led the little animal out into the yard.

Logan handed his reins to Tamhas.

'Take the horses to the stables, if you please. Then

join me in my study. We'll go over the accounts before dinner.'

He stood for a moment, drawing off his gloves and watching his cousin ride away. It had been a good day and surprisingly enjoyable, riding over his land, checking the provisions for the winter. He and Tamhas had also talked to the tenants, explaining how the agreement with Contullach should make them more secure, but reassuring them that he would not be withdrawing his patrols of the outlying pastures and homesteads until he was confident there would be no more raids upon the livestock.

He turned and walked towards the house. The late afternoon sun had turned the pale lime-harled walls pink, while the windows gleamed like gold. The beauty of it caught him unawares and he felt a sudden rush of satisfaction. He had been back at Ardvarrick for a month and he was beginning to settle into his new role as Laird. He grinned, remembering how reluctant he had been to return, but now he was looking forward to his first winter here for ten years.

Logan had enjoyed his travels on the Continent, but looking back he could see that his life in England had settled into a comfortable but aimless pattern. The endless round of balls, card parties and visits to the theatre had been merely an elegant way to pass the days, to keep at bay the ennui of an indolent and indulged lifestyle. Ardvarrick was very different. Every day brought a new challenge. He was responsible for the lives not only of his household, but his tenants. He ran up the shallow steps and into the house. The thought of such responsibility was sobering, but he relished it.

* * *

'So, we are agreed.' Logan tapped the map with his finger. 'We'll drain the southern slopes and plant more barley, and we can build the new barn here.'

'Aye, that will work.' Tamhas nodded. 'And are you wanting me to draw up plans for a new jetty in the loch?'

'I think so. The old one was perfectly adequate in my father's day, but it is too small to handle extra trade. We have timber from our own forests we can cut down for it.' He straightened. 'A good day's work, Cousin. Come into the drawing room and we'll take a glass of wine before we eat. I vow I am so hungry now. I hope Norry has a good dinner for us.'

Tamhas laughed 'Have you ever known her not? I—'

A knock on the door interrupted him.

'There's a young person asking for you, master.' The manservant looked disapproving. 'A female.'

'Is there indeed?' Logan raised his brows. 'What sort of female, William? A lady? Is she young, old?'

The manservant frowned. 'She is so wrapped up that I cannot tell you, master. And she'll not give me her name. From her voice I'd say she's a gentlewoman.'

'A mystery, then.' Logan glanced at Tamhas. 'We are going into the drawing room, William. You may show her in there.'

Logan had given orders that a fire was to be kindled of an evening and the room was warm and welcoming when William showed in their mysterious visitor. She was shrouded in a voluminous striped plaid in shades of purple and green and it was not until she lifted her head and the evening sunlight fell on her face that Logan recognised her. He concealed his surprise and dismissed the manservant before turning to greet her.

'Mistress McInnis. Set a chair for the lady, Tamhas, by the fire, if you please.'

She nodded and said softly, 'Thank you.'

Ailsa pushed the folds of plaid from her head and stood, irresolute. All her attention had been on getting to Ardvarrick as quickly as possible, urging the little pony to an unaccustomed canter for much of the way. Now that she was here, she felt dazed and needed time to collect her thoughts.

Logan Rathmore was holding out his hand to her. 'Will you not remove your *arisaid*, mistress? You will be more comfortable without it.'

Silently she unfastened the brooch and slipped off the plaid, handing it to Logan, who placed it carefully over the back of her chair.

'There. Now sit down and warm yourself.' As she did so, he took a glass of wine from Tamhas and placed it on a little table at her elbow. 'Drink this, when you are ready.'

She ignored the wine and gripped his arm, saying urgently, 'I came to warn you. About Ewan Cowie. He is planning mischief!'

Logan frowned at the dainty fingers clutching his sleeve. 'Tonight?'

'No.' She shook her head. 'Tomorrow, possibly the following night.'

She was very pale, there were dark smudges beneath her eyes and Logan's first instinct was to reassure her. He smiled and covered her hand with his own.

'Take your time and tell us everything.' She was still clutching him tightly and he said gently, 'Mistress McInnis, you are safe here, I promise you. Trust me.'

His calm tone had the desired effect. Ailsa released her grip on his sleeve and folded her hands together in her lap. He waited quietly while she composed herself. Then, haltingly, she told him all she had overheard from the stable. When she had finished, her anxious violet eyes moved from Logan to Tamhas and back again.

She said, 'He wants you to think my uncle is not to be trusted.'

'You have taken a great risk, coming here. Why did you not send a note, or go to Fingal with this?' Logan asked her.

'There are so few people at Contullach I could trust with such a task and certainly no one who would not be missed. As for my uncle—' a faint crease furrowed her brow '—I am not sure he would believe me. Ewan would deny it, or laugh it off as a prank, but it is not, I know he means you harm!' Her hands twisted together in her lap. 'He is against any agreement between you and my uncle.'

'I had already gained that impression,' replied Logan.

She picked up her wine and sipped at it, her hands clasped about the glass as if she did not trust herself to hold it with just one.

'The lifting of cattle is a very old practice,' she murmured. 'I am aware of that and I know it has been going on between clans for generations. My uncle is not entirely innocent and, although he no longer goes out himself, I think he has been turning a blind eye to

Ewan's thieving.' She drew a breath. 'I also believe my cousin has been taking some of the beasts for himself, picking out the strongest and healthiest and moving them to his own lands.'

'What makes you think that?'

'Often, when I am playing in the hall, people say things as they pass. They can be...indiscreet.' Her shoulders lifted a fraction. 'No one pays any heed to a harper.'

'And you think Cowie is playing a double game,' said Logan. 'You think he is lifting my cattle on your uncle's orders, but keeping some for himself.'

'I do.' Her frown deepened. 'But not only from Ardvarrick lands, from my uncle's tenants, too. There have been many reports of cattle going missing.'

Logan's lip curled. 'And, of course, it is easiest to blame the Rathmores!'

'Who would suspect Ewan of thieving from his own kin?' She turned her face up to him, her eyes dark and troubled. 'I have no proof of it, only snatches of conversation. My uncle would want a great deal more from me before he could be made to believe ill of Ewan and his friends.'

'I, on the other hand, have no difficulty in believing ill of them.' Logan smiled grimly. 'I had already decided I would not relax my vigilance just yet, even though the most valuable beasts have already gone to market.'

'But Ewan knows you will be guarding the farms bordering Contullach land. I believe he means to attack your own cattle, the ones you keep closer to this house.'

'The devil he does!' exclaimed Logan. She watched

him exchange a glance with his cousin, 'Fortunately, that is easily remedied. Thank you for warning us of the danger.'

Ailsa acknowledged his thanks with a nod. Her business here was done. She suddenly felt very tired and not a little dispirited. She put down her glass and pushed herself to her feet.

'I should go.'

'Will you not dine with us?' Logan glanced towards the window. 'It will be dark in an hour. You had best wait and ride back when the moon has risen.'

The thought of a hot meal was very tempting and Ailsa hesitated. The Laird decided it for her. He took her silence for acceptance and nodded.

'Good. Tamhas, go and ask Norry to have a third place set at table, if you will, and I will pour Mistress McInnis another glass of wine.'

Tamhas went out and Logan turned back to Ailsa.

'Will you not sit down again, mistress?' He watched her sink down again, her whole demeanour suggesting fatigue. 'You have gone to a great deal of trouble to warn me. One might ask why.'

One small, white hand fluttered. 'I had to do something. I do not want Ewan breaking the peace before it is even begun. He speaks for only a few of my uncle's people, but he could ruin it for everyone.'

'Which I think is his intention,' muttered Logan, drily. 'Who knows of your coming here?'

'No one. I left word that I was going to Loch nan Clàrsairean to practise. I left the *clàrsach* under bushes there so that I could use the pony to ride to Ardvarrick.'

He glanced again towards the window. 'It will be very late when you return.'

'I often practise at the loch until the sun is setting. If anyone should notice my absence, I will say I forgot the time.'

'But surely you will be missed.'

'Oh, no. Fingal is away from home tonight and will not require his harper. No one else at Contullach will *miss* me.' The bleak note in her voice smote him. Did no one value her, save for her musical ability?

He said, 'I will ride back with you.'

'Oh, no! I pray you will not, sir. It is quite unnecessary. I can find my way.'

'Perhaps you can, but I will not allow you to return unaccompanied and in the dark.' His tone was firm to show he would brook no argument. She glared at him, a stubborn set to her mouth that made his own lips twitch. 'Do not look so mutinous, mistress, I am doing this for my own sake as much as yours. If any harm should befall you on the way back to Contullach, the blame would surely be laid at my door.'

He waited, observing her inward struggle, and after a few moments she capitulated with a murmur of thanks.

'Good.' He refilled her wineglass and handed it back to her. 'I shall put you on one of my own horses, too. Your pony will travel faster without you on its back.'

'That is very true. The poor beast is unaccustomed to moving at more than an ambling walk and I pushed him most shamefully to get here.'

She gave him a wan smile, trying to make light of the situation, and his admiration for her grew. The ride here must have been difficult enough, but he could only imagine how long it would take her to get back on the little pony.

Tamhas returned and Logan thought his young guest might feel awkward to be in the company with two men, both relative strangers. He did his best to put her at her ease, but it was when Tamhas joined in, mentioning the recent ceilidh and mutual acquaintances that she truly began to relax. Logan was content to sit back and listen as she chattered away, talking of people and events he did not know or barely remembered from his youth. For the first time he felt a slight pang of regret that he had stayed away so long.

Ailsa sipped at her wine and felt her anxiety lessening. She had arrived at Ardvarrick with only one thought, to warn the Laird, but once inside the house she had become all too aware that it was a much finer building than her uncle's stark castle. Polished wainscoting and oil paintings covered the walls of the entrance hall and the panelled doors were decorated with gleaming brass handles.

She had been shown into the drawing room, where there was more gleaming woodwork and the wide sash windows made the most of the remaining light. She had noted, too, that the room was filled with the most elegant furniture, including the comfortable satin-covered chair where she was now resting. At first such grandeur had threatened to overwhelm her, but the warm fire, the wine and the kind attentions of her companions combined to soothe her nerves and, although she knew she must return to Contullach Castle at some point, she was not sorry to put off the moment of leaving.

When a servant came in to announce that dinner was ready, the Laird rose and held out his arm to her.

As if I was a fine lady, she thought, feeling a warm blush spreading up through her body.

However, even though she had not been reared in such a grand house as this, Ailsa's upbringing had not been totally lacking. She knew what was required of a lady. She rose and placed her fingers lightly on the proffered sleeve, marvelling at the softness of the wool beneath her fingers, but even more aware of the strong arm beneath the cloth. She felt a strange mixture of comfort and excitement when she was with this man. He had asked her to trust him and she did. She knew in her very bones that Logan Rathmore would look after her.

Ailsa had thought the drawing room sumptuous, but the dining room made her stop and catch her breath. The curtains had been pulled across the windows, shutting out the night, and the room glowed with golden candlelight. A long table was covered with such an array of silver that the snowy white cloth was almost obscured. There were no benches around the table, only a set of elegant walnut chairs with padded seats and carved legs. Places had been set at the foot and head of the table, with a third place on one side.

Beside her, she heard Logan give a soft laugh. 'My housekeeper appears to think we need to impress you, Mistress McInnis. You should be honoured, madam, I doubt we could do better if the King himself were to dine with us! However, I would rather not stand upon such ceremony and, if you do not object, Tamhas and I will move the place settings to one end of the table, so we may eat and converse more easily.'

The change was soon accomplished and Ailsa was persuaded to sit at the head of the table, with Tamhas and Logan on either side. The servant's startled look when he returned with the first dishes caused Ailsa to giggle. She stifled it, but not before her host noticed.

'Just so, mistress.' He cast her a look brimming with laughter. 'However, I think we can all agree that this arrangement is much more comfortable.'

The last shreds of reserve fled. They set to work on the dinner with an ease that Ailsa would not have thought possible. Logan and Tamhas served her with the daintiest morsels from the silver dishes and would have refilled her wine glass regularly, if she had not decided it would be wise to drink sparingly.

Logan wanted the conversation to flow as easily as the wine and he was quite prepared to work at it, but it proved unnecessary. Ailsa had a lively mind. She asked him about his time in England and listened avidly as he described to her the London Season with its balls and entertainments. Tamhas was more interested in the sport to be had at his uncle's establishment in Hampshire, which led to a discussion of hunting and fishing before they moved on to his plans for Ardvarrick and the preparations for the coming winter.

'After what you have told us tonight, I shall put an extra guard on the fold,' said Logan, helping himself to more of the venison. 'There are a number of heifers that look promising for breeding next year, is that not right, Cousin?'

'Aye, there are. And I'd not want to lose that bull calf your father bought, either,' Tamhas answered. His face became more serious and he added, 'It was his final purchase before he took to his bed for the last time.'

Ailsa felt the change in the air. She glanced at Logan and was pained by the bleak look in his dark eyes.

She said quietly, 'I am very sorry for your loss, sir, and that you did not get here in time to speak with him before the end.'

'Thank you. The end was quick and that is a mercy.'

He was resting one hand on the table, the fist clenched, and impulsively she reached over and clasped it.

'I am very sorry, truly.'

His eyes fell to where her hand covered his, then he looked up, the ghost of a smile touching his lips.

'I believe you are and I thank you.'

The air changed again. The sorrow was replaced by a tension and something sparked between them, an understanding of loneliness. An affinity that defied explanation, but sent shockwaves through Ailsa.

She quickly withdrew her hand and turned her attention to the food in front of her as she tried to make sense of what had occurred. Nothing tangible, no words, merely a look, a meeting of eyes, but it had set her heart thudding like a wild animal's. Her whole body tingled. She had felt nothing like it before and it frightened her.

'Will ye take more wine, Logan?'

Ailsa almost jumped as Tamhas asked his cousin the question. She stared down at her plate, conscious of the fire in her cheeks. How long had she and Logan been staring at one another? It felt like a lifetime, but surely it could only have been a few moments.

And yet.

Logan was holding his glass out for Tamhas to refill it, talking normally, as if nothing out of the ordinary had happened. She kept her eyes lowered, listening to the two men. It occurred to Ailsa that Logan was consciously deflecting his cousin's attention away from her, giving her time to compose herself. Fanciful nonsense, surely, she told herself, but when at last she felt sufficiently composed to look up again Logan met her eyes, such warm understanding in his own that her world was once again shaken to its core. No one had ever looked at her in that way. No one had ever made her feel so…so alive.

By the time they had finished their meal the moon was already rising over the hills.

'It is time we were leaving,' Logan told Ailsa. 'Your homeward journey will be a long one in the dark. I will send word to the stables and have them look out for my mother's saddle for you.'

She said quickly, 'I would rather ride astride. I have never learned to ride side-saddle.'

She was looking a little self-conscious and he made no comment, merely sent William off with his instructions.

It was less than half an hour later they were ready to depart. Logan escorted Ailsa to the stables and threw her up into the saddle. It took all his willpower to ignore the neat ankle and shapely leg she displayed as she made herself comfortable on the mare. She had been uneasy, constrained, at times during the dinner and he had no wish to make it worse.

After what she had told him of Cowie's plans, Logan arranged for four of his men to accompany them, but apart from a stag and several hinds, they encountered no one as they rode through the moonlit glens to Contullach. Even pushing the horses as fast as they dared, it took them over an hour to reach Contullach land, but Logan barely noticed the time. He enjoyed riding on such a night as this, with the landscape bathed in moonlight and no biting wind to chill the skin. His pleasure was enhanced by the woman riding beside him, straight-backed, at home in the saddle, even with her skirts tucked up in a most unladylike way! She was unusual, this harper of Contullach, and she intrigued him.

They followed the winding track through the woods for another mile until they reached the loch and Ailsa directed him to the spot where she had left her harp, hidden among bushes at the side of the road. She jumped down and ran to retrieve it while Logan fetched the pony and helped her to secure the precious instrument to its back. When she had checked the fastening, she bade him farewell.

'I thank you for your help, sir, but you need not accompany me further. It is but a mile from here to the castle and I have the moon to light my way.'

'I will walk with you until the house is in sight.'

'Truly, there is no need.'

He ignored her protests. Ordering his men to wait

for him, he took the pony's reins and set off along the narrow track that ran between the pine forest and the loch. Ailsa fell into step beside him. They walked in silence, but he was all too aware of the woman at his side, so much so that his skin tingled. Occasionally her fresh, flowery scent came to him on the night air. Whether it was a concoction of the dried seeds and plants stored in her linen press that had scented her clothes or the herbs she used for washing her hair he had no idea, but the fragrance reminded him of a summer's day.

It was so different from the strong, cloying perfumes favoured by the English beauties. He recalled they had been especially pungent in the suffocating heat of the theatre or a crowded ballroom. He put his mind to trying to recall the perfume Lady Mary had used, but strangely it eluded him. He could not concentrate on anything but the moonlight and the dainty figure beside him.

When Ailsa stumbled, he was quick to reach out and catch her. The contact brought a sudden heightening of his senses. The moon shone brighter, the scents of the night, of pine trees and damp earth, were more defined. And Ailsa leaning against him felt like the most natural thing in the world. He was aware of every beat of her heart, of the warmth of her skin, her ragged breathing.

She looked up at him, her eyes shining like stars in the dim light. Only by a supreme effort of will did he resist the temptation to kiss her, but he knew that if he did so he would not want to stop. She was an innocent. She had put herself under his protection and he must not abuse that trust just because the moonlight had made him lose his wits.

Steeling himself against the screaming protests of his body, he set her on her feet.

'Careful now.'

Surprisingly, his voice sounded normal, even indifferent. However, he could not deny himself the pleasure of keeping hold of one dainty hand.

'I will help you,' he said, tucking it into the crook of his arm.

'I am perfectly capable of walking unaided!'

Her independence was entrancing, but he dare not tell her that.

'You have just demonstrated that to be untrue,' he drawled. 'This is no time for stubborn pride, madam.'

She gave a little huff of indignation, but did not pull away from him. They walked on a few yards and her silence was as eloquent as any diatribe. Logan, his momentary weakness now under control, found himself smiling in the darkness.

He said, 'I know you would dearly like to tell me to go to the devil, madam.'

'I should not be so uncivil,' she retorted. 'It is merely that I hardly know you.'

'How so?' he teased her. 'Have you forgotten we danced together on the night of the ceilidh?'

Was it his imagination or did her hand tremble on his arm?

'You are no gentleman to remind me of that, Logan Rathmore!'

'Did you not enjoy it?'

'Yes. No!'

He heard a hissing intake of breath and laughed,

but at the same time his conscience smote him and he said penitently, 'Forgive me, Ailsa McInnis. You are quite right, I should not have mentioned it.'

'No, you should not.' They continued on in silence. Then, 'Let me tell you, sir, that I had quite forgotten all about that encounter.'

Ah, so now it was *she* who could not let the matter drop!

'Had you, now?' A grin tugged at his mouth, but he replied gravely, 'Then I am mightily cast down, mistress, because I cannot forget it. It is etched in my memory for ever.'

'Oh.'

'Yes, indeed,' he continued. 'Because I enjoyed it, very much.'

'You…you did?'

'I did. In fact, I—'

She interrupted him. 'I can see the castle before us.'

They stopped. In the distance he could see the black outline of Contullach Castle against the night sky. Faint lights twinkled from the houses without its walls, but two brighter torches flared on either side of the gates leading into the castle yard.

'This is where we must part.' She pulled her arm free and turned to face him. 'I thank you for your care of me, Ardvarrick.'

He held out the reins to her. 'And I must thank *you* for your warning, Ailsa McInnis. I shall be on my guard now for any raids on my cattle.'

She seemed to struggle with herself. Then she burst out, 'You will take care? What I mean is, I would not have anyone hurt.'

'I can make you no promises, mistress. If Ewan

Cowie is bent on mischief, it may be impossible to avoid it.'

Even in the moonlight he could see she was distressed at his answer. He put the reins into her hands, giving her fingers a comforting squeeze before he stepped back.

'I will do my best to avoid violence, Ailsa, you have my word on that.'

She hesitated, as though she might speak again, but instead she tugged on the pony's rein and hurried off towards the castle.

Logan watched her until she had entered the gates and was lost to sight before he turned away. As he made his way back to his waiting men, he went over the last few moments of conversation they had shared. It was just as well she had stopped him when she did, for he had succumbed to the temptation to flirt with her and she was too innocent to know that. What might she have thought if he had told her how much he had enjoyed that dance in the moonlight? What hopes might it have raised within her breast? Hopes that he could not fulfil because he had left his heart in England.

To mislead her in such a way would not be the actions of an honourable man. It would be the actions of a scoundrel.

Chapter Five

Ailsa coaxed the pony into the stable, where a lamp was burning and in its dim light she noticed someone sleeping just inside the doorway.

'Rab! What are you doing here?'

The young man sat up and stretched. 'I was waitin' for ye, mistress.'

'Has anyone been asking for me?'

She looked about her anxiously and was relieved when he shook his head.

'I knew you'd need my help when you got back,' he told her with simple pride.

'That was very clever of you, Rab, thank you.'

Once the pony had been settled in its stall, she watched Rab pick up the harp and asked him to carry it to her room. They met no one on the stairs and Ailsa was hopeful that her long absence would have gone unnoticed. She had told Ardvarrick that no one would miss her and that was true: when Fingal was away, she was left very much to her own devices, her aunt and cousins having little interest in music. They were content for her to keep to her room, or to join the women servants who gathered in the warm kitchens on winter nights.

Her thoughts returned to the dinner she had shared at Ardvarrick. She knew the two men were only being polite because they were grateful for her warning, but they had made her feel welcome, not merely useful. It was a short step from the dinner to thinking about Logan escorting her back to Contullach. Riding through the dark with the moon rising over the trees had been strange enough, but when the Laird had accompanied her on the final part of their journey and they had walked alone towards Contullach, Ailsa had been beset by unfamiliar and disturbing emotions.

She had wanted Logan Rathmore to think her strong and capable, but then she had been foolish enough to trip up. She would never forget how he had caught her, his grip firm yet gentle. She remembered the scent that had assailed her as she leaned against him. Not just the familiar mix of soap and leather and wool, but something specific to the man himself. It had assaulted her senses and rocked her even more off balance. She had found herself wound tighter than a harp string, breathless as she tried to steady her nerves and regain her composure.

She quickly shed her clothes and slipped into her night shift. How right her aunt was to say she must be wary of all men. She had liked Logan Rathmore's company from the first. She had thought they could be friends, but she knew now that was not possible. One moment she was enjoying his teasing banter then, without warning, a look or a touch would leave her breathless and she would feel an almost overwhelming desire to throw herself into his arms.

Just the thought of it made Ailsa feel hot. She went over to the window and opened it, resting her chin on her arms as she stared out. Sailing high above in the clear sky, the moon cast harsh black shadows across the blue-grey landscape. Somewhere in the far distance Logan and his men would be making their way back to Ardvarrick, but everything within her view was still and silent.

A new tune began to form in her head, soft and sweet. A lullaby, perhaps. A soothing melody inspired by the night. Smiling, she shut the window and tried to hum a few bars as she slipped into her bed, but it was as yet too imprecise. She needed to relax, to let the music form in her head as she went over her journey back to Contullach tonight. Of walking beside a tall and handsome man, whose eyes glowed in the moonlight and whose touch made the blood sing in her veins. Smiling to herself, she cradled her cheek against her hand and closed her eyes.

Not a lullaby, a love song.

In the morning, no one mentioned Ailsa's prolonged absence. She breathed a sigh of relief over that, but her more pressing concern now was to discover if Ewan meant to carry out his plan to plunder Ardvarrick. To this end she made sure she was in the parlour with the ladies to await her uncle's return.

'Come and sit you down by the fire, Husband. You are looking exhausted.'

Morag fussed about him and Kirstin added another cushion to his chair while Màiri brought him a tankard of ale.

'I am,' he replied. 'Tired as a dog.'

'I think 'tis time you left these journeyings to the younger men,' Morag suggested

'Aye, Father, Ewan could have done it on his own,' said Kirstin. 'After all, this time next year we will be married and he will be your son and heir.'

Ailsa said nothing, but she was watching Fingal carefully and saw the tightening of his jaw.

'I know he is to be your husband, lass. 'Tis why I take him with me when I make my visits, but I vow he shows little interest in the running of Contullach. I wanted him to come back and go through the rents with me tonight, but he has gone off on his own business.'

'Oh.' Kirstin looked up, surprised. 'He did not return with you?'

'Some tale of Castle Creag needing his attention.' His scowl deepened. 'Lord knows what it can be, the last time I saw it the place was almost a ruin!'

'Aye, Husband, and you have been pressing him to refurbish his old home in readiness for his taking a bride.' Morag shook her head at him. 'Fie on you, sir, sometimes I think there's no pleasing you! There is time yet for him to learn your ways.'

'And he'll have ideas of his own for what he wishes to do here,' muttered Kirstin, but Fingal was talking to his wife and did not hear her.

Sitting quietly in one corner, Ailsa listened and grew anxious. She had no doubt that Ewan and his friends were going to Ardvarrick. She wondered now if she had been foolish to warn the Laird. A sudden and unexpected raid would result in the loss of a few cattle, but if Logan Rathmore was lying in wait, then there could be bloodshed. She shivered at the thought, but it was too late to do anything now. She could only sit and wait.

Two days later Ailsa was wakened by a hasty banging on her door.

'Up you get, Ailsa, I need you to help me in the kitchen!' She opened her eyes to find Jeanie Barr standing over her. 'The mistress has given leave for Peggy to go and stay with her sister, who has been brought to bed of a baby girl. Which would be all very well if Ilene had not slipped on the stairs and cut her head last night. It is that sore this morning the girl is fit for nothing save the simplest of tasks.'

'I will help you by all means.' Ailsa jumped out of bed and reached for her clothes. 'Although you know I have had little practice in the kitchen.'

'You have a quick mind and will soon pick it up. Another pair of hands is what I shall need most today.'

Ailsa dressed quickly and made her way to the kitchens, glad of the distraction. Keeping busy might give her something to think about other than Ewan stealing Ardvarrick cattle.

It was late morning and she was making girdle scones when she heard Jeanie exclaim sharply, 'Mercy me, what in heaven's name has happened to ye, Ewan Cowie?'

She looked round quickly. Kirstin was guiding a rain-soaked Ewan through the doorway. His two friends followed, looking equally dishevelled.

'They were attacked on their way to Castle Creag,' Kirstin explained, tearfully. 'We need to clean them up and then we must find something for their cuts and bruises, Jeanie.'

The older woman was already inspecting Ewan's bloodied brow.

'Tincture of yarrow will do it,' she declared, wiping her hands. 'Now sit ye down over there, the three of you, and Mistress Kirstin can find a cloth for you to dry your faces while I fetch the jar.'

'Ailsa can help me,' said Kirstin.

'That she will not,' retorted Jeanie. 'She is watching the scones for me and, if I am not mistaken, that first batch needs to come off now, before they burn!'

Ailsa quickly turned back to the fire and busied herself with moving the scones from the girdle on to a rack to cool. From her brief glance, all three men looked to be badly bruised. Consistent with a beating, she thought, but at least none of them was seriously hurt. She listened intently as Kirstin demanded why they had not returned yesterday.

'We would have done so,' muttered Donal, one of the three, 'only they turned our horses loose. It took us most of the day to catch them.'

'Aye,' added Ewan, 'and then it came on to rain, so it was as black as pitch. It took us all the night to get back.'

'Villains!' exclaimed Kirstin. 'What a trick to play, with you all so beaten and sore.'

'Whisht, lassie, you should be thankful they escaped so lightly,' retorted Jeanie, coming back in at that moment with a small stone jar in her hands. 'It surprises me they did not take the horses to sell.'

'And you have no idea who did this, Ewan?' Kirstin persisted. 'Did you not recognise any of them?'

'I've already told ye, no.'

'It must have been Ardvarrick's men,' she continued. 'Who else would do such a thing? Father will have something to say about it—'

Ewan stopped her, saying hastily, 'No, no, there is no need to trouble Fingal with this.'

'But he must be told of it!'

'And I say he does not!' snapped Ewan. 'I forbid any of you to mention it to Fingal. Coll and Donal will be leaving as soon as Mrs Barr has applied her lotions so Fingal won't see them. And I shall say my horse threw me.'

'But, Ewan—'

'Do not fuss me, woman. It was not so very serious.' He glared around the kitchen. 'You are none of ye to mention this, is that understood?'

'Well now, I wonder what mischief those boys have been up to?' mused Jeanie, when she and Ailsa were alone again in the kitchen.

'Did you not believe them?'

'If those three were attacked, I'd wager they deserved it,' retorted the older woman. 'If I am honest with you, Ailsa, I would not trust any one of them out of my sight and so I tell you!'

Secretly Ailsa agreed with her. She was convinced they had tried to lift cattle from Ardvarrick. Their temper suggested they had failed and taken a beating, but at what cost to those on guard at Ardvarrick? Her stomach gave a sickening lurch. Had Logan been hurt? The questions rolled around in her head, causing Jeanie to scold her when she allowed the next batch of scones to scorch.

'Heaven knows but you are in a dream today, madam! Head full of music, I don't doubt. Och, away with you, girlie, out of my way now. I shall do better without ye!'

She flapped her hands and Ailsa went away, as she was bid. It was raining too hard to go out of doors so she took her harp up to the little solar to practise, but even then she could not concentrate. Her mind kept wandering to the day she had found Logan in this very room. She remembered how he had read to her from his book. And it was not only the poems, she had enjoyed the way Logan read the words, his voice smooth and melodic, wrapping around her like a warm cloak. Her mind kept wandering back over that encounter even while her fingers plucked at the strings and by the time hunger drove her back to the hall for dinner, she realised she had played only old, familiar tunes and worked at none of the newer pieces at all.

When everyone was gathered for the meal, Ailsa held her breath when Fingal drew attention to Ewan's battered face, but he accepted his nephew's explanation that he had taken a tumble from his horse on the way home from Castle Creag. Ewan responded in vague terms when Morag asked him about the work to be done there and Kirstin, anxious to deflect attention away from her betrothed, quickly changed the subject. Nothing else was said of it and Ailsa thought it was unlikely she would ever know the truth.

When the meal was over the family went into the parlour, but they had barely closed the door when it opened again and a servant came in.

'A messenger from Ardvarrick has delivered this.'

Ailsa did not miss Ewan's sudden wariness. He moved towards the fire, his eyes regularly darting towards Fingal as he took the letter and read it.

At last Fingal grunted and handed the paper to his wife. 'Here. He addresses both of us, but you may have it, Morag. Damned fop, to be fussing over trifles, I'd not have sent a man out to spend a full day riding in this weather merely to thank us for our hospitality.'

Morag smiled. 'Do not be so hard on the new Laird, Fingal. It was a fine, gentlemanly thing to do.'

'Nay, I agree with my uncle,' cried Ewan. 'No *real* man has time for such niceties. That's for his wife, when he has one.'

Fingal chuckled. 'Now he is Laird, I've no doubt Logan Rathmore may well be taking a wife before too long.'

'She will not be anyone we know,' said Morag. 'Ardvarrick is not a poor man and, with his upbringing he will want a bride from the first circles of society.'

Ailsa felt her aunt's eyes upon her. She knew Morag would be thinking of the ceilidh and Ailsa's dance on the terrace with the new Laird. If her aunt was trying to warn her that nothing could come of such a brief encounter, it was unnecessary. Ailsa was well aware that she was no fit bride for Rathmore of Ardvarrick.

'Mayhap he will take an Englishwoman, like his mother,' put in Ewan, his lip curling in contempt. 'Rathmore has grown soft with his southern living. He'll not stay long in the north and good riddance to him, I say.'

He was smiling, his confidence clearly restored, and conversation moved on. Ewan was so much at his ease, teasing Kirstin and laughing with Fingal, that Ailsa began to wonder if she could have been mistaken in him. Perhaps he had not ridden to Ardvarrick and had been telling the truth about being attacked. After all, young men were prone to exaggerate, weren't they? It was possible what she had overheard had been nothing more than bluff and bluster. However, she could not quite bring herself to believe that and was still trying to decide upon the matter when she retired to bed.

Ailsa went quickly to her room, but it was not until she crossed to the bed that the light of her candle fell on the small folded paper lying on her pillow. She snatched it up, noting the single letter A on the front before she broke the plain seal. At first the words danced before her eyes and she had to read it again to make sense.

Mischief makers sent away with nothing but bruises to show for their trouble. I doubt they will try again. No harm done here and nothing taken. A thousand thanks.

She sat down on the edge of her bed, staring at the writing. There was no signature, nothing to indicate the sender, but it could only be from Logan. Relief flooded through her, together with a sudden elation and she wanted to laugh out loud. The polite message to her aunt and uncle had been a ruse to send a man to Contullach and let her know what had happened. She closed her eyes and pressed the paper to her breast.

The note must be destroyed, of course. She dared not keep it, any more than she dared think too much about the writer. She did not need Morag's warning to tell her the Laird of Ardvarrick was not the man for her. Why, she could not even ride a horse properly. She had seen the look of surprise on his face when she had refused to use the lady's saddle and how he had turned away after throwing her up on to the horse. She had no accomplishments, save her harp-playing, and she would not even have that if she married.

No, at Contullach she was valued. She had a purpose. Much better that she concentrate on her music and forget all about Logan Rathmore.

The last flush of autumn gave way to bitter winter. The ladies of Contullach remained indoors for the most part, wrapped up warmly against the cold draughts and the icy chill that lingered in every corner of the stone building. They spent their days and the long dark evenings in the parlour, while the menfolk preferred the hall, where they did not need to mind their language and might enjoy more boisterous entertainments.

Whenever Ewan was present Kirstin kept to his side like a leech, glaring at Ailsa as if daring her to come between them. For her part, Ailsa was glad Ewan had little opportunity to speak to her. She misliked the way he stared when she was entertaining the family with her music and she was at pains to avoid his company.

Winter tightened its hold. Snow covered the mountains and gradually moved down to the lower slopes until even the most sheltered glens were white with frost. Ailsa threw herself into her music. She could no longer take her harp to the loch and the old solar was too cold so she played in her room, practising old favourites and working on new ones, such as the lilting tune that she thought of secretly as 'Ardvarrick's Air'.

She heard no mention of Logan Rathmore, but she

could not forget him. His voice and his handsome face haunted her dreams, even more so as spring approached and she remembered he had promised to call again upon her uncle. There had been no news of a marriage at Ardvarrick and she thought they would have heard if the Laird had taken a bride. Not that she had any hopes in that direction, of course, but she had liked the man and wanted to see him again.

As the days warmed and lengthened, Ailsa's spirits lifted. She hummed merry tunes as she went about her business in the castle and there were occasional April days when it was fine enough for her to take her harp to Loch nan Clàrsairean. There she could allow the calm beauty of the hills and the water to inspire her music. Her aunt insisted again she should not venture out alone and Ailsa agreed to take Rab, aware that Ewan Cowie was still casting resentful looks in her direction.

She hoped, when Logan Rathmore called again, Fingal would allow her to play for the company. Even though she must keep her distance from the Laird, she remembered how much he had enjoyed her music and she wanted to play for him, to see the warm light of approval in his eyes. She knew her uncle too well to mention the matter, but as the time approached for Ardvarrick's visit she found her hopes growing, only to have them dashed when Fingal told her she would not be at the castle for the Laird's visit.

'Not be here?' Ailsa frowned at him. 'I do not understand.'

'The village women are off to the shieling at Beltane and you are going with them,' Fingal told her.

'No need to look so down-hearted, lass, it is a chance for you to spend time in the hills and enjoy the fine weather.'

'But...but what of my music?'

'It will do you no harm to practise other skills for a few weeks,' said her aunt, smiling. 'You will return to us, and to your harp, refreshed.'

'Who will play for you, while I am away?' She looked at her uncle. 'How will you amuse your visitors?'

'Old Iain will be here. He can entertain us with his fiddling.'

It was only then that Ailsa realised how much she had been looking forward to seeing Logan Rathmore again.

She said, recklessly, 'I could remain, at least until Ardvarrick has been here to see you. I could join the women once he has gone.'

She knew immediately she had made a mistake. Fingal's face darkened.

'I will not have you here, flaunting yourself before young Rathmore, and that is final! Now get ye to bed, girl, and let us hear no more about it.'

Her cheeks on fire, Ailsa fled to her room, where she paced the floor, her hands clenching and unclenching in anger and bitter disappointment. She wanted to scream and rant. In frustration she swept up the pewter cup beside her bed and hurled it at the wall, where, apart from splattering water on the floor and denting the rim, it did little damage. However, it did relieve her feelings and she threw herself down on her bed, burying her face in the pillow to stifle her angry muttering.

Her initial rage had calmed by the time someone

entered the room. She felt a gentle hand on her shoulder and heard her aunt's voice.

'Do not take it so hard, my dear. Your uncle is concerned for your well-being.'

'How could he say such things?' Ailsa whirled. 'I would never flaunt myself! I only want to play for the Laird.'

'Are you sure that is all you want? Be warned, Ailsa, Fingal had it from the man himself that he does not want a wife.' Morag sighed. 'But it is not merely Logan Rathmore we must consider. You have grown into a very pretty young woman, Ailsa. Other men have noticed you, including my nephew. That, in turn, has distressed Kirstin.'

Ailsa sat up. She said stiffly, 'I am sorry for that, Aunt, but I cannot help it. I avoid Ewan whenever I can.'

'I know, my dear, but we must face facts. You are nineteen now. A woman. Many men will be tempted by you. That is of great concern to your uncle. He is anxious for you.'

'He should not be! I know my duty. I know full well what will befall me if I—if I *succumb* to any man's attentions. You may be sure I have no intention of doing so.'

Smiling, her aunt sat down on the edge of the bed. 'Alas, my dear, sometimes one's feelings can be far stronger than any duty. In the spring it's not only the animals who are moved to find a mate. Believe me, you will be safer at the shieling with the womenfolk.'

Her temper cooling, Ailsa acknowledged the truth of her aunt's words with a sigh. 'Must I go?'

'Yes, you must. Not merely for your own sake, but

Kirstin's.' Her aunt stopped and folded her hands together in her lap. 'She has set her heart upon marrying Ewan and will not rest until she is his wife. Your uncle wants it, too. He has always regarded Ewan almost as a son.'

'And you do not?' Ailsa had not missed the heartbeat's hesitation.

Morag would not meet her eyes and appeared to choose her next words with care.

'I grant you he is a little wild, but it is a good match for Kirstin. Ewan has land of his own, even if Castle Creag is in need of some repair. With that, and what he will inherit from Fingal, his lands will be second only to Ardvarrick in this area. As his wife, Kirstin will want for nothing. And once they are married, Ewan will settle down.'

Ailsa did not believe that and she guessed her aunt felt the same, but neither of them could say so. Morag continued.

'Fingal and I are agreed that if you are away at the shieling for the summer, it will give Kirstin and Ewan time to grow closer.'

Ailsa nodded miserably. She did not want to go away, but neither did she want to come between Kirstin and her betrothed.

'When do I leave?'

'Beltane. The first day of May. When the women take the cattle up to the higher ground for the summer grazing you will go with them. You must leave your music behind, but I think you will have little time to miss it. You will be busy with making butter and cheese, spinning, looking after the children—oh, there are so many things for you to learn, Ailsa. Fingal

is convinced that a period away from your harp will have you pining to return to it.'

'He is right,' muttered Ailsa, already growing cold at the prospect.

'And perhaps,' continued her aunt, 'when you see how hard they work, you will realise how you have been blessed by this gift for music. Harpers are much respected. It means you can lead a life of comfort and ease.' She reached out and touched Ailsa's face. 'And a little more sunshine will put the colour back in your cheeks, my dear. You have grown very pale this winter.' She rose. 'Now. You must get some sleep. To-morrow Rab will escort you to the shieling with the other women. Jeanie Barr will take care of you while you are there.'

Ailsa nodded and resigned herself to her fate. It would not be so very bad if she was with Jeanie Barr— the widow had proved herself a good friend in the years since Ailsa had lost her mother.

I must make the best of it, she thought as she pre-pared to go to bed. *I will work hard and enjoy the novelty of being with the women, doing things other than music.*

As she settled down to sleep she uttered up a final hope that she would be too busy to think about the Laird of Ardvarrick.

Chapter Six

The small calf was lying beside the path, its thin
flanks heaving. Ailsa crouched beside it, saying en-
couragingly, 'Come, sweeting, up you get. Just another few yards.'

Jeanie plucked at her sleeve. 'Come away, Ailsa,
we have tarried too long here. She was a late baby
and by rights should not have survived this long. She
is too weak for the journey. It cannot be helped. You
must leave her.'

Ailsa straightened, but remained standing over the
calf. She shook her head. 'No. Rab will carry her. You
could do it, could you not, Rab, if I carry your pack
for you?'

He took off his bonnet and scratched his head. 'Aye,
I could, I suppose,' he said doubtfully. 'If 'tis what ye
want, Miss Ailsa, but my pack's fair heavy, mind.'

'I have been shifting the *clàrsach* back and forth
since I was a child, I will manage,' she replied with
great determination. 'I will not leave this poor creature here to starve.' She waved the older woman away.

'We will be obliged to stop often, Jeanie, so you go on with the others. We do not want to hold you back.'

'I do not like to leave you, Ailsa.'

'Whisht, now. We will not be far behind and what harm can come to me walking up the shieling track? I have Rab with me, too. We will be safe enough.' She hugged Jeanie and kissed her cheek before giving her a little push. 'Off you go now. It is not that far and we will have the wee beastie on the high pasture with the others before sunset, I promise you.'

Jeanie hurried away to catch up with the other women walking up the hill and Ailsa turned back to her companion.

'Very well, Rab. Give me your pack and we will be on our way!'

But although Ailsa carried Rab's bag on her shoulders, it was slow going, even along the valley bottom. By the time they began to climb away from the burn and up the hill path to the summer pastures, everyone else was out of sight. The track was well worn and covered in stones and they had not gone far when Rab stepped on a loose rock and stumbled. The lad recovered, but Ailsa could see he was sweating profusely and she touched his arm.

'We should bide here a while, Rab.'

He did not argue, but put the calf down carefully and they sat beside it, allowing the fresh breeze to cool them. It was then that Ailsa saw two riders in the valley. A frisson of excitement went through her. They were coming from the western end of the glen, the most direct route from Ardvarrick to Contullach. She put a hand up to shield her eyes and stared at the figures as they cantered along beside the burn. Very few of her uncle's people owned horses and she knew Fingal was expecting the Laird to call any day.

Rab had also seen them and he said anxiously, 'Who is it, Mistress Ailsa?'

'It is Logan Rathmore and his man Tamhas,' she said, trying to keep her voice calm. 'They must be on their way to Contullach for the meeting with my uncle. Keep still, Rab, perhaps they will not see us and ride on.'

She knew it was a vain hope. The men could not fail to spot them on the exposed hillside. She felt a little guilty, as if she had deliberately put herself in the Laird's way, but what could they do, short of diving off the path and hiding in the heather?

Ailsa knew the moment Logan Rathmore saw her, for he checked his horse and soon the two men turned off their track and crossed the burn to ride up towards them.

'Mistress McInnis!' Logan called to her as he approached. 'Is anything amiss, can I be of assistance?'

When she did not reply he dismounted and handed the reins to Tamhas before scrambling up the rocks and on to the track. She moved away.

'Pray continue on your way to Contullach, sir. My uncle will be waiting for you.'

'I am sure he would not wish me to abandon his niece without attempting to help.'

His smile set her heart fluttering, just as it had last year. She recalled her aunt's words, that feelings could be stronger than duty. It was her duty now to assure the Laird of Ardvarrick that she did not need assistance. It was her duty to send him on his way. She should do so. She *must* do so.

She remained silent.

Logan knelt down beside the calf. 'What have we here?'

'The wee beastie canna walk up to the shieling,' offered Rab, responding to the friendly question. He added proudly, 'I've been carrying her.'

'They said to leave her,' Ailsa explained. 'But there's no grazing left here and I know she will recover, once we get her to the higher pastures.' She glanced fleetingly at Logan and flushed. 'I could not leave her to starve for want of a little effort.'

'No, indeed. I will take her for you. We can put her across my saddle.'

'What? No! We will manage well enough.' Ailsa was panicking now. 'Rab, get up, we must be on our way.'

'No, I insist. Rab, stay there while I fetch my horse.'

Ailsa was mildly annoyed that the simple lad recognised the voice of command and remained where he was while Ardvarrick ran nimbly back to his companion. She watched him lead his horse up the stony incline to re-join them on the track.

He turned to Rab. 'Now, lad, the calf knows you, so it would be best if you held her. Up you get and I will pass the poor creature up to you.'

Ailsa knew she should object, but Rab was already scrambling up into the saddle, highly delighted with this rare treat. Once the calf was safely laid across the boy's lap, Ardvarrick insisted on shouldering Rab's pack, then he took the reins and invited Ailsa to lead the way. She made one last, half-hearted protest.

'But my uncle is expecting you.'

'I have told Tamhas to go on and give my apologies.' She could not prevent a little gasp of alarm and he gave her a reassuring smile 'Have no fear, mistress, he will merely say I have been delayed. Tamhas will be discreet.'

Ailsa could not deny that the horse would carry the calf up the hill much more quickly and easily than she and Rab could ever manage, so she accepted the inevitable and turned to walk alongside Logan Rathmore.

'I should thank you for your efforts,' she told him.

'You should,' he replied gravely, 'but I can see it is causing you some difficulty.'

She choked back a laugh. 'I *am* grateful, sir, but I am also conscious that you should not be doing this.'

'Why not?'

She hesitated, then decided it would be best to be honest.

'Because Fingal is sending me to the shieling to keep me out of your way.'

'Does he think me such a danger, then?' He glanced back at Rab, then asked her quietly, 'Did Contullach learn of your coming to Ardvarrick last September?'

'No, no one knows of that.' She flushed a little. 'Fingal does not want my head turned by you.'

'I am flattered he thinks so highly of me.'

'Or by any man,' she added quickly. 'I am a harper. Music is my life,' she added, so there could be no misunderstanding, 'to the exclusion of everything else.'

'Except helpless animals.'

'Now you are making fun of me!'

'No, no, I assure you I am not. I admire your efforts to save the calf. I presume everyone else had given up hope?'

'The weakest animals starve in the winter, I know

that, but this calf has survived thus far, so I know she is a fighter.'

'Then we shall get her there.'

She stopped 'I cannot have you do this for my sake!'

He slanted a wry look at her. 'Put down those hackles, mistress, and keep moving. I have cattle of my own. Every animal is an investment for the future. As you know full well.' He lowered his voice so only she could hear him. 'Why else would you have come to warn me of that impending raid last year?'

It was a rhetorical question and she was glad he did not require an answer. It was true she wanted to maintain the peace between Ardvarrick and her uncle, but that had not been the principal reason she had made such efforts to warn him. That was something she could not admit, even to herself.

He said, 'Perhaps this will go some way to repay the debt I owe you.'

'There is no debt,' she said fiercely. 'I did what was right. I did not want your agreement with my uncle to fail.'

Mentioning Fingal brought back Ailsa's worries. He would be furious when he learned of this encounter, but it was too late to do anything about that now.

They walked on in silence for a while, Ardvarrick leading the horse carrying Rab and the calf along the rocky path. It was a crisp, sunny day and the Laird seemed to be enjoying himself, humming softly as he went.

'I know that tune,' she said, when she recognised one particular melody. 'I play it often.'

'Do you? It is well known in the Isles, I believe.'

'It is.' Ailsa nodded. 'My father's family came from the Isles.'

'But it was your mother who taught you to play? She was Contullach's harper, too, was she not?'

'Yes, but that was before I was born. She died when I was a baby.' Ailsa did not wish him to offer sympathy so she continued quickly, 'It was her sister—my aunt—who taught me, at first. When it was seen I had the gift, I went first to a family in Dingwall and then my uncle sent me to Skye, to study with the finest harpers.'

'Their teaching is rewarded. You play very well.'

'Thank you. However, it is the only thing I know how to do.'

'Do not forget you told me you could read and write.'

'I can,' she conceded. 'And I can reckon a column of figures, but I know little else that is of any practical use in running a household. That is another reason I am going to stay with Jeanie Barr at the shieling, to learn such things.'

In the past few days Morag has told her many times how fortunate she was and it was so, Ailsa knew it. There was no denying she loved her music, but recently she had been aware of a growing dissatisfaction, a feeling that there was something missing from her life. Quickly she pushed the thought aside and sought to turn the conversation away from herself.

'You must find life at Ardvarrick very strange, after England.'

'It is certainly different.'

'You do not like it here?' He had spoken lightly, but she had detected a bitterness in him.

'It is not a question of liking. My father left me Ardvarrick and all the responsibility that comes with it.'

She sighed. 'Then we are both of us bound by our duty.'

'We are, but that is not to say duty must be unpleasant. On days such as this, there is nowhere better.'

Ailsa nodded. If she had not been ordered to go with the women and children to the shieling today, she would have taken the *clàrsach* to the loch, adding her music to the sigh of the wind, the song of birds. She would have played to the accompaniment of the gentle lap of water against the shore.

A sudden ache of regret welled up that it would be months before she would be able to return to her harp. Perhaps Fingal was wise to send her away, perhaps he knew it would convince her that without her music she was nothing.

'You are silent,' he interrupted her thoughts. 'Do you not agree with me?'

'On the contrary. There is nothing I enjoy more than being out of doors on a sunny day.'

'It is even better when one can spend it in good company.'

He smiled down at her and she felt a familiar flutter of alarm. She had to remind herself that Logan Rathmore had been schooled in Edinburgh and lived ten years in England. He was Laird of Ardvarrick, a man of considerable wealth and power. What would he want with a female who had seen so little of the world? She had nothing to offer him, except perhaps a flirtation to pass the time and that could prove dangerous, at least for her.

Your worries are foolish, Ailsa. He has asked you for nothing. As long as you keep a guard on your heart there can be no harm in talking with him.

The tiny whisper of rebellion would not be silenced. Worse, she wanted to believe he liked her company. So she returned his smile and decided to enjoy this time, ruthlessly quelling the positive clamour of voices in her head that warned her there could be a great deal of harm in it.

The sun was low by the time they reached the huddle of low buildings that provided summer quarters at the shieling. Smoke was already issuing from some of the bothies and it was quiet, most of the children already sleeping after their long walk. Jeanie Barr was standing at an open doorway and as soon as she saw Ailsa, she hurried towards her.

'The Lord be praised you are here, lass. I was about to set out in search of you.'

She was frowning at Logan Rathmore, but the Laird appeared unaware of her disapproval. He held the calf while Rab dismounted, then watched as the lad carried it away to join the other cattle. Only then did he turn back to address Jeanie.

'You must be Mistress Barr. My apologies, madam, if our late arrival caused you concern.'

Ailsa noted with amusement that her friend was in no way immune to that charming smile. Jeanie shook her head and tried to look stern, but she was blushing like a young girl.

'Aye, well, Ailsa is here now and that is all that matters.' She folded her arms. 'I suppose you'll be needing supper?'

His smile grew. 'I confess a bite to eat would be welcome, mistress.'

'You had best come away in, then. 'Tis only the bannocks and goats' cheese I brought with me,' she continued, ushering them inside. 'I've not had time yet to get the broth pot on the fire.'

'I shall be glad to share whatever you have,' he told her. 'But only if there is sufficient. I'd not have you go short.'

Jeanie gave him a baleful look. 'And I'll not have it said anyone was turned away from my table, Logan Rathmore.'

Ailsa wondered if the Laird would take offence at her friend's speech, but at that moment he met her eyes and she saw only warm amusement in his own.

Ailsa would never forget sharing a meal in the small dark bothy with Jeanie and Logan Rathmore. She struggled to eat the food on her plate, her stomach knotted with nerves. She reminded herself that she had dined with him and his cousin at Ardvarrick, but somehow this felt much more intimate and even Jeanie's presence as chaperon made little difference. It was not that the Laird paid her any special attention, he addressed most of his remarks to Jeanie, but his very presence unsettled her. She wanted him to go, but as the evening wore on another worry surfaced and by the time they had finished eating, she felt compelled to speak.

'The light is fading rapidly now and the path will be treacherous in the dark. Is that not so, Jeanie?'

The older woman pressed her lips together. She

looked at Ailsa for a long moment, then finally she nodded.

'Aye, it will be dangerous to set out now.' She sighed, making it plain she would rather their guest did not stop the night but felt obliged to offer hospitality. 'We will find room for you in the old bothy, if you do not mind sharing quarters with Simple Rab. He is a good lad and quite harmless.'

'Thank you, that will suit me well enough.'

Jeanie pushed herself to her feet. 'Then if you have finished your meal, I will take you across now and show you where you can stable your horse for the night. Ailsa, you will stay here and clear away.'

Logan rose and followed Jeanie, but at the door he stopped and glanced back.

'Perhaps I shall see you in the morning?'

Ailsa turned away. All evening she had been praying for him to leave, but now the moment had come she would give anything to keep him with her a little longer, but he must never know that.

She said, 'I fear not, sir. There is much to be done here.'

'Then I will bid you goodnight, Mistress McInnis.'

She kept her back to him, unable to trust herself to reply and after a moment she heard the door close. He was gone.

'Well, he is settled,' said Jeanie, when she returned a short time later. 'though I doubt the Laird is accustomed to sleeping on a heather mattress. And I found him a blanket, too.' She scowled. 'Which I would not have to do if he'd only wear the plaid like a proper man.'

Ailsa did not think there was anything unmanly

about Logan Rathmore. True, his leather top boots might be more suited to a town gentleman and they were beginning to show signs of wear after the long winter's use, but the dark riding jacket was serviceable enough and fitted smoothly across his broad shoulders. His muscular thighs were plainly apparent, too, beneath the buckskin breeches. However, Ailsa knew it would be unwise to say as much. She merely smiled and changed the subject. She pointed to the corner of the room.

'You see I have made up the box bed that we are to share. I hope I have done it aright.'

'Aye, it will do.' The older woman nodded in approval. 'And you've cleared away everything, too. Let us to bed, then, and leave the morning to look after itself.'

Jeanie had been snoring gently for a long time before Ailsa finally fell asleep. Fingal had sent her up here to keep her away from Logan Rathmore. What would he say when he knew the Laird of Ardvarrick had accompanied her to the shieling? That he was even now sleeping in a neighbouring hut? She shifted restlessly, wondering if Logan, too, was lying awake, recalling every moment of their day together. Reliving every word, every look. She pressed her hands across her stomach, which suddenly felt light with a strange excitement. There was an unfamiliar ache in her body, a yearning for she knew not what, except that it had something to do with Logan Rathmore.

Enough! Ailsa turned on her side and pulled the rough blankets a little tighter around her. She must stop this madness. She resolutely turned her mind to what she would be doing for the summer months. Life at the shieling would be very different for her. There would be no music to practise. Instead, she must help the women with their summer tasks: milking the cows, making the cheese and the butter which was too precious to use, but would be stored ready to sell at the market. She might also become proficient at spinning, which would be done during the long, light evenings with the women sitting in their doorways when the weather was fine.

Ailsa knew she would miss playing the *clàrsach*, but if she kept busy the summer would soon pass. After that she could return to her beloved music. It was time to remind herself that if she gave her heart to Logan Rathmore, she would lose that precious gift for ever, as her mother had done. Best to forget him. He would ride away to Contullach Castle in the morning and, after his meeting with Fingal, he would return to Ardvarrick. It was unlikely they would meet again for at least another twelve months. She told herself she did not care, but as she hugged herself in the darkness, she felt a sudden and quite foolish urge to weep.

Ailsa woke very early in the unfamiliar surroundings. Jeanie was still snoring gently beside her, so she slipped out of bed and dressed quickly. They would need fresh water and she decided this was a good time to fetch it. The man who had haunted her dreams was unlikely to be about at such an early hour. Alas, as she approached the burn, she saw that Logan was already on the bank, sleeves rolled up, splashing his face in the ice-cold stream. She hesitated, but it was too late, he had seen her. He bade her a cheerful good morning.

'I decided to make an early start.'

'Oh. I hope your bed was not too uncomfortable,' she replied. 'Or perhaps Rab's snoring disturbed you—'

'I am an early riser, that is all. Do not look so anxious, I am not grown so soft that I am easily disturbed.' He noted her confusion and laughed. 'I am well aware of what is said of me.'

'I doubt anyone still thinks that, sir.'

'It does not matter if they do. As long as you do not despise me.'

'No, no.' She was afraid that saying more might suggest she was encouraging him and she busied herself filling the buckets.

'I thought Mistress Barr would keep you hidden until I had gone.' She heard the teasing note in his voice, but maintained her silence. He tried again. 'Rab told me the calf was grazing happily when he left her last night. We went up to check her at dawn and she looked well enough.'

Ailsa thought it would be impolite not to respond, when he had gone out of his way to help them with the calf. She said quietly, 'I am glad.'

He wiped his face and hands with a strip of linen. 'How long do you stay here?'

'Three months, perhaps a little more.'

'You did not bring your *clàrsach*?'

'I shall have no time for it.' She hesitated. 'It is in part why Fingal sent me here. To remind me how much I love my music. I shall return to it refreshed and eager to practise again. And I shall appreciate how fortunate I am to be a harper. You will not know how much work the women undertake while they are here.'

She had filled the second bucket and turned to carry them away.

'Let me do that.'

He had shrugged himself into his coat and stepped closer to pick up the buckets. Silently, Ailsa stood aside. Perhaps Jeanie would say she should have refused his help but the leather buckets were heavy when full and Ailsa knew she would slop much of the water over the sides before she even reached the bothy. By contrast, Logan carried them easily. She had nothing to do but to walk beside him.

'You are mistaken,' he said, as they moved away from the burn. 'I do know what goes on in places such as this. As a young boy I used to spend weeks each summer on the shieling at Ardvarrick. I recall how hard the women worked. For the children it was more of a holiday, although we did help to mind the cattle and gather the plants to dye the wool.'

'I thought you would have been at home, with your parents.'

'My father had little patience with young children.' His mouth twisted. 'Or with very young men, it seems. When I finished my schooling in Edinburgh at sixteen, after a couple of months here, he packed me off to England to…er…continue my education.'

She turned to stare at him. 'You were still studying while you were in England?'

'Aye.' He laughed, but there was no humour in his tone. 'I learned the niceties of being an English gentleman. I did the Grand Tour and learned how to take snuff elegantly, how to behave in a ballroom or drawing room. Nothing of any use to me here.'

Her brows rose. 'Are we all such savages, then?'

'No, no, of course not. But life here is…different.'

'You did not wish to come back to Ardvarrick.'

'Very perceptive of you, mistress. I did not. I enjoyed my life in the south. I knew I should have to return at some point, but my father was supposed to live for years yet and there would be plenty of time for me to learn what is required of a laird.' He shrugged. 'To be just to my father, my mother had always wanted me to become better acquainted with my English relatives and Father could not have foreseen that he would be struck down so suddenly. Alas, I returned to Ardvarrick in the autumn, ill prepared to take his place. I have had to learn a great deal, very quickly.'

'But you have your people around you,' she reasoned. 'They will be able to advise you.'

'With the exception of my cousin, they are entrenched in the old ways. My suggestions for the running of Ardvarrick are resisted and they blame my desire for change on the fact that I have been away for so many years. I am now thought to be more Englishman than Scot.'

Ailsa had heard as much at Contullach. She glanced across at him, taking in the fine wool riding jacket, the yellow satin waistcoat and soft buckskins.

'Perhaps there is some truth in that,' she murmured. 'Are you not enjoying your new life?'

'This past winter has been difficult, coming to terms with my father's death, taking up the reins of management. Tamhas supports me—the others, I fear, resent my new ideas.'

'It is a common problem. Even my uncle has had to spend a great deal of time during the winter, convincing his tenants that your new agreement will benefit them.' She smiled at his look of surprise. 'I told you I hear a great deal of talk at Contullach. People speak quite freely when I am playing. They quite ignore me.'

'Truly? I cannot believe that.'

His smile made her blush and she quickly averted her eyes. This flattery was something he would have learned in England, where she had no doubt it was considered a harmless enough diversion, but it was not so here. Not for her. She walked on in silence, staring rigidly ahead, and after a moment he continued.

'And now they have had time to consider, is there more opposition to Contullach moving his cattle with mine? That is, if you can tell me without breaking a confidence.'

'Most of my uncle's tenants think it a good thing, to put aside the rivalries of the past.'

'And Cowie?' he asked her. 'Is he still against it? There have been no more attempts to take our cattle, so I hope the beating he received has taught him a lesson, but I doubt it has made him look more favourably upon the plan.'

She said cautiously, 'When he sees the extra revenue to be gained, he will be persuaded, I am sure. And he is to marry Kirstin this summer. My uncle believes his hot temper will be cooled, once he has a wife.'

'I pray you are right, Mistress McInnis.' They were approaching the bothy and he said suddenly, 'I shall miss your playing while I am at Contullach.'

'And I shall miss playing for you.' Ailsa had not meant to say it aloud and she looked up at Logan in alarm. 'Forgive me! I did not mean—that is, I should not have spoken. Pray forget I said it! Forget *me*.'

'Do you truly wish me to forget you?'

He was looking at her, his dark eyes were serious, but there was a glow in them she could not mistake. She knew then, with terrifying certainty, that this was no mere flirtation. Panic flared and she dragged her gaze away.

'This is wrong!' She forced out her words, even though they cut like a blade as she spoke them. 'There can never be anything between us, Logan Rathmore.'

'I see.'

Ailsa dug her nails into her palms to prevent herself from uttering the words that were on her tongue. She did not want him to *see*. She wanted him to argue with her, to sweep her into his arms and declare undying love. To behave like the heroes of the songs and poems she had learned all her life.

They had reached the bothy and Jeanie was standing there, her arms folded and a frown darkening her brow when she saw Ailsa was not alone.

It is for the best, Ailsa McInnis. He might promise to love you for ever, but you know it would not last. How can it, when you have so little to offer him? If you give in to this passion now, you would lose more than your heart. You would lose your music.

Ailsa looked away from the older woman's frown of disapproval, but Logan appeared in no way discomposed. He placed the buckets carefully on the ground beside the door and straightened.

'There, not a drop spilled.' He smiled at Jeanie. 'I thank you for your hospitality, Mistress Barr. I shall go on my way now and leave you to your summer work. May the weather be kind to you.'

His farewell nod was to them both. He made no

effort to meet Ailsa's eyes again and she felt it like a stab wound.

Forget him now, as he will you.

'Logan Rathmore has a smooth tongue, I'll give him that,' muttered Jeanie, as she and Ailsa watched him walk away. 'But what Contullach will say when he knows Ardvarrick spent the night up here I do not know.'

'Perhaps he will not hear of it,' murmured Ailsa, hopefully.

Jeanie snorted. 'Someone will tell him, you may be sure of that! And I've no doubt he will blame me for it, too, although what I can be expected to do when the man turns up here, bold as brass, I don't know. But there's no harm done. I hope?' She bent a frowning look on Ailsa. 'You didn't let him touch you?'

'No, no.'

But oh, how she had wanted him to touch her, she thought, as she followed Jeanie inside and sank down on a little stool. How she had wanted him to take her in his arms and kiss her.

'Well, thank heaven for that, 'Jeanie went on. 'The consequences of any lass giving herself to a man can be severe, but for you the penalty would be so much worse.'

'You think it is true, then, that the Contullach harpers cannot marry?' Ailsa clasped her hands together and fixed her anxious gaze upon Jeanie. 'Do you not think it could be an old wives' tale?'

'It is not what I think,' said Jeanie, grimly. 'It is what has happened to the harpers I have known in my lifetime, including your mother. And to all those that went before, if the legend is to be believed. Whatever the truth of it, the risk is too great.'

The two women were silent, lost in their own thoughts, until at last Jeanie shrugged and beckoned to Ailsa.

'Worrying about it will not help. Come along, lassie, there is work to be done!'

Chapter Seven

Logan rode slowly down the hill, allowing his horse to pick its own way along the rocky track. The May sun was warm on his back, easing the mild ache he felt from spending the night on a thin mattress of heather and bracken. He had told Ailsa McInnis that his years in England had not made him soft, but perhaps that was not the whole truth. Ailsa. Seeing her again, talking to her, had been an agreeable interlude, he could not deny it. He admired her stubborn determination to take the ailing calf up to the summer pasture and he had been pleased to help. He also admired her honesty in telling him why she had been sent to the shieling and could only hope she would not suffer because he had been there.

Once he reached the valley track, Logan pressed on as quickly as he could. He wondered how his failure to arrive at Contullach Castle yesterday had been received. Fingal Contullach might well think he was putting on airs, sending his man ahead of him as if he was some high and mighty prince.

* * *

He found his cousin waiting in the castle yard.

'I was looking out for ye,' said Tamhas. 'Contullach wants me to take you to him directly.'

'Very well.' Logan handed his reins to a waiting stable hand and strode into the house. 'Is he angry with me?'

'He appeared to take your delay in good part. Of course,' muttered Tamhas mischievously, 'I didna' tell him you had broken your journey to rescue a pretty maiden.'

'Mighty good of you! Come along then, let us get to business.'

The hall was filled with Contullach's clansmen, who had gathered to witness this historic moment and, with the exception of Ewan Cowie, they all appeared to look favourably upon the new agreement that had been drawn up after a flurry of messages between Logan and his host. The two men sat down at the long table to sign and add their seals to copies of the document. Once the business was concluded, Fingal invited everyone to stay and eat together.

'You'll be giving us the pleasure of your company tonight, I hope, Ardvarrick. My wife and daughters are keeping to their parlour while most of the women are away at the shieling, so we'll not need to mind our language.' He clapped Logan on the shoulder. 'You've no need to rush away, eh?'

'None at all.'

'Good, good. It will be simple fare tonight because there's only Peggy and Ilene in the kitchens, but I'll wager they'll feed us well.'

* * *

Logan found himself sitting between two of Contullach's men. There was little conversation between them and, glancing down the table, he observed Tamhas talking quite freely to his companions. Logan knew that his years away from the Highlands had put him at a disadvantage. It would take some time before he was regarded as anything but an outlander.

He was content to listen while the conversations flowed around him. The topics were familiar, the concerns similar to those of his own people at Ardvarrick. Would the weather be kind this summer, would the harvest be a good one. It was a far cry from his life in Hampshire, where he had had no responsibilities except to enjoy himself. He had learned the arts of duello and dancing, joined the gentlemen in the hunting field or at the gaming tables and he was equally at his ease whether he was conversing with highborn ladies or low-born servants. It was no surprise his Highland neighbours thought him soft.

This last winter, his first at Ardvarrick for ten years, had reminded him how different life was here. In the Highlands, survival was a great deal more important than social graces. He had much to relearn but he would do it. He *must* do it, for this was his life, his inheritance.

He had no choice.

With the business concluded, Fingal Contullach was in a genial mood and the meal was a protracted one. Logan stifled a yawn and wished he had slept better at the shieling, but although his bed had been comfortable enough his rest had been disturbed by thoughts of

Ailsa. The shy smile in those entrancing violet eyes, the curtain of red hair that glinted like fire in the sun. He thought it was fortunate she was not playing the *clàrsach* for them tonight, for he feared he would not be able to keep his eyes off her.

It was growing dark and Logan was wondering how soon he might retire without giving offence when Fingal called for more ale to be brought in.

'We will take another toast to our arrangement. What say you, Ardvarrick?'

'By all means,' he answered politely.

'Hah, Simple Rab!' Contullach's cheerful shout caught Logan's attention and he looked up, immediately recognising one of the young men carrying in more jugs of ale. 'So, you are come back from the high pasture now.'

'Aye.' Rab came up, beaming. 'I escorted Mistress Ailsa safe to the shieling yesterday, as you said I should.'

'And is all well with the womenfolk?' asked Contullach, holding out his cup to be refilled. 'Do they have everything they need?'

'Oh, aye, they're settled now.' Rab turned his innocent, smiling face towards Logan. 'And the young coo we carried up, sir, she's doing well now. I took another look before I left at noon. Quite sturdy on her legs, she was.'

There was no sudden silence, no one stopped their conversation to stare at him, but Logan was aware of Ewan Cowie glaring at him and, at the head of the table, Fingal had tensed. He leaned forward, his fierce eyes glaring at Logan from beneath their shaggy brows.

'What's this?' he growled. 'You were at the shieling, Ardvarrick?'

Contullach's ominous tone brought a hush to those sitting nearest.

'Aye.' Logan kept his tone light, casual. 'I saw the boy struggling to carry the calf up the hill and I put the creature over my saddle.'

'The devil you did!' Cowie muttered angrily.

Logan ignored him and addressed his host. 'I may have been away in England for years, Contullach, but I know the value of cattle. You will be looking out for every last beast to fatten for market.'

Cowie gave a savage laugh. 'And I'd wager it was the women *you* were looking out for, Ardvarrick! A chance for a little wenching, eh?'

The sneering remark silenced everyone around the table. It was a calculated affront and Fingal swore at his nephew.

'You'll apologise to my guest, Ewan Cowie. Now.'

It was a half-hearted command and Ewan paid him no heed. Logan pushed himself to his feet, his hand going to the hilt of his sword.

'I'll not take that insult from you or anyone, Cowie.'

They were both standing now, eye to eye across the table. It had gone too far for reason and Logan was not sorry. He disliked Cowie and was in no mood to accept an apology.

'Well?' he addressed the man, his scathing tone nicely judged to inflame a hot temper. 'Shall we settle this now?'

'You mean to fight me, with that?' Ewan waved a hand towards the elegant Italian small-sword at

Logan's side and laughed. 'Away, man, 'twould not be a fair fight.'

'It has served me well enough in the past. Furthermore—' Logan's eyes moved to the broadsword hanging from Cowie's belt '—it has the advantage of being legal.'

'It will take more than an Act of the English Parliament to prevent Highlanders carrying their weapons,' declared Cowie, his lip curling. He jerked his head toward Tamhas. 'Your man has one, I saw it when he rode in yesterday. Ask him to lend it to you.'

'That I shall not!' declared Tamhas. He turned to Logan, saying with quiet urgency, 'Whisht, now, master, you'll be out of practice with the broadsword.'

'You may well be right, Cousin,' Logan drawled. 'In fact, I am sure you are and for that reason I shall use my own sword. However, I would borrow your shield, if you would run and fetch it for me.'

Logan flicked a smile at his cousin, who looked helplessly towards Fingal Contullach, but although their host was scowling, he remained silent. Tamhas tried one final argument.

'You have both been drinking,' he muttered. 'At least leave this until the morning!'

But Logan was not to be moved. He said quietly, 'Oblige me in this, Cousin.'

Frowning, Tamhas threw himself out of the room. Fingal rose and strode off to the dais while his men cleared the furniture and moved the candles and lamps to make a well-lighted space in the centre of the hall. Without haste, Logan removed his coat and laid it gently over the back of a chair, followed by his sword, still in its scabbard. When he turned, he saw

Cowie had stripped to his shirt and trews. He already had his sword in one hand and his *targe*, the small round shield, on his forearm. As soon as Tamhas returned, Logan drew his own small sword and took up the *targe*, balancing it on his arm to accustom himself to the unfamiliar weight. He glanced at Fingal.

'To first blood?'

The old man nodded. 'Aye, if you must fight. To first blood.'

Ewan Cowie bared his teeth in an unpleasant smile. 'When my blade catches ye, Ardvarrick, it might well be your last blood, too!'

They began, circling warily, Logan's fine blade dancing. It looked thin and almost ephemeral compared to the wider and longer broadsword. The company had fallen silent and Ewan was grinning, thinking the fight as good as won. He lunged, but Logan was ready for him. He sidestepped, catching his opponent's weapon upon the *targe* and pushing it away. At the same time his thin blade slipped beneath Ewan's defence and nicked his side. With an oath, he jumped back, eyes wide with surprise.

Logan lowered his sword. 'Ready to apologise, Cowie?'

The man glanced down at the small red spot on his shirt. 'I was caught off guard.'

'First blood,' declared Fingal. 'We agreed.'

'*I* agreed nothing!' cried Cowie, raising his sword.

Logan only just managed to block the slashing blade and throw his opponent off. They began to circle once more. Ewan went on the attack, his broadsword flashing in the candlelight, but every blow was blocked by Logan's shield or caught upon the small-sword's hilt.

Silently, Logan called down thanks for the Italian fencing master who had drilled him so thoroughly. He danced around his rival, deliberately taunting him, provoking him to waste his energies in wild swings and desperate lunges. The broadsword began to look heavy and unwieldy compared to Logan's thin blade, which darted about, evading Ewan's attempts to parry. It flicked at his shirtsleeves, slashing the linen and occasionally pinking the flesh beneath. Tiny blood-red flowers began to bloom on the pale linen.

Another wild slash of the broadsword was caught on Logan's sword hilt. Cowie closed in. They grappled, the two men evenly matched for weight, but Logan had been conserving his strength and he used it now to thrust his opponent away. Ewan staggered back and crashed into a chair. Fingal Contullach let out a roar.

'Enough!' He strode between the two men. 'Enough, I say! You have drawn blood, Ardvarrick. Can ye not be satisfied?'

'Easily,' replied Logan, breathing hard, 'if this damned hothead will admit he is defeated.'

'He does.' Contullach grabbed Cowie's arm and prevented him from returning to the fray. 'He does admit it.'

'That I do not! Let me at him, Fingal, I am not finished yet!'

'And I say you are. Damme, Ewan, can ye not see Ardvarrick is playing with you? He could have finished you at any time, had he so wanted.' He pushed the young man towards the door. 'It is over, man. Go and tend to your cuts and get yourself a fresh shirt.'

With a final, vicious glance towards Logan, Cowie stumbled away and was helped out of the room by two of his friends. At a gesture from Contullach, the other men began to put the room to rights. Tamhas picked up Logan's coat and held it up for him.

'You're a damned fool, Cousin, takin' on the fellow like that!'

'I know and I have suffered for it,' replied Logan mournfully. 'I have ruined my waistcoat.' He ran a hand over the yellow satin, indicating where one of the cloth-covered buttons was missing. His eyes swept around the floor. 'I cannot see it, no doubt it has been trodden beneath an unsuspecting foot. Ah well. I suppose I could replace them all with brass, engraved with my initials...'

'Will ye stop your funning!' exclaimed Tamhas, angrily. He helped Logan into his coat and muttered, 'Have a care where Cowie is concerned, I did not like the look he gave you.'

Logan sobered immediately.

'If I am truthful, neither did I. He will do me mischief, if he can. But not here and not openly. I do not think he will risk Contullach's wrath.'

Order was restored in a very short time. More ale was brought in, but Ewan Cowie and his friends did not reappear. Contullach touched Logan's arm.

'You'll take a glass of wine with me, Ardvarrick.' he said, 'I have it shipped in from Burgundy.'

It was late and Logan would have preferred to retire, but he recognised the offer as a gesture of peace and accepted with a word of thanks.

'We'll drink in private, if ye'll come with me.'

Logan handed his weapons to Tamhas and followed

Fingal to his private chamber, where he was invited to sit in one of the chairs flanking the hearth.

'Here, try this.' The old man handed him a glass. 'I want to show you we aren't all savages, despite the behaviour of my wife's nephew.'

'I never thought it,' Logan replied mildly.

They sat in silence, savouring the wine.

'That was a fine display of swordsmanship,' said Fingal at last.

'I would rather it had not occurred.'

'So, too, do I. But Cowie insulted you.' The old man paused to study his glass. 'You could have killed him a dozen times.'

'That was not my intention.'

'Instead you humiliated him in front of his friends and his kin. He will not forget that, Ardvarrick.'

'He questioned my actions and cast a slur upon my honour.'

'Did he?' Fingal sat forward in his seat. 'Was there not a wee grain of truth in his accusation?'

Logan sensed the danger in the air and did not answer immediately. Only the truth would serve him here. At last he raised his eyes to meet Fingal's stern gaze.

'I came upon a lass and a young man struggling with the calf and went to help them. If they had been obliged to leave the beast behind, it would not have survived. You know that, Contullach.'

'Aye, I do, but would you have done the same if it had not been my harper with Simple Rab?'

'It would have made little difference to me who she was, I would still have helped. As for Rab, you assigned the lad to protect her and he did not fail you.

He will tell you the lady was never out of his sight until he handed her into the keeping of Mistress Barr.'

Logan kept his gaze steady. All he had said was true, but he thought it wiser not to mention this morning's encounter with Ailsa McInnis. That was a different matter altogether. At last the old man nodded and looked away.

'Aye, Rab is not able to lie.' He sat back in his chair, gazing into the fire for a long, long moment, then with a sigh he drank the last of his wine. 'You'll forgive me for questioning you, Ardvarrick, but good harpers are hard to come by and I do not want to lose mine. I'll not stand by while anyone trifles with Ailsa McInnis, you understand me?'

He was about to make a stinging retort to remind Contullach that he had been born and bred a gentleman, then he remembered Ailsa this morning, begging him to forget her. He did not *want* to forget her. He liked her, he enjoyed talking with her and saw no reason why they could not be friends, but there was no doubting the fear in her eyes. Was she afraid of losing her heart to him? He, of course, had no heart to lose, he had given it to Lady Mary Wendlebury years ago, but Ailsa, innocent that she was, might easily tumble into love with any man who showed her a little kindness.

All this rattled through Logan's head in a heartbeat. It explained Fingal's concern and his anger melted away.

'Aye, I understand,' he said quietly. 'I would never do anything to harm the lady.'

For a long moment the two men looked at one another, then Contullach nodded. He pushed himself out of his chair.

'I believe you, Ardvarrick, and I'll bid ye a good-night. No, no, don't ye stir, man. Stay and finish your wine in comfort.'

'So, we have the agreement, signed and sealed.' Tamhas chuckled and patted his saddlebag. 'I confess I never thought you'd get old Contullach to the sticking point.'

'He knows full well it will mean more money for his people as well as ours.'

'Aye, but that fool Cowie almost ruined everything.'

'And he could still,' said Logan. 'He has tried to do so before.'

'You should have run him through when you had the chance.'

'And risk the old man tearing up our agreement? No, I could not do that, but I fear I have made an enemy there. He will cause trouble for us if he can.'

'Nothing we can't handle,' replied Tamhas comfortably.

'I pray you are right,' said Logan, but as they rode back towards the coast and Ardvarrick, he was unable to dispel his sense of unease.

Chapter Eight

Logan stood at his study window, staring out. He had forgotten just how glorious Ardvarrick could be in August. The sun was making the purple heather glow on the hills and, on the blue waters of the loch, fishing boats were returning with the tide. The tall masts of a larger vessel were visible, too. It would be one of the merchant ships, offloading iron ore for smelting at the nearby furnaces. A second ship was anchored in the loch, waiting for its turn to dock. By next summer he hoped the new jetty would be in place and his plans to increase trade could really begin.

If he was still here next summer.

He glanced down at the paper in his hand. His aunt's letters from Hampshire were infrequent, gossipy affairs and he usually gave them no more than a cursory glance, but this one carried information that had stopped him in his tracks. The Earl of Fritchley was dead and his aunt suggested that his widow might now look favourably upon his suit.

All the old feelings he had suppressed for so long resurfaced. He was sorely tempted to try his luck again. Mary had been married to the old Earl for five years and, according to his aunt, there were no children from the match. A distant cousin had inherited the title and the young widow had returned to her father's house. His eyes came to rest upon a phrase that his aunt had underscored.

No one expects Lady Fritchley to remain in mourning for very long.

Was it worth risking another disappointment? She might refuse him again. But on the other hand, he argued with himself, she might not.

The sunny view from the window faded. He was no longer seeing the loch and mountains and sunshine. He was in a grand house in London and dancing beneath glittering chandeliers, whisking Mary around the floor. He had just returned from his Grand Tour and it was the first time they had met since her marriage to the Earl of Fritchley. She was as beautiful as ever and looked every inch a countess, jewels winking at her throat and nestled in her golden curls. She greeted him with unalloyed pleasure, they danced twice together and afterwards remained talking for a full half an hour. She even flirted with her fan, their eyes meeting over its lacy edge. Was she regretting her marriage to the aged earl? She did not say and he could hardly ask her.

For the rest of the evening Logan had watched her, his heart sore with longing, as she moved from one adoring partner to the next. But at the end of the evening she sailed out of the ballroom on the arm of her husband with never a backward glance. Logan had decided then that in future he would avoid parties where they might meet. He had no intention of joining the coterie of her besotted admirers, preferring to nurse his broken heart in private.

And he had done so, for five long years, but now there was the possibility that he might achieve his heart's desire. The woman who had filled his dreams was free to marry again and his aunt had written that Lady Fritchley had already made it clear that her next husband would be a younger man.

In birth Logan knew he was not ineligible and his estates at Ardvarrick were sufficient to provide him with a comfortable income. If she did not wish to live in Scotland, then that was possible, too. He would not be the first Laird to make his home in England. And a wife might be what was needed to ease the restlessness that had been growing on him since his return to Ardvarrick.

He looked again towards the loch. Tomorrow the merchant ship would be reloaded with pig iron and sail off to the markets in the south. It could take him as far as Bristol and from there he could get a passage to Portsmouth. He sat down at the desk and drew a fresh sheet of paper towards him. With luck and a fair wind, he could be in Hampshire in little more than a se'ennight.

He had not written more than a few lines before he was interrupted by a servant at the door.

'Your pardon, master.'

He looked up impatiently. 'Well, what is it, William?'

Before the man could answer, he was pushed aside and Fingal Contullach strode in, two burly henchmen at his shoulders. Logan got to his feet, his brows raised at such a precipitous entrance. Contullach was scowling, one hand resting on the hilt of his broadsword.

'Where is she?'

'She?' Logan regarded him coldly. 'To whom do you refer?'

Contullach moved closer, his chin jutting pugnaciously. 'Ailsa McInnis. My harper!'

'I have no idea. The last time I saw her was in May, at the shieling.' His eyes narrowed. 'If you do not believe me, Contullach, feel free to search the house.'

They locked glances, then Fingal grunted, as if satisfied with something, and he relaxed a little.

'We'll talk alone.'

'I am at your service.' Logan's bow was all icy courtesy.

Fingal jerked his head and his companions turned to leave the room. Logan addressed William, who was still hovering anxiously in the open doorway.

'Take them to the kitchen and find them some refreshment. And send Tamhas in with ale for us.'

Logan waited until the others had withdrawn.

'Trouble, Contullach?' He waved his guest towards a chair.

The other man nodded, but remained on his feet. 'Ailsa is gone. I heard of it this very morning.' He kept his eyes on Logan. 'I was told that *you* had taken her, Ardvarrick.'

'You do not wholly believe that, or you would not be standing here talking to me.'

'True. I should have come here with an army and torn this house apart!'

'That I can well believe.'

There was a scratching at the door and Tamhas

came in with a jug of ale. He served the two men silently, then withdrew again. Logan took a draught of ale, watching his guest. The man had slumped on to the chair, frowning into his tankard.

'Tell me what you know,' said Logan. 'Mayhap I can help.'

Contullach sat forward, the tankard clasped between his hands. 'Jeanie Barr came down from the shieling to tell me Ailsa had gone to fetch water at dusk and did not return.'

'When was this?'

'Two days' since. Jeanie had gone to bed and did not notice she was missing until yester morning.'

Two days! Logan hid his dismay.

'And why did you think *I* had a hand in her disappearance?'

'They found this by the burn, near the abandoned buckets.'

Fingal held out his hand. Resting in the palm was a small round button, grubby now, but its covering of yellow satin was unmistakable.

Logan said carefully, 'I lost that when I was fighting with Ewan Cowie.'

'Aye, I heard you say so at the time.'

'I have not worn the waistcoat since. It is still missing the button, if you would like to see it?'

'No, no, I believe ye, Ardvarrick.'

Logan frowned. 'Someone is trying to foist the blame for this on to me and I'd wager it's Cowie, although you may not wish to believe that.'

'Of course I do not wish to believe it!'

'But you cannot be sure he is innocent.'

'No, I cannot be sure.' Contullach scowled into his

tankard. 'That is the reason I did not come here to hang ye today and say to the devil with our agreement!' He broke off, his jaw working as he wrestled with some internal struggle. When at last he spoke again, it was with a visible effort. 'Cowie has taken agin' you, Ardvarrick. I think he might have made off with Ailsa to spite ye.'

'I know he hates me, but to use the lady in such a manner—! Would he harm her?'

'I cannot think so.'

'You do not want to think so.'

'Damnation, Ardvarrick, he is engaged to marry my daughter!'

'Tell me what worries you,' Logan pressed him.

'Last autumn, Ailsa accused Ewan of trying to force his way into her bed. He denied it, said she was jealous. I accepted his word, but—och, 'tis not unusual in a young man to try his luck with a pretty woman. That is in part why we sent the lass away to the shieling. Kirstin was mad for Cowie and we thought she would fare better with him if Ailsa was out of the way for a while.'

'That did not work, then.'

'It would seem not.' Contullach's shoulders sagged. 'Ewan left a week ago. He told us he was going to visit friends in the Black Isle.'

'And have you sent someone after him, to confirm that he is there?'

'No. I came first to see you. I would much prefer to believe it was you who has done this, rather than my own kin.'

'I'm obliged to you,' Logan retorted, his impatience

growing with every heartbeat. 'But this will not get
her back. Cowie has land of his own, does he not?'

'Aye, Castle Creag.'

'And have you sent men to search for them there?'

'Not yet. Confound it, what if I am wrong? Ewan
Cowie is my heir. He already has the loyalty of many
of the younger men, some of whom think the peace between our lands is a mistake. If I accuse him unjustly,
they may well take his side against me.'

Staring at Fingal Contullach, Logan thought the
man suddenly looked very tired.

'Very well.' Logan drained his tankard and put it
down. 'If you are reluctant to tackle him, then let me.
Where is he most likely to be?'

'He might have made up the story of the Black Isle
to cover his tracks, because that is the opposite direction to his own land. Castle Creag is at the head of
Loch Tarin, some fifty miles to the south. Kirstin has
been asking Ewan to show her the castle, but he keeps
putting her off. It is isolated and remote, little chance
of anyone happening upon the place.'

'Then that is where I shall go.' Logan pushed himself to his feet, eager to be moving. 'Go home, Contullach. Send your men to search elsewhere and leave
me to ride to Castle Creag.'

He went to the door and held it open for his guest,
but before passing through, Contullach stopped and
looked up at him.

'If you bring me proof that Cowie is behind this,
Ardvarrick, then I will act.'

'That might not be necessary,' barked Logan. 'If he
has taken Ailsa, then I may well bring you his corpse!'

* * *

Ailsa stirred. She was lying on a hard board and covered in rough blankets. Opening her eyes, she gazed at the bare stone walls with dismay. This was no nightmare, it was all too real, and when she stirred, her bruised body confirmed it. There was no mattress on the bed, only a rough blanket beneath her and an old and noisome plaid, thrice folded, to cover her.

She was still in the kersey gown she had been wearing when Ewan had snatched her up from the side of the burn and ridden off with her across his saddle bow. How long ago was it, how long had she been here? She tried to think. They had travelled from dusk until dawn for two nights, making the most of the moonlight and stopping to sleep in the woods during the day to avoid being seen. She frowned, trying to concentrate. They had arrived at this fortified house yesterday, so she had been missing for three full days.

Her wrists were chafed and sore where Ewan had bound them. The only reason they were not tied now was because she was a prisoner in this room. A shudder ran through her. Ewan had not forced himself upon her yet, but she had no doubt he would do so, as soon as he was rested. He had told her as much before he left her yesterday, when he had dragged her close for a goodnight kiss.

Ailsa climbed off the hard bed and began to pace the stone floor, trying to ease the stiffness in her muscles. The room was bare, save for the wooden platform bed she had slept upon, a chair and an old table pushed into one corner. At least she had been provided with a chamber pot to relieve herself. It was cold, too. There was an arched window, but it was not glazed, although the remains of metal hinges in the walls suggested there had been shutters across the opening at one time.

When she had been locked into the room last night, she had noted that the window was unbarred and large enough for her to climb through, but any hopes of escaping that way were soon dashed. The walls descended in a sheer drop of twenty feet or more to a narrow grassy ledge, from which jagged rocks disappeared into the dark waters of the loch.

'Scream as much as you wish, Ailsa,' Ewan had told her, as he left the room. 'The walls are so thick no one inside this place will hear you. And outside, there is no one to come to your aid. The village is abandoned and no one fishes the loch now.'

He had told her there was no one to hear, but still she had stood by the opening, shouting until she was hoarse, but to no avail. The long summer twilight had faded to dark, but no one responded to her calls and at last she collapsed, exhausted, on to the hard bed, where she fell into a troubled sleep.

Ailsa heard the scuff of leather on the stone steps outside her room and quickly moved to the window. Remembering how her skin had crawled yesterday when Ewan kissed her, she was determined to hurl herself out on to the rocks before she allowed him to touch her again. The key turned in the lock and Ewan came in. She glared at him.

'How long do you mean to keep me a prisoner?'

Her furious demand elicited little more than a sneer. 'As long as it suits me to do so.'

'It has been three days already,' she retorted. 'My

uncle will be searching for me and when he discovers what you have done—'

'He won't. I have seen to it that Fingal believes it was Ardvarrick that took you from the shieling.'

'Why should he think that?'

'I have left proof of it. And knowing Fingal, he will be swift to exact his revenge.' His cruel laugh made her blood run cold. 'I would not be surprised to find he has razed Ardvarrick to the ground by this time.'

'But they signed a pact. What of that?'

'Fingal should have torn it to shreds by this time. But if he hasn't done so already, if he is growing faint-hearted in his old age, I will soon persuade him. That is why I must return to Contullach today, to make sure that foolish peace my uncle brokered with Logan Rathmore is over. Ardvarrick is not Laird of our clan and I'll be damned before I will bow to that cowardly Sassenach.'

Ailsa was shocked at the venom in Ewan's words. There was a wild, maniacal gleam in his eyes that frightened her.

'Is it so wrong to want to live in peace with your neighbour?' she asked him, trying to speak rationally. 'You cannot go back to the old ways of our grandfathers, always fighting. It is madness to think it. Since the Rising in fifteen, the government has been sending more troops to the north.'

'Hold your tongue, woman, you know nothing about it!'

'I know a great deal,' she flung back at him. 'I know the government plans to subdue the Highlands. Even now they are building new roads and new barracks for the soldiers. They will not go away, Ewan.

You know that as well as I. The King is determined to enforce the law here.'

'King!' He gave a savage laugh. 'That Hanoverian usurper is not *my* king, nor ever will be! But enough of this! I must go.'

'So, you are going back to Contullach where you'll pretend you know nothing of what has happened to me.' Her lip curled. 'Fingal believes you are his loyal heir.'

He grinned. 'Aye, that he does, the old fool. I shall go back and help him to search for you. And if he hasn't murdered Logan Rathmore yet I will help him with that, too!'

'And you are leaving me here, a prisoner.'

'I have not finished with you yet.' Ailsa's blood ran cold at the look he gave her. 'You will be perfectly safe. I am leaving two women here to take care of you. There is a well in the undercroft and they have food enough for more than a week, so there will be no necessity for either of them to leave the castle while I am gone, just in case you are thinking you might escape.'

'And what of Kirstin? Do you think she or Fingal will forgive you, once they know what you have done?'

'How will they ever know? Who is going to tell them? No one knows you are here, save the women downstairs and they will not speak against me. Everyone at Contullach will think Ardvarrick has taken you for his pleasure.' Ewan gave her a sneering smile. 'No need to look so anxious, my dear, you are safe enough here, as long as you please me.'

'And if I do not *please* you?'

'Then your body will be found on Ardvarrick land. More proof that that preening fool of a laird is guilty.'

He reached out and gripped her chin. 'So, you would do well to keep me sweet, Ailsa, and I will teach you what is required of a mistress.'

She slapped his hand away. With a laugh he caught her wrists and forced them behind her back. Ailsa turned her head as his mouth descended and it fell on her neck. A shudder of pure revulsion ran through her and she closed her eyes tightly, bracing herself for what was to come.

The shock and surprise when he let her go made her stagger and she clutched at a chairback for support.

'If I had time, I'd teach you not to be afraid of me.'

'It is not fear,' she flashed back. 'It is disgust.'

He shrugged. 'You will get over that.'

'Why?' she asked him. 'Why are you doing this to me, Ewan?'

'Because you have grown into a beautiful woman, Ailsa McInnis, and if I do not take you, Ardvarrick will.'

'Fingal would never allow—'

'He cannot stop it! I have seen the way Ardvarrick looks at you. In time he would take you, whatever Fingal says, and I won't have that. I'll not have Logan Rathmore bedding a Contullach woman, especially not one that I have not yet enjoyed.' She saw the lustful gleam in his eyes, then it faded. He shook his head as if to clear it and sucked in a breath. 'I must go. I have waited a long time for you, sweeting, and I can wait a little longer for our coupling. I want to savour the moment when I take your maidenhood.' He went to the door. 'Consider that, Ailsa McInnis, while I am away.'

He went out and she heard the key turn in the lock. Suddenly her limbs were shaking too much to support her and she sank down on to the bed. He could never let her go, he could not risk her telling their uncle what had occurred. Her only chance was to escape, and quickly, before Ewan returned. Once he had bedded her she would be ruined. It would not only be her virginity that was lost. Fingal would have no use for her if she could no longer play the *clàrsach*. She was nothing without her music.

Logan moved quickly. He gathered six trusted men and set off for Castle Creag within an hour of Contullach's departure. Tamhas had looked at Logan in surprise when he emerged from the house.

'So you still have your plaid,' he remarked as Logan strapped the roll of woollen cloth to his saddle.

'What of it? I thought it would be useful if we sleep out of doors.'

The old Laird had given it to Logan for his sixteenth birthday, but he had left it at Ardvarrick when he had gone to England. He had discovered the plaid stored away in the oak chest in his room, along with the rest of his Highland clothing, including a jacket and trews that he had never worn because they had been far too large for him at the time. Now, however, they fitted him perfectly and were well suited to this venture. He braced himself for some remark upon his choice of clothing, and Tamhas did not fail him.

'So, we are making a Highlander of ye again!' he declared, a gleam of satisfaction lighting his eyes. 'And about time, Cousin.'

With a growl Logan climbed into the saddle. 'Stop your talking and let us get on!'

* * *

They travelled fast, stopping only to snatch a few hours' rest when it was too dark to continue. They found a sheltered spot in the lee of a rocky outcrop where they tethered the horses securely and made themselves comfortable on the heather, which grew thick and fragrant. Then they settled down to wait for the moon to rise.

'Well, I am thankful 'tis a clear night for sleeping under the stars,' remarked Tamhas, dropping down beside Logan. His teeth flashed in a grin and he looked as if he might say more, but Logan stopped him.

'Hold your tongue,' he commanded. 'I'll not have you mention my Highland clothes again!'

'What?' Tamhas spread his hands, feigning innocence. 'I was merely going to say you are well prepared for the weather.'

Not only the weather, thought Logan, wrapping himself in his plaid. The jacket had a sheath sewn into the lining and Logan had slipped into it the *sgian dubh*, the small dagger with its black handle that his father had carried at all times. He felt the hardness of the dagger now against his ribs as he rolled on to his side. He might have need of it as well as his sword, before too long. Ewan Cowie was unlikely to give Ailsa up without a fight.

He pulled the plaid tighter about him. He thought sleepily that being Laird of Ardvarrick was never going to be easy, but swordfights and abductions—it was a far cry from Hampshire.

Lady Mary, as she then was, had called it a savage land, when he had tried to describe it to her. They had been at Lady Templesham's rout, where the gentlemen were dressed as peacocks and the ladies in their frills and furbelows were patched, powdered and pomaded until they resembled nothing more than waxed effigies.

'La, sir,' she had trilled, plying her fan, 'I cannot imagine how any gentleman can live in such an outlandish place. From what you tell me, there are no roads and carriages, and little good society, certainly not enough to sit down to an elegant dinner!'

At the time he had accepted her strictures meekly enough, but he should have made more effort to defend his homeland. Here in the Highlands life was much harsher, it was true, but there was so much less pretence. Here, a woman did not hide from the sun. Instead she turned her freckled face to it and let her red hair hang loose around her shoulders, where it rippled in the breeze in a shining curtain.

His tiredness disappeared with a jolt. This was not just any woman he was imagining, nor was it Lady Mary Wendlebury. It was Ailsa. The sudden desire that gripped him was quickly replaced by a sickening apprehension. She had been missing for three days. Who knew what might have happened to her in that time? If Ewan Cowie had harmed her, he would tear him limb from limb.

Fear such as he had never known before gnawed at Logan. He did not doubt for one moment that Cowie had abducted her, but what if Fingal was wrong, what if he had *not* taken her to Castle Creag? A moment's reflection told him it was unlikely he had gone elsewhere. Cowie would not risk carrying Ailsa away over Ardvarrick land, nor could he keep her anywhere near Contullach. Unless he was prepared to carry her to the Isles, then the old home of the Cowies was his only refuge.

Logan closed his eyes and forced himself to breathe deeply, slowly. He must sleep. As soon as the moon rose, they would set off again. Tomorrow they would reach Castle Creag and then he would need all his wits about him.

Unable to come up with a plan of escape, Ailsa slept most of the day, waking in the afternoon when the two women left to guard her brought in a small bowl of stewed bones and oatmeal and put it on the table. It looked unappetising, the fat already congealed on the surface.

Ailsa glanced at it in distaste. 'I thought you might leave me to starve.' They stared at her with dull, uncaring eyes. She tried again. 'You might as well have done, rather than serve me cold stew.'

'We cannot light a fire until after dark,' said one of the women.

Ailsa glanced towards the window. 'You could have waited another few hours, then, and brought me a hot meal!'

'Ewan Cowie said no lights,' retorted the woman. 'How would you see to eat it?'

'Aye,' said her companion. 'No one is to know there is anyone here.'

'You expect someone to come looking for me, then?'

'No! Why should they seek you here?'

Ailsa did not miss the quick, furtive glance that passed between the women and the little seed of hope inside her was not quite extinguished. As soon as the women had left the room she ran to the window. There was no one in sight, nothing moving. She tried shouting, screaming, but apart from sending several crows flapping from the roof there was no other response. Sighing, she went back to the table. The stew looked no more appetising, but she knew she should try to eat it.

Surprisingly, the food put more heart into Ailsa. Instead of taking to her bed, she went back to the window, an idea forming in her head. The sun had dropped behind the hills, putting them into deep shadow, and she could see little save the restless waters of the loch, ruffled by the fresh breeze. Quickly she struggled out of one of her petticoats and tied it to the remains of the hinge that protruded from the wall. When she pushed the white linen out of the window, the breeze caught it and it flapped merrily against the stone. It was a small thing, but it was all that she could do.

She paced up and down the room, listening to the snap of her makeshift flag outside the window. Anger and frustration welled up, but also fear of what would happen to her. Ewan could not let her go. He would take his pleasure, but then he would dispose of her and lay the blame on the Laird of Ardvarrick.

The thought of Logan Rathmore was like a physical pain. He could not come looking for her, she should not expect it. He would be too busy defending himself against Fingal's wrath. Dejected, she threw herself on to her bed and stared into the growing darkness until finally, she fell into the blessed oblivion of sleep.

The day was far advanced by the time Logan and his men reached the rocky track that wound its way through the ruins of old houses, long abandoned, to the shores of Loch Tarin. Tamhas, riding beside him, responded to his questioning look.

'Aye, this was a thriving township until a few years back.'

'What happened?'

'Too many poor harvests and harsh winters.' He pointed to a bothy on the edge of a small inlet. Its walls were intact, although the heather roof had almost disappeared. 'No doubt some managed to cling on for a while. That old fishing hut looks as if it was occupied until recently.'

Looking around him, Logan could still see the outline of a cattle fold and signs of the old lazy beds on the slopes of the hill, where a few vegetables would have been coaxed to grow.

'And this is Cowie's land?' he asked. 'What did his family do to help the people?'

'They were happy enough to take the rents, but when the cottars could no longer pay, they threw them out.' Tamhas turned his head to spit. 'In the end there were no rents to collect.'

Logan's mouth tightened. His contempt for Ewan Cowie grew.

The old track meandered along beside the water and at last Logan had his first view of Castle Creag. It was built upon a small promontory and surrounded on three sides by jagged rocks that protruded like monstrous black teeth from the waters of the loch. A formidable dwelling, he thought, watching the crows wheeling and circling around the roof. Easy to defend, although there were signs of dilapidation, even from here.

Their path swung inland, away from the loch shore

and through rocky woodland until at last they were approaching the castle from the landward side. Logan could see the curtain wall had mostly collapsed, exposing the small courtyard and ruined outbuildings. The walls of the house itself showed signs of repair and the roof above the stepped gables was in place, but as they approached, the air of neglect about the building intensified.

The ground was covered in stones, marking the outline of old black houses that had long since rotted away. Inside what was left of the curtain wall, grass and weeds pushed up between the stones of what had once been a courtyard. The house itself was built so close to the edges of the rock that it was impossible to walk around three of the walls and the fourth, facing the courtyard, had been built for defence, with several arrow slit windows high up in the walls and the only entrance a sturdy oak door set several feet above the ground and reached by a flight of stone steps.

'It would seem they do not encourage visitors,' murmured Logan. He handed the reins to Tamhas and jumped down to inspect the remains of the outbuildings. 'But there *are* signs that at least one horse has been kept here recently.'

He ran up the steps and hammered on the door.

'There is no one here,' declared Tamhas, after they had strained their ears for any sounds within the castle.

'It would appear not.' Logan climbed back into the saddle and looked up at the castle walls. No smoke issued from the chimneys. Nothing moved. The sun was so low now that they were in the long shadow of the hills and the chill did nothing to improve his mood.

'I hate to admit it, but mayhap Fingal Contullach was wrong. If Ewan did take her, he did not bring her here.'

He turned and rode away from the castle with Tamhas riding at his shoulder. Neither of them spoke until they were emerging from the woods and back out on to the loch.

'What next?' asked Tamhas. 'Do we return to Ardvarrick?'

'I am not going to give up yet,' said Logan. 'We will go back to the abandoned village and bed down for the night. If there is anyone in the castle, we will see the lights in the windows. If not—' a black cloud was descending upon his spirits, but he was not yet ready to acknowledge it '—we will search the area. Enquire of anyone we can find.' He glanced at Tamhas's grim face and sighed. 'I know, it is unlikely we shall discover Cowie or the lady by such means, but we must try. After that, I must speak to Fingal Contullach before—'

He broke off when one of his men shouted out to him.

'Ardvarrick, look. Look back!'

He swivelled in the saddle to look back at Castle Creag, standing squat above the loch. It was little more than a grey shadow in the failing light, but something fluttered from the walls, like a white pennant.

When Ailsa woke again the moon was rising and relieving the darkness with a grey-blue light. The scratchy plaid that acted as her blanket was pulled up around her face and smelled even more malodorous. Her nose wrinkled. These plaids were worn by men for days on end. During the day, half of it was fastened with a belt around the waist as a kilt and the rest thrown over the shoulder, to be used as a cape in bad weather. At night it could be wrapped around its owner if they were obliged to sleep in the open. No wonder, then, that it smelt so bad.

She sat up suddenly, her mind racing. Dragging the makeshift blanket from the bed, she pulled the edge of it through her fingers, counting the lengths. It was what, four, five yards long? She tugged at the woven material. Could she trust it?

Ailsa dragged the plaid across to the window, where she took one of the ends and forced it several times over the spike where she had tied her petticoat. Then she bundled up the rest and threw it out of the window. The plaid dangled down, shifting slightly in the breeze. It stopped several feet short of the narrow grassy verge. It was impossible in the gloom to work out just how far from the ground it ended. She would have to let go and hope she did not break a bone when she landed.

A sudden laugh shook her. What was she thinking? It was most likely she would lose her grip while climbing down and tumble to her death. She should worry about the final drop if and when she reached it. And even if she did survive the fall, she could not swim. She would have to make her way over the jagged rocks and hope the water was not too deep for her to wade through it and reach land. Another problem that must wait until it arose.

Hitching up her skirts, she scrambled on to the window ledge.

Chapter Nine

Logan hunched at the prow of the small rowing boat as it moved almost silently through the dark waters, making slow but steady progress towards Castle Creag. The moon was rising but had not yet cleared the hill and they stayed close to the bank, within the shadows, although the risk of detection was not their only reason for keeping to the edge of the loch: there was a very real fear that the skiff might not be watertight.

They had found the boat upside down and abandoned beside the fisherman's bothy, two sets of oars stored tidily beneath. They had placed her in the loch immediately and by the time the moon had risen sufficiently for them to set off she had not shown too much sign of leakage. Nevertheless, Logan had ordered Tamhas and one other of his men to bring the horses and follow as far along the bank as they could.

Trying not to think of sinking, Logan kept his eyes fixed on the castle. The white pennant still fluttered, catching the moonlight. It was not until they had left the shadows and were rowing directly towards the teeth-like rocks guarding the castle that he saw something else below the window. At first it was merely a grey smudge against the darker walls. Only when they drew closer could he see the figure, pale arms clinging to some unseen rope and swinging precariously against the castle walls.

'By heaven, Ailsa! She is climbing down.' He knelt up in the prow, every sense alert. 'Faster, lads. Row faster!'

They were cutting through the water, heading towards the promontory, and he could only pray that the skiff did not catch on some sharp and unseen rock submerged beneath the water. The castle loomed above them and the men lifted their oars, allowing the little boat to drift closer until it was scraping on the tumbled boulders. Logan jumped out and scrambled over the rocks to the base of the castle. The descending figure was just out of his reach, feet scrabbling and failing to find purchase on the rough wall.

'Ailsa, let go,' he called up to her. 'Let go, I will catch you.'

He barely had time to brace himself against the wall before she tumbled into his arms. He was winded, but he held her tight, dropping beneath her weight to sit on the narrow ledge. He hugged her to him, his eyes closed, not quite believing what had happened.

'Logan?' She wriggled in his arms. 'Is it really you?'

He opened his eyes and gazed at her, his throat too constricted to speak. When he loosened his grip, she raised one hand and laid it against his cheek. He turned his head to plant a kiss in her palm.

'Yes, it is I,' he murmured, his voice ragged.

She buried her face into his shoulder. 'Oh, how I prayed you would come!'

Her words were muffled, but they made his heart swell.

'And I prayed I would find you.' He wanted to sit here for ever with her in his arms, but there was more to be done. He said, 'We must move. Are you hurt?'

'A few scratches and bruises, that is all.'

'Truly, is that all?' He held her away from him, straining to see her in the darkness.

'Truly, I am unharmed.'

Relief overwhelmed him and found expression in an angry outburst.

'Then why in heaven's name did you risk your life climbing out of that damned window?'

A shudder ran through her. 'Because of what he s-said he would do.'

Anger gripped Logan. A cold rage against the man who had taken her, but it must be subdued, controlled. At least until Ailsa was safe.

'Can you walk?' he asked her.

'I believe so.'

To prove it, she extricated herself from his grasp and rose to her feet, shaking out her skirts.

'We need to get you into the boat.' He jumped up and took her hand. 'The rocks are slippery, but my men will help you.'

Logan held her firm as she stepped off the ledge and moved with care over the tumbled rocks. Below her, one of the men was holding the boat steady against the rocks while a second had clambered out and was reaching up towards them.

'If the lady would give me her hand...'

Logan did not want to let go but he knew he must. He relinquished her hand and held his breath as the men helped her into the skiff. Once she was safe he followed quickly and soon they were moving almost silently away from the castle.

Ailsa shivered uncontrollably as the boat skimmed across the water. She could not quite believe that she had managed to climb down from the window. She had clung so tight to the plaid that her fingers ached with the effort and she opened and closed her fists to ease the joints. Her elbows and knees were hurting where she had grazed them on the rough stone and she relived the panic she had felt when she realised there was no more plaid beneath her, that she would have to drop into the darkness.

She had still been summoning up the courage to let go when she had heard Logan's voice, as if she had conjured him by sheer force of longing. She heard it again now, as he put his jacket around her.

'Here. There is a cloak for you, but it is still strapped to my horse, so you must wait until we reach the shore for that.'

'Thank you.'

Her hand came up and covered his where it rested on her shoulder. His grip tightened, sure, comforting, and it was that as much as his jacket that eased her trembling.

They reached the shore and Logan swept her into his arms. He carried her through the shallow water to the bank, where Tamhas and his companion were waiting for them with the horses.

Logan set Ailsa on her feet, but kept a grip on her.

'I must know, I must be sure,' he muttered. 'It was Cowie who snatched you from the shieling, was it not?'

'Yes.' She gave a slight nod of her head and he glanced back at the castle.

'Is he in there?'

'No. Only the two women who he paid to guard me. Ewan has gone back to Contullach.' She added bitterly, 'To help in the search for me.'

'Then the sooner I get you back to your uncle and you tell him the truth, the better.' He turned to his men. 'I do not want anyone to know how she escaped, so we had best sink the boat.'

In the near darkness, someone laughed. 'The wood is so rotten that won't be difficult.'

They watched the skiff disappear beneath the inky black water before mounting their horses. Ailsa rode with Logan, sitting across the saddle in front of him with her head on his shoulder. She felt very safe, wrapped in the promised cloak and held secure between his strong arms.

She said, as they set off, 'Fingal will believe this was your doing.'

She felt Logan's scornful huff reverberate through his body. He said, 'Cowie tried to make out that was the case, but your uncle is no fool. Rather than laying siege to Ardvarrick, he came to talk to me. It was he who told me where I was most likely to find you.'

She gave a tiny gasp of outrage. 'If he knew, why did he not come after me himself?'

'He suspected, but could not be sure.'

'And if he had accused Ewan falsely it would cause a rift.' She nodded sagely. 'Fingal dotes on Kirstin and she will admit no fault in her betrothed.'

'But not only that. Your uncle is growing old. He knows many of his people look to Cowie as their next leader. I think he feared he would lose their support.'

'That is possible, sadly. Ewan attracts the young hotheads to him, those who would rather rule by fear and violence.'

'Most of them will change their minds when they see the advantages of working with a neighbour rather than against him.'

Logan spoke calmly, but inside his anger against the man simmered. For all that he wanted peace with his neighbour, he knew he would be sorely tempted to put a sword through Ewan Cowie when he next saw him.

They rode through the night, making the most of the moonlight until their route took them through the trees, where the thick canopy of leaves obscured the sky and they were obliged to stop. Then they slept until dawn.

Unlike Ewan when he carried her off to Castle Creag, Logan saw no need to hide away during the daylight hours but even so Ailsa knew they would be obliged to spend another night on the road. Their route took them through a long, winding pass where they came upon a small homestead that sold them butter, cheese and oatcakes to eat once they stopped for the night.

'There is a shepherd's hut in the glen yonder,' said Tamhas, pointing away into the distance. 'It is only a little way off our route.'

Logan nodded. 'Very well, let us try it.'

They were fortunate to find the hut empty and set-

tled down within its walls with their supper. 'We will collect fresh bracken and heather for you to lie upon and you shall sleep alone in the bothy,' Logan declared, when they had eaten.

Ailsa felt a little shy in the company of so many strangers and did not argue, but when they had fashioned her makeshift bed and Logan sent them all outside, she felt obliged to remark that it seemed a little unfair for her to have the hut to herself.

'It is a dry night and we will come to no harm outside,' he told her. 'We all have our plaids to keep us warm.'

'Even you,' she murmured.

'Even I.'

His smile made her heart beat a little faster. When he bent and kissed her cheek she closed her eyes and fought down the urge to reach out for him.

'Sleep now, Ailsa.'

He went out and she wrapped her cloak about her before making herself comfortable on the makeshift bed. She could still feel the touch of his lips against her cheek. Such kindness from a man she barely knew.

In my heart I have known him for ever.

She closed her eyes, smiling at such foolishness. Logan Rathmore was doing this as much to clear his name as to help her, but that did not lessen the warm glow that spread through her when she thought of him.

Even in the height of summer the Highland nights could be cold, but Logan was warm enough, wrapped in the thick plaid. The exertions of the last few days had taken their toll and he fell asleep quickly, only to wake with a start a short time later. At first he thought

it was the light of the rising moon that had disturbed him. Then he heard it again. A whimper from inside the bothy. Ailsa was dreaming. He lay very still, listening to the soft sounds. She was talking in her sleep, although he could not make out the words. He frowned as she became increasingly distressed, but when she cried out he could resist no longer. Gathering the plaid around him, he scrambled to his feet and went to the door.

Inside the hut there was enough moonlight to show him that Ailsa had thrown off her cloak and was thrashing restlessly on the bed. She appeared to be struggling with some unseen enemy. Logan knelt beside her, catching her hands and holding them between his own.

'Ailsa, hush now. You are safe.'

At first, she fought against him and he was obliged to speak again before she roused enough to open her eyes.

'You were dreaming.'

'A nightmare. I was so afraid.' She dragged her hands from his grasp and reached for him. 'Hold me, Logan!'

He took her in his arms, holding her close while she shook with terror. He rested his cheek against her hair, ignoring the small pieces of bracken and heather that had become tangled in her curls. At last she stopped trembling and her breathing steadied, but when he tried to release her, she clung to him.

'Stay with me!' Her whispered plea struck Logan like a knife, slicing through his determination to protect her honour and behave like a gentleman. To steady himself, he breathed deeply, inadvertently filling his head with the scent of her. It reminded him of the open moors, of fresh breezes and sunshine, but it did nothing for his resolve to move away.

Ailsa wound her arms about his neck and pulled his head down to hers. 'Kiss me.'

'Ailsa—'

'Don't leave me now, Logan.' Her breath was warm on his cheek, fanning his senses, arousing him as much as the warm, soft body pressing against him. Dear heaven, how he wanted her! He had always wanted her, from that very first meeting.

Her lips brushed his. 'I *need* you to kiss me.'

Logan gave in to his desire. He kissed her, gently at first, but her eager response shattered his self-control and put all sensible thought to flight. He lay down with her and gave himself up to the embrace, measuring his length against hers, the blood singing in his veins as the kiss deepened and her body moulded itself to his. When at last he raised his head, he was shaking and breathless. Ailsa stared up at him, her face pale in the moonlight, her eyes black pools that threatened to drown him. He drew in another ragged breath.

'Ailsa, I must go.'

'No, please, stay.' She reached up and cupped his face. 'I want you to stay with me.'

He closed his eyes, hoping he might defeat this temptation if he could not see her.

'That is not possible, sweetheart.' He tried to make light of it, although he had never been more serious. He said, 'If I stayed, I should want to do more than kiss you.'

'I know. I understand that and—' her voice was

hardly above a whisper as she went on '—I would like that, too.'

He was undone. His iron will liquified when faced with the double assault of her words and her beseeching look. Still he struggled to withstand the desire raging through him.

'Please stay.'

The quiet plea and the way she moved her body against him was slicing through the final shreds of his resolve. He must give her one last chance to save herself.

'Tell me to go before it is too late,' he muttered. 'Tell me to go and I will leave you.'

'But I do not want you to go.'

Her arms slid around his neck and she began to cover his face with quick, urgent kisses. He was almost lost.

'Oh, Ailsa, there can be no going back from this!'

She gave a shuddering sigh. 'I do not want to go back, Logan. I want to be with you. Always.'

Always! His heart swelled and soared as he heard her. She should have her wish. He could think of nothing better than to have her at his side for ever. He wanted to tell her so, but he could not speak, he could not think of anything except the delicious ecstasy of her touch and the desire blazing in him. He could only manage a few, final words before their lips met for another explosive kiss.

'With my body, I thee worship…'

Ailsa opened her eyes. The silence and the grey light coming in through the unglazed window told her it was not yet dawn. She was wrapped warmly enough, but not in the noisome blanket of her prison. And she was not alone. This was Logan's plaid and he was beside her. They were both naked, but she could not recall undressing. All she could remember was the comfort of his arms, the taste of his kisses and the feel of his hands roaming over her skin, bringing her body alive.

Contentment filled her. A feeling that she was complete. She turned to watch him as he slept, noting the dark lashes, the strong nose and sensuous mouth. This was where she should be. Where she wanted to be, wrapped together with the man she loved.

Love! Ailsa gazed at the sleeping man beside her and was filled with wonder when she thought of what had happened between them. She had given herself to him and he had rewarded her with such ecstasy as she had never known before. Even her music had not afforded her such pleasure.

The thought of losing her music sent a trickle of fear running through her newfound contentment. Logan stirred and looked at her.

'You are still here,' he murmured. His dark eyes warmed her, dispelling the momentary panic. 'I thought you were a dream.'

She smiled at him. 'No, I am here.'

He pulled her close and kissed her and she felt again the delicious ache deep inside. He ran his hands down her back, cupping her bottom and pressing her against his body. He was hard, aroused and a little shiver of excitement ran through her.

'Afraid?' His eyes searched her face anxiously. 'Did I hurt you last night?'

'Oh, no,' she disclaimed quickly, afraid he might move away from her. She saw the relief in his eyes.

'Sometimes, for a maid, I believe it can be frightening. The first time.'

'Not with you,' she told him, blushing. 'I did not know anything could be so, so wonderful.'

His smile grew and he pulled her closer.

'Then perhaps we should do it again, before we get dressed.'

Grey skies accompanied them on the final part of their journey but Logan barely noticed. His heart was singing as he rode with Ailsa sitting before him. She was safe and she was his. A joyous laugh bubbled up and a line from Robert Herrick came into his head.

Thou art my life, my love, my heart

It would be more correct to say that he was hers!

When Tamhas came alongside, saying he thought they would reach Contullach by dusk, he corrected him.

'We are not going to the castle. I am taking Ailsa directly to Ardvarrick. She will be safer there.'

He heard a gasp from Ailsa, but she waited until Tamhas had dropped back before speaking.

'You are taking me to your own house?'

'I am. Did you not say last night you wanted to be with me, always?'

'Yes, but…'

He murmured in her ear. 'Surely you did not think I could let you go, after what occurred last night?'

Her reply was cautious. 'I believe men say many

things they do not mean when they are in the throes of passion.'

Logan laughed. 'What a strange mixture of wisdom and innocence you are, Ailsa McInnis! That is true, but I am not the sort of man to bed a maid and then leave her. No, I will put you into the care of my housekeeper and you shall live at Ardvarrick until I can arrange everything with the minister. We shall be married—'

'Married!'

Her evident shock made him smile.

'Aye, what else should we do? It is very likely our companions have guessed what occurred last night, although we may be sure of their discretion. If you agree, we shall be wed with due ceremony at Ardvarrick, as my parents and grandparents were before us. As my lawful wife you shall have the full protection of my name and my fortune.'

Ailsa listened, hardly daring to believe what Logan was saying. Could he truly wish to marry her? Could he really love her? His next words brought the dream crashing down.

'We shall invite everyone to celebrate with us afterwards and you shall play your *clàrsach* for our guests!'

'Oh, Logan, no!'

'But of course you must, I love to hear you play. I am very proud of your talent, it is part of who you are.'

'But I c-cannot.'

Her misery increased. It was her musical ability that he loved and she had forfeited that for a moment's passion.

'What is it, sweetheart, what have I said to upset

you?' Logan was looking at her in concern. 'If you do not like the idea of playing at your own wedding, then you need not do so.'

'Thank you,' she replied quietly.

He took one hand from the reins and hugged her. 'Pray do not upset yourself,' he said, kissing her cheek. 'I know how much you love your harp and I thought you would wish to play, but it is of no matter. There will be plenty of time for music when we are wed.' He stopped. 'Ailsa? You are very stiff, very silent. What is wrong?'

She could not bring herself to tell him that she could no longer play for him. Not here, where she could not study his reaction when he learned the truth. She shook off the dark thoughts and glanced back with a smile.

'Nothing is wrong, nothing at all, save that this is all so sudden.'

'My poor sweeting, what a time you have had of it! First you are abducted and locked in a castle and then, when you have been free for barely a day, I expect you to make decisions about our wedding.'

'Yes, how very unkind of you to propose to me in this fashion.'

She managed to give a little laugh. It sounded hollow, but she hoped Logan would put that down to exhaustion, after all she had gone through.

They rode on in silence and Ailsa's mood grew ever more gloomy. She had given herself to Logan quite freely and she could not regret that. Last night the choice had been so simple, her desire for him had far outweighed any thoughts of the future. There had been no question of holding back when her whole body had been screaming for his touch, but she had loved him, too. She realised now it was quite different for Logan. He liked her, yes, he found her attractive, but it was her music he loved.

What would he say when she told him she could not play the harp ever again? And she *must* tell him, she could not allow him to marry her without knowing the truth. He would be angry that she had deceived him and she would face that. They must be honest with one another, whatever the consequences, and she feared the consequences for her could be grave indeed.

If Logan decided he no longer wished to marry her, she did not know what she would do.

As the day wore on and the weather improved, so did Ailsa's spirits. Riding with Logan, sitting before him and with his arms keeping her secure, the future did not look quite so bleak. She would tell him she could no longer play the *clàrsach*, but she did not need to do so just yet. She would wait and convince him that she could be a good wife in all other ways, then perhaps he would still wish to marry her. It was a risk, but she thought it worth the attempt. After all, what else was there to be done?

His arms tightened. 'Was that a sigh, Ailsa?'

'Only a little one.' She leaned against him, taking comfort in the solid wall of his chest against her back and yet already feeling like a fraud. 'I was reflecting upon how good you have been to me, risking your life to rescue me, taking me to your home. I do not deserve you, Logan Rathmore.'

* * *

The humble note in her voice plucked at Logan's heart and he dropped a kiss upon her hair.

'Hush, sweetheart, I am no saint, I promise you.' He lowered his voice. 'If I was, I would not have taken advantage of you last night.'

She trembled against him and, although he could not see her face, it was easy to imagine the blush painting her cheeks.

'You did not take advantage of me, I begged you to stay with me.' She twisted around towards him, saying urgently, 'I did not do it to trap you into marriage, Logan, please believe me. I would never do that to you.'

'I never thought it, lass, you may be easy about that.' He used one arm to pull her closer while he stole a quick kiss, then said with mock severity, 'Now stop wriggling. You are fretting my horse and he will unseat us both if we are not careful!'

Obediently she turned back and Logan settled his arms more securely around her again. They were travelling over Ardvarrick land now and he could relax his vigilance a little and consider the situation. He had spoken true, Ailsa had not trapped him, but by giving in to his desire he had committed himself to a marriage. It was not what he had planned and he almost laughed aloud when he thought of how he had considered returning to England to see the widowed Lady Fritchley. He knew now that what he had felt for her had been calf love, little more than infatuation. It was nothing compared to what he felt for the woman riding with him today. He no longer dreamed of celestial blue eyes and guinea-gold curls, he was not interested in a society that talked of nothing but the latest gossip and fashions and had nothing to do but enjoy themselves.

He glanced down again at the red-gold head just below his chin. If Ardvarrick and everything else was to disappear this very moment, he would not care. This woman was his world. He needed no other.

It was evening when they arrived at Ardvarrick and Ailsa's first thought was that the house was on fire, but it was the setting sun making the windows blaze with light. When she had ridden here in the autumn, to warn Logan about Ewan Cowie, she had seen only the grandeur of her surroundings. Now she tried to take in every detail of what could be her new home.

Ardvarrick House was charmingly situated against a backdrop of a wooded hillside and it was approached by a short, curving drive. The house itself had two rows of large windows that looked across the meadows to the sea loch. More windows pierced the stepped gables of the two wings and a series of ornamental chimneys rose from the roof. It was as different from Contullach as it was possible to be and Ailsa loved it.

Logan dismounted by the shallow steps leading to the door and reached up to lift Ailsa down.

'Can you stand, or shall I carry you?'

'I can walk perfectly well, if you will give me a moment.'

But she was obliged to cling to him. After riding for so long her legs felt very weak, but she would not suffer the indignity of being swept up into his arms in front of his household.

'Take as long as you wish,' he told her.

Keeping one arm around her, he handed the reins to Tamhas and ordered the others to go on to the stables.

'There you are, Master Logan. I was looking out for you.'

Ailsa looked up at the sound of the soft voice and saw a grey-haired woman in a black stuff gown hurrying down the steps.

'This is Norry, my housekeeper,' Logan told Ailsa. 'Although she prefers me to call her Mistress Noranside when she is angry with me!'

'Now you stop your teasing, Master Logan, and bring the young lady inside. Poor thing, she looks worn out. Come along in, both of you. I have some broth ready and perhaps a piece of chicken, mistress, if you are up to it.'

Ailsa allowed herself to be shepherded up the steps and into the hall, where Logan released her.

'If you will take Mistress McInnis with you and look after her, Norry, I have matters I need to attend to.'

'But of course, Master Logan!' Mrs Noranside took her arm. 'Come along, we will wait for the Laird in the drawing room. Bless you, my dear, there's no need to be afeared, he'll be along soon enough. And you are perfectly safe in this house, no one will harm you here.' She chuckled as she gently urged Ailsa forward. 'Oh, yes, mistress, the master told me all about it before he left. He said how you had been carried off and that he was going to find you.'

'He—he did?'

'Aye, and I'd have had a bedchamber ready for you, too, if he had sent word of when he meant to return! Heaven bless you, I confess I did not expect him quite so soon. Why, I only had time to tell Shona to run up and prepare a room when I saw you walking up the path.'

'But he said he would bring me here?' Ailsa pressed her.

'Not exactly, but I could see he was in a rare taking over you, so he'd want to keep you under his eye once he had you safe. Master Logan has few secrets from me, you see. I looked after him until he went off to school and then, when he was no longer in need of a nursemaid, I stayed on to be housekeeper here. And he has never forgotten his old nurse. Even when he was on his Grand Tour, he found time to write to me.' As she talked, she led Ailsa through the hall to the drawing room, where a cheerful fire was burning.

'I know it is summer, but the evenings can be chilly here and a body feels it more, I find, after a long journey. Come and sit here in this armchair, my dear, and I'll fetch a tray for you and the master and you can eat in here, before the fire.'

She chattered on, settling Ailsa in her chair and bringing a stool for her feet before bustling away and leaving Ailsa with only the sound of the crackling fire to keep her company. She closed her eyes. She felt quite bewildered by the events of the past few days and not least by the fact that she had been spirited into this luxurious house.

If she needed anything to remind her that Logan Rathmore was out of her reach, it was Ardvarrick. She remembered visitors to Contullach telling her uncle that his neighbour's new residence had been built for a gentleman. And Logan Rathmore *was* a gentleman, she knew that. He was cultured, educated and, while she could read and write, and keep accounts, she knew nothing of the world. Nothing of *his* world. How could she possibly make him a good wife?

'My poor love, you are exhausted.'

Her eyes flew open to find Logan smiling down at her. He bent and kissed her brow.

'I would carry you to bed this minute, but Norry says your room is not yet ready. Besides, she will be bringing a meal to us any moment.' He knelt beside her, taking her hands in his firm, warm grasp. 'I have sent word to Contullach, telling them you are safe. First thing in the morning I will visit the minister. To ask him to marry us. He may wish to call upon you here, to speak with you. Would you mind that?'

He had changed out of his travelling clothes and was now wearing a brown wool coat over a russet-coloured waistcoat and breeches. She guessed he would call it plain country wear, but it was a stark contrast to her own gown, which bore the ravages of her ordeal.

She bit her lip. 'You do not have to marry me, Logan. In fact, I would r-rather you did not.'

He looked at her, brows raised. 'Now, what is this, are you rejecting my offer? Am I so repulsive to you?'

He was making light of it, but that only added to her confusion.

'No, no! It is just that…' She paused, deciding how best to explain. 'Your life has been so…so different to mine. You have lived in Edinburgh and seen London. You have travelled on the Continent. I have not been further than Skye.'

He smiled at her. 'And that is somewhere I have never been.'

'It is not just that.' She bowed her head, her cheeks on fire with mortification. 'I…am not your equal.'

Silence followed. Ailsa gently disengaged her hands and clasped them tightly together in her lap. She expected Logan to walk away from her. Instead he sat down on the footstool.

'Ailsa, look at me. Look at me. Both the Rathmores and Contullachs can trace their lines back generations, perhaps even to the Lords of the Isles, if legend is to be believed. As Contullach's niece you are equal to me in birth, if not in fortune, so let me not hear any more nonsense about that.'

The look in his dark eyes was grave, but not unkind.

'Thank you,' she murmured, 'But there is more. I am unused to society's ways. I… I do not want you to be ashamed of me.'

'I could never be ashamed of you, sweetheart.'

Logan saw that she was not convinced and he took her hands again. They trembled in his grasp and he squeezed her fingers.

He said gently, 'I have been away for ten years, Ailsa. There is much about living here that *I* do not know or have forgotten. Your knowledge will be invaluable to me. We have much we can teach each other.' He pulled her hands to him and kissed them. 'Now—' he smiled at her '—do you think you could put up with me as a husband?'

He saw her eyes widen and a tear trembled on her lashes.

'Oh, Logan, I will marry you, if you are sure it is what you want. And I promise you that I will do everything in my power to be a good wife to you.'

He pulled her close and kissed her. 'You have made me the happiest of men! I—'

Logan broke off as Norry came bustling in with a supper tray and ordered him to place a little table beside Ailsa's chair. He complied, resigned to the fact that it was beyond him to make a declaration of love in front of his old nursemaid.

They shared a light supper together. Ailsa was almost too tired to eat, but Logan coaxed her to take a little soup and a glass of wine. When a serving maid came in to remove the dishes, he ordered her to send Mrs Noranside to him.

'You need to sleep,' he told Ailsa. 'Norry has prepared the yellow guest room for you and she will help you undress.' He pulled her to her feet and into his arms. 'Much as I would like to take you to my own bed, the people here look to me for an example. I am afraid that we must be models of propriety until we are lawfully wed.'

He kissed her then, in a fashion that was anything but proper, and she responded instinctively. Her bones melted as their tongues danced together and when he raised his head she lay passively in his arms, her head thrown back against his shoulder, gazing up at him. His eyes were blazing and she did not doubt he wanted her as much as she wanted him. She put a hand to his cheek.

'I cannot believe I deserve the good fortune of becoming your wife.'

'You deserve far more,' he murmured, brushing her lips with his again.

Her body responded immediately, but they were

interrupted by the opening of the door. Ailsa felt the blood rushing to her face, but Logan was not a bit put out. He smiled down at her, his eyes glinting.

He said lightly, 'Here is Norry interrupting us again. This time to take you up to bed. Sleep well, my dear, and I shall see you in the morning.'

Ailsa was conscious of a small stab of loneliness as she left the drawing room. She was aware of a disappointment, too. Her body yearned for Logan to hold her, to kiss and caress her as he had done in the shepherd's hut. He had said he wanted her in his own bed, but if that was so, if he wanted her as much as she wanted him, could he be so restrained?

Her observations of the men at Contullach—and her own experience with Ewan Cowie—told her men were unable to control their passions. She had also heard that English society was rife with scandalously licentious behaviour. Could Logan Rathmore be so very different? She thought it more likely that, having bedded her once, his lust for her was sated, but he felt honour bound to marry her.

With such a tangle of emotions and ideas running riot in her head, Ailsa accompanied the housekeeper up the stairs to the yellow guest room, a delightful chamber, prettily decorated in straw satin and flowered chintz.

'Now, I have searched out one of my nightgowns for you,' said Mrs Norris. 'It will be far too big, but better than nothing for tonight. Once I have helped you into bed, I will fetch up a cup of hot chocolate, or would you prefer a little more wine?'

Ailsa had never drunk hot chocolate, but she liked

the idea of a warm drink and said so. Mrs Noranside beamed at her.

'My late mistress loved her chocolate and I was always partial to a cup, too, which Master Logan remembered and he brought me a supply when he returned home last year. Such a thoughtful boy he was and he hasn't changed a bit!'

In no time Ailsa was sitting in bed, propped up against a bank of soft feather pillows and Norry was pressing a cup of hot chocolate into her hands.

'Now, you drink that, mistress, and I will sit here with you until it is finished.' She pulled a chair beside the bed and sat down, folding her arms across her ample bosom.

'Oh, please, I do not want to keep you,' Ailsa began, but the housekeeper stopped her.

'Whisht, now, you are keeping me from nothing, mistress. Tomorrow I will send up Shona to wait upon you, but tonight I wanted to look after the lady my master has set his heart upon.' Ailsa's eyes flew to her face and Mrs Noranside beamed at her. 'It does my own heart good to see the young Laird about to marry at last, that it does.'

'He has told you?' Ailsa blushed. 'And you do not object?'

'Object? Bless you, mistress, what have I to say to anything? Master Logan is his own man and will go his own way, as he always has.' The old woman settled herself more comfortably in her chair and smiled at Ailsa. 'I cannot think that anyone at Ardvarrick will object, mistress. We shall all be glad to see him settle down with a good Highland lass.'

Here in this cosy room, nestled against the soft pillows, Ailsa was beginning to feel more comfortable. She even felt she might broach a subject she dared not put to Logan. She chose her words carefully.

'It surprises me that the Laird of Ardvarrick has not married before now.'

'Aye, well…there *was* talk of a lady. In England. Daughter of an earl or some such, but it came to nothing.'

'Oh.' Ailsa plucked at the sheet. 'When was this?'

'Let me see, it must have been four, five years ago. Master Logan wrote to his father about it. That set the household by the ears, I can tell you!'

Ailsa sipped her chocolate, but its warmth could not reach a sudden cold spot in her heart.

'Was—was he very much in love with her?'

The housekeeper shook her head. 'Nay, 'twas no more than a boyish fancy, which was fortunate, for his parents were not at all happy to think of Master Logan coming home with a wife they had not even met!'

Ailsa stared at the covers, the chill in her heart growing. If the old Laird and his lady had been upset at the thought of an earl's daughter, what would they think of her?

She asked, 'What happened?

'In the end it all came to nought and the lady married someone else. Which I can now see is a good thing, because the master has fallen in love with you, my dear!'

Ailsa paid no heed to the last part of the housekeeper's speech. She could not bring herself to believe Logan truly loved her. Perhaps he was the kind of man who fell in and out of love easily.

She said now, 'Did you learn why it came to nothing? Was his suit rejected? Or perhaps he realised he had mistaken his heart.'

'He never gave a reason, and if he had told the mistress I should have known about it, believe me.' Norry rose and took the empty cup from her hands. 'In any event, Master Logan has never mentioned the matter since. Well, it was years ago, now. I expect it is all long forgotten.' She smiled and said comfortably. 'First love never lasts, eh?'

Ailsa kept silent and settled down to sleep, but it nagged at her that Logan should have wanted to marry someone else, even if it was five years ago. And as for first love, Logan was *her* first love and she was as certain as she could be that it would last for ever.

Chapter Ten

Ailsa slept late in the morning and was brushing her hair when Logan came into her room.

'Norry told me you were dressed or I should not have dared to disturb you.' In two strides he had crossed the room and pulled her up into his arms. He took the brush out of her hand and threw it aside as he kissed her. 'I could not leave without saying goodbye.'

She was inordinately pleased at his show of affection and laughed up at him.

'But you are only going to the Kirk to see the minister.'

'I know, but I wanted to see you first. To assure myself that you are really here.' He kissed her again. 'You should make yourself familiar with Ardvarrick while I am gone. You will soon be mistress of everything I own and you must feel free to go where you will.'

'I would rather you showed me over the house,' she said shyly. 'I would not be wanting to put myself forward in your absence.'

She waited for him to chide her for being foolish and tell her that a true lady would have no such qualms. Instead he smiled.

'Very well, it will be my pleasure. But I'd advise you to ask Norry to show you the lower rooms, the kitchen and the like. They have always been her domain and while they will naturally be part of yours, she does not like me, a mere man, wandering around there!'

With that he left her and Ailsa went in search of the housekeeper, who was only too delighted to show her the service rooms situated in the basement and also the servants' quarters on the upper floor. Ailsa was pleased that the luxury of the house was not confined to those rooms used by the master and mistress. Her own position had always been something between a servant and a member of the family and after the chilly cell-like bedchambers of Contullach Castle, the painted walls and sash windows in Ardvarrick's attics looked very comfortable. It whetted her appetite for exploring the rest of the house with its master.

Logan returned to Ardvarrick shortly after noon and as he stepped into the hall, he saw Ailsa coming down the stairs. There was no mistaking the delight in the shy smile that lit up her face when she saw him. It gladdened his heart.

'You are back!' she cried, hurrying towards him.

He threw aside his hat and swept her up into his arms.

'Well, well, if that is the sort of welcome I can expect from my wife, I am a very lucky man!'

'I was looking out for you.' Blushing, she took his

arm and went with him to the dining room, where a cold collation was set out.

'We did not know quite when you would return,' she explained, sitting down with him at the table. 'Mrs Noranside said you would be hungry.'

'I am. Ravenous!' He laughed, tearing a hunk of bread from the fresh loaf and helping himself to a piece of the cheese rolled in oatmeal. 'The minister is well known for his frugality. But he redeemed himself somewhat in my eyes because he has agreed to marry us in four weeks' time. If that is agreeable to you?' He watched as Ailsa poured him some ale. 'For myself I would like it to be tomorrow, but I must first write to my family in Hampshire about you. I doubt they will be able to make the journey, but I should at least advise them of the wedding. And I shall ask my aunt for advice on the latest fashions for you.'

When Ailsa blushed scarlet, Logan cursed himself for a fool and wished his last words unsaid. She was wearing the gown she had arrived in yesterday and he had reminded her of it. Norry had done her best to clean and repair the damage overnight, but it still showed signs of its ill use.

He said quickly, 'You will feel more comfortable once you have a fresh gown to wear. I ride to Contullach tomorrow to see your uncle, so I shall bring your clothes back with me. They will suffice for the moment, but you must have new gowns as befits the Lady of Ardvarrick. I should very much like to take you to London and let you choose everything from the finest establishments, but there is no time to do that before we are wed.'

'No indeed,' she murmured, taking a little bread and cheese for herself.

'We could travel to Inverness, to see what they have there, but I think I should write to my aunt. If I give her your description and measurements, she can send up whatever she thinks suitable. What do you say to that? No need to colour up, Ailsa, I have no doubt she will be delighted to help.'

'Will she?' Ailsa was tearing her bread into small pieces, but she was not eating them, merely dropping them back on her plate. 'She is more likely to think you are marrying beneath you.'

'Never. Not once I have told her all about you.'

She smiled at that and Logan hoped he had set her mind at ease. He continued with his own repast, his mind filled with plans for the wedding. There was much to be done, but before anything else he must go to Contullach. He had no doubt Ewan Cowie would be there, trying to lie his way out of trouble, now his scheme had been thwarted.

His heart contracted painfully when he thought of what might have happened to Ailsa and he glanced across the table, thankful to have her safe under his roof. She looked a little thin. Unusually pale, too, but he had no doubt that under his care and the watchful eye of Mrs Noranside she would soon recover her bloom.

He was shaken by a sudden, overwhelming need for her to be happy here. He wanted her to be happy with *him*. It was important that she knew that.

'Ailsa, if there is anything at Ardvarrick that does not suit you, if there is anything I can do to make you happier, you must say so. Promise me!'

'Why, of course I would tell you.' She smiled at him, putting to flight the shadows in her eyes that worried him so. 'I am happier here than I have ever been, I assure you. Now, finish your meal, sir!'

Some half hour later, Logan drained his cup and pushed it away from him with a sigh of satisfaction.

'I feel better for that. Now, madam, I am at your disposal for the rest of the day. I said I would show you over the house, did I not?'

'Yes, you did.' She brightened immediately. 'And I should like to see it as soon as maybe.'

Logan smiled. 'Very well, if you do not object to my travelling clothes, we can begin immediately!'

After a brief inspection of the drawing and dining rooms, which Ailsa had seen already, Logan opened one of the doors at the far end of the hall and ushered Ailsa into the shuttered interior.

'This is the morning room,' he said, crossing to the window and folding back the shutters. 'It was designed for my mother, but she died before the house was finished. You see the windows face south and allow in a good deal of light. You may have it for your own, if you wish. We can decorate it afresh and you can choose new furnishings.'

'Oh, no.' Ailsa had walked to the middle of the room and she was looking around, her hands clasped together. 'I like it very much as it is. Once the wainscoting and furniture has all been polished, it will be very comfortable.'

'I thought it would do very well for your music room.'

Logan felt the change in the air immediately. Ailsa was standing very still. It was as if she had become stone. He took a step towards her.

'Have I said something amiss?'

'No, not at all.' She appeared to shake off some troubling thought. 'I am sure I shall be able to make good use of this little chamber. Are there any more rooms on this floor that I should see?'

She was smiling at him, but there was a wariness in her eyes. He thought her tone a little brittle and suspected there was something she was not sharing with him, but he was reluctant to press her. She would confide in him when she was ready, he was sure of it, so he concentrated on answering her question.

'The only other room is the one I have taken for my study. Would you like to see that?'

'Very much.'

Ailsa followed him out of the morning room, relieved he had not questioned her. She would have to tell him about her music, but not yet. Not yet.

He led her to the very end of the passage. It was a corner room, sparsely furnished with two chairs and a few items of furniture. A handsome walnut knee-hole desk was positioned to make the most of the light flooding in through the windows set into two of the walls. Unlike her uncle's writing table at Contullach, the top of Logan's desk was almost bare. A single piece of paper bearing a few lines of writing lay in the centre of the desk and there was a neat pile of folded letters to one side, weighted with a pretty pebble. The only other items on the desk were a silver standish and a branched candlestick, both polished until they gleamed.

Logan scooped up the half-written sheet and screwed it into a ball.

'I apologise for the room being so untidy.' He threw the paper into the fireplace. 'This is my private room. Norry is allowed in to clean it, but only occasionally. No one has been in here since I left to come after you.'

'I think it is exceedingly tidy,' she told him. 'And very comfortable, too.'

She trailed a hand across the pretty veneered top of the desk as she moved past it to one of the windows that looked out over the approach road.

'It is a fine prospect, is it not?' Logan came to stand beside her. 'With the sun glinting on the loch waters and the changing colours of the surrounding hills, it is better than any painting.'

She laughed. 'It is a wonder you get any work done here.'

With him standing so close she suddenly felt very shy. Quickly she moved on. There was a map of Scotland on one wall and a small press that she presumed held the papers and ledgers pertaining to the household. On a side table she spotted a small pile of books. She put out a hand, then stopped and looked towards Logan, who nodded.

'Go on,' he said, smiling. 'You may look at them.'

Logan watched her as she picked up the books one at a time and carefully turned them between her dainty hands. Finally, she took up the smallest volume, the Lovelace poems he had taken with him to Contullach. He remembered he had been reading the poet's lines to his mistress when she had come into the solar and he had looked up to see Ailsa standing before him, the sun glinting on her red hair and enhancing the delightful sprinkling of freckles across her dainty nose.

He had been captivated, as he was now, and equally reluctant to show it. *Then* she had been almost a stranger and he had not wanted to frighten her away with even a mild flirtation. Here, today, she was his future wife and he had to rein in the urge to pull her into his arms and cover her face with kisses.

His throat felt very tight and he was obliged to clear it before he could speak again.

'I brought these books with me from Hampshire, but I shall buy more now. And I shall purchase a press to store them. My uncle had a fine one, with glass doors and a lock. Not that anyone here is likely to want to steal books.'

'And will you allow me to read them?'

'Of course.' He took her hand and kissed it. 'Everything I have is yours, Ailsa.'

The pressure of his lips on her skin was lighter than a feather, but it sent the blood racing through her veins. Gazing up into his face, seeing the warm glow in his eyes, Ailsa wondered how on earth this miracle had occurred. How had such a man come to care for her?

'What have I done to deserve such happiness?' she murmured.

'You have agreed to marry me,' he replied. 'Besides, you play the *clàrsach* like an angel, and that, surely, deserves a great deal!'

He spoke warmly, but the effect upon Ailsa was like the winter wind. Somehow, she managed not to flinch, to keep her smile in place, but an icy hand was clutching at her heart now and her blood was no longer singing. Her gift for music was gone. She should tell Logan. He deserved to know before they were committed irrevocably to a marriage. She opened her mouth, but the words she needed would not come. Some demon in her head argued that she should not risk losing him now, she should wait and make him love her for her own sake. Logan was still smiling at her and her uncomfortable conscience surfaced again.

Coward. Tell him. Tell him!

She swallowed and took a little step away from him. 'Shall we continue our tour?'

Ailsa was at her dressing table the next morning when Logan came in. She put down her hairbrush and rose to greet him. She did not resist when he took her in his arms and kissed her, but when he raised his head she put her hands against his chest and gazed up at him.

'You are dressed for riding. You are going to see my uncle?'

'I am.' He brushed a wayward curl from her cheek.

'And if my cousin is there?'

'I have no doubt he will be.' Logan frowned, his eyes dark and brooding. 'God knows what lies he has been concocting.'

'But you will be able to lay the truth before my uncle.'

'Aye, that I will.' His mouth hardened. 'Cowie must not be allowed to get away with this.'

Ailsa clutched his jacket, chilled at the thought of a duel. 'You will not fight him?'

His face softened a little as he realised how anxious she was. 'Not if you do not wish it.'

'I do not.' She clung to him. 'Ewan cannot harm me now that I am here and you should leave Fingal to deal with him.'

'I wish I could be sure he would punish Cowie as he deserves. I should much prefer to take my own revenge.'

Ailsa shivered, not for what might happen to Ewan Cowie, but hating the thought of Logan suffering the slightest hurt.

'Let me write to my uncle,' she suggested. 'I will explain to him how badly Ewan treated me. Let me do it now, Logan, it will not take me long and you may take it with you. When he knows how Ewan ill used me and how well you have behaved, Fingal will act accordingly, I am sure of it.'

She held her breath. The men at Contullach would think it beneath them to be advised by a woman. They were quick to draw their swords and mete out vengeance, but Logan was different. He treated her with respect and listened to her arguments. The band around her heart tightened. It was one of the reasons she loved him.

At last he nodded. 'Very well. I will fetch up paper, pen and ink while you finish arranging your hair.'

Logan and his men reached Contullach Castle just as the household was gathering for dinner. He pushed his way past the servants at the door and strode directly into the great hall. His entrance, followed by half a dozen men bristling with arms, caused an outcry. Benches were overturned as everyone jumped up from the table and Contullach came forward with a roar of anger.

'What the devil do you mean by bursting in like this, Ardvarrick? I overlooked your coming in here wearing that wee sword o' yours in the past, but your men know to leave their weapons at the door!'

'Not this time,' barked Logan. 'You had my message yesterday. I explained everything so you know precisely why I am here. I want justice for your niece.' He looked the older man in the eye, saying slowly, deliberately, 'For my future wife.'

'Your what?'

Contullach's astonishment echoed in the muttering that went around the room. Logan ignored it.

'You have proved you cannot keep her safe, so I must.' He drew a folded paper from his jacket and held it out. 'This is a signed and witnessed deposition from Mistress McInnis, describing her abduction.' His eyes swept over the company. Ewan Cowie was standing with one arm thrown around Kirstin Contullach's shoulders. Logan walked up to him. 'By this rogue!'

Cowie sneered. 'I've already told ye, Uncle, Ailsa was very willing to come away with me. In fact, I'd say she was desperate to be bedded. With almost twenty years in her dish, she is becoming a dried-up old—'

Logan silenced him with a blow to the jaw. Cowie staggered back. Kirstin screamed and threw herself between the men, but by that time Tamhas had grabbed Logan's arm and pulled him away.

'Steady, man.'

Logan shook him off, his blazing eyes fixed on Cowie. 'I made Ailsa a solemn vow that I would not kill you, but by God, do not push me too far!'

'Enough!' roared Fingal. 'I'll remind ye you are not the Laird here, Ardvarrick. And you are not the only one with a grievance. I have lost the best harper I ever had through this business. Unless you want to drag our names and that of your future wife through the courts, then you will leave me to punish my own!'

Tamhas touched his arm again. 'He is right, Logan. 'Tis better that we keep this matter between ourselves.'

'Your man speaks wisely,' said Fingal. 'If the girl was not harmed, as you and my nephew both assert—'

'Harmed!' Logan rounded on him. 'What would you call it? The villain carried her off against her will, imprisoned her in a ruinous castle and threatened her with the very worst of fates so that she risked her very life to escape him!'

Ewan Cowie uttered a curse and turned towards Fingal. 'But I did not touch her, Uncle! On my life, I did no more than steal a kiss from the wench. She was still a maid when *I* saw her last!'

The implication in this final sneer was unmistakable. It was only Tamhas's grip on his arm that stopped Logan drawing his sword and running the man through where he stood. Fingal Contullach was aware of it, too. He stepped in front of Logan, waving Ailsa's letter in his face.

'She is not your wife yet, Ardvarrick, but she was the Contullach harper and she *is* still my niece. Ailsa demands that I deal with the matter and I will. Damnation, man, I will flog Cowie as he deserves.'

'Father, no!'

The strangled cry brought Contullach's eyes to his daughter. She ran forward and clasped his arm.

'Ewan confessed everything to me. He told me how bitterly he repents what he had done. We had quarrelled, you see, and he was angry with me. I drove him into her arms! Please, Father. The intimation has already been read out in the Kirk. In a week we will be husband and wife.'

'Aye, you will,' growled Contullach, scowling. 'But because of what he has done, there will be no harper to play at your wedding. He deserves a whipping, if only for that!'

Logan watched through narrowed eyes the little scene playing out before him. Kirstin hung on her father's arm, pleading for her man. Ewan Cowie stood behind her, looking for all the world like a repentant sinner, except for the cunning look in his small eyes. Logan felt a sudden stab of sympathy for the woman, if she could not see the sort of man she was marrying.

'Well, Ardvarrick?' Fingal turned back to him. 'Will a flogging satisfy you? We'll do it now, here in the hall where it can be witnessed by your people and mine. And afterwards, you will stay and eat with us, to seal the peace.'

The cold-blooded barbarity of it chilled Logan, but he knew better than to protest. This was a harsh land and it bred harsh people with their own ideas of justice. Tamhas stepped closer and murmured in his ear.

'You should accept, man. Ailsa has always thought of Ewan Cowie as her cousin. She would not want his murder on your hands.'

Logan frowned. He had given Ailsa his word. It had been an easy enough promise to make when she was safe in his arms, but here, face to face with Ewan Cowie, he wanted nothing more than to put an end to the rogue.

'Very well, we do it your way, Contullach.'

His reluctant consent was enough for Fingal, who

called for his whip to be brought in. Ewan Cowie had grown pale, but he did not move, neither did he complain when two of Fingal's men helped him out of his jacket and tunic. Logan turned away.

'We have ridden a long way. Perhaps, Contullach, you can tell me where we refresh ourselves before we sit down to dinner with you.'

Fingal looked surprised. 'You will not stay to see justice administered?'

'I am content to leave that to you,' he replied coldly. 'Those of my men who want to stay and watch may do so. I shall not.'

With a shrug, Contullach barked an order. Logan and Tamhas followed a servant to a small chamber, where they found a pewter dish and jugs of water.

'I am going back to the hall,' said Tamhas, after quickly washing his face and hands. 'I'd not put it past our host to go easy with the lash.'

Logan shrugged. 'Not too easy. Fingal Contullach knows the rest of our party is watching. Also, he needs to show Cowie that he is still master.' He dried his face and threw down the cloth, saying irritably, 'What galls me is that he is angrier over losing his harpist than any harm that might have come to the lady herself.'

'Contullach would say your years in England have made you soft.'

Logan scowled. 'If he crosses me in this, he will find that is far from the case.' He pulled off the black ribbon that confined his hair at the back of his neck and turned to the looking glass propped up on a chest of drawers. 'Off with you, then, and watch Cowie take his punishment, if you so wish. I will return once I have made myself more presentable. I only hope they will mop up any blood before we dine!'

By the time Logan returned to the hall, all evidence of the scuffle and any subsequent punishment had been cleared away. Of Ewan Cowie and Kirstin there was no sign. The long table gleamed with pewter dishes and Fingal Contullach called to him from one end of it.

'Come and sit beside me, Ardvarrick.'

Logan glanced at Tamhas, who nodded. The matter was dealt with, finished. The flogging had been administered, the culprit punished and life continued, although Logan was surprised at his host's good humour. However, that was soon explained.

'I met with the drovers two days ago,' said Contullach, filling Logan's tankard with ale from a leather blackjack. 'The price they are offering for my cattle this year is pleasing. Very pleasing indeed.'

Logan's brows rose. The meeting must have taken place before he had known that Ailsa was safe.

'Why were you not searching for your niece?'

The old man shrugged. 'I was fair certain you would find her. And you can rest easy now, Ardvarrick. Ewan Cowie will give you no more trouble.'

'You can be sure of that?'

'Aye. He confessed to me he allowed his ballocks to rule his brains.' Contullach saw Logan's look of polite cynicism and added, 'The boy is young, Ardvarrick.'

'Not that young,' Logan flashed back at him. 'He is barely a year younger than I!'

Fingal shrugged. 'He has strong passions and has been too long without a woman. He has been waiting for my Kirstin, you see. Another week and they will be wed. Oh, I see what you are thinking, man, that I shouldn't let him marry my daughter, but she is still mad for him and I cannot deny her what she wants. Besides, the match secures a strong leader for Contullach when I am gone.'

'A strong leader, aye, but not a wise one.'

'Nay, you are wrong. The boy will learn wisdom. Especially when he sees in his purse the extra money we get for our cattle this season.' He grinned and lifted his ale cup. 'To the peace, eh, Ardvarrick?'

Logan touched his tankard to Contullach's, hoping rather than believing he had heard the last of Ewan Cowie.

After Logan had left, Ailsa was at a loss to know what to do with herself. She made her way to the housekeeper's room in search of company and was grateful when Mrs Noranside invited her to take a dish of tea.

'It has rarely been used since the mistress died, but I have the occasional cup and it is still good to drink,' she said, setting a chair for Ailsa before she began preparing the tea.

'When did Lady Ardvarrick die?' asked Ailsa. 'I beg your pardon if I appear too curious, but I am eager to learn as much as I can of the master's family and little is spoken at Contullach about the Rathmores, save when there is something wrong, such as a cattle raid that can be blamed upon them.'

'It has been much the same here at Ardvarrick,' replied the housekeeper with a sigh. 'The late mistress and Morag Contullach did try to bring the families together, when Master Logan was a boy, but I fear Fingal Contullach always resented Ardvarrick's prosperity. It is true that my lady's fortune accounted for some of it, but even more was down to years of good management.' She sighed and looked a little wistful, then shook it off and smiled at Ailsa. 'But what was it you asked me, my dear? Oh, yes, Lady Ardvarrick. Now, let me see…it must be all of four years since she passed on. A lovely lady she was. English born and well connected, too, but not too proud to make her home at Ardvarrick.'

'Did she not miss England?' asked Ailsa.

'A little, but she wrote letters all the time to her family in Hampshire. She sent Logan to live with them, when he had finished his schooling in Edinburgh. That was just before the rising of fifteen and I think my lady was anxious he should not get caught up in that. She was also eager that he should know his relatives and something of the world other than Ardvarrick, so he went south. And he could not have disliked it, for he stayed there until last autumn, when he returned to take up his duties here.' She gave a little laugh. 'He was reluctant when he first came back, we could all see that. He clung to his English ways, but by the end of the winter you could tell he was becoming more at home here. I am hopeful that we might yet see him in the belted plaid, for I recall even as a boy he looked very grand in it.'

Ailsa sipped her tea and imagined Logan's tall, broad-shouldered figure in Highland dress. He had looked very handsome as they rowed away from Castle Creag, standing in the prow of the little boat in his tartan trews and jacket, his head up, hand on the hilt of his sword. Her saviour. Her protector and perhaps—a delicious frisson of excitement ran through her—soon to be her husband.

The day stretched out before Ailsa. Logan's parting words had been that she should explore Ardvarrick and make herself familiar with her new home. She was a little shy of wandering around the house alone, but after spending a comfortable hour drinking tea with Mrs Noranside, the bright sunshine was irresistible and she went out to explore the grounds.

Everything at Ardvarrick delighted Ailsa. She loved the walled kitchen garden, where the air was redolent with the smell of herbs, but it was the terraces on the south front that she liked most. There was a paved walkway all around the house, but on the south side it led down via shallow steps to a terrace containing formal parterres full of lavender, pansies and primulas, as well as tall blue spiky flowers and other colourful blooms that were unfamiliar to Ailsa.

The plant beds were surrounded by low hedges of clipped box or yew and separated by well-drained gravel paths where she could walk out after a shower without having to change into sturdy footwear. Ailsa loved the neatness and order of the parterres and she was intrigued by the imposing statues that stood sentinel over the paths. More steps descended to a narrow strip of sloping lawn. A low wall defined the boundary of the garden and beyond it the meadows led down to the sea that glittered like silver in the sunlight. Colourful flowers had been coaxed to bloom in the borders and more marble statues graced the lawn.

After Contullach with its stark stone walls and cobbled yard, Ardvarrick was luxury indeed.

She whiled away the afternoon out of doors, talking to the gardener who had been brought in by the late Lady Ardvarrick, when the new house had first been conceived, to transform the grounds. Ailsa learned that the statues dotted around the gardens were Italian, shipped over at great expense. Sadly, Logan's mother had died before she had seen her designs realised, but the old Laird had ordered that the gardens should be completed and maintained, as a memorial to his wife.

After finishing a tour of the gardens Ailsa continued her exploration, finding her way to the well-appointed stables, where the head groom was happy to regale her with stories of Logan as a young boy, running wild around the estate. The time flew by and when at last a chill wind sprang up and she returned to the house, she was surprised to see that it was almost time for dinner.

She ran up quickly to her room. Logan had promised to bring her clothes back from Contullach, but he would not return until tomorrow and in the meantime, she must make do with her one gown. The housekeeper had done what she could to clean and mend it, but once she had something fresh to wear Ailsa was determined to throw it away. It held too many horrid memories of her imprisonment at Castle Creag.

She washed her face and hands and tidied her hair and was about to leave the room when she noticed the writing implements were still on the table by the window. Logan had told her that only the housekeeper was allowed into the study and that would explain why

Shona, the maid assigned to look after her, had not returned them. Well, that was something Ailsa could do. She picked up the pen and the silver inkwell and made her way quickly to Logan's study. The room was as she remembered it and Ailsa paused for a moment, imagining Logan here, poring over his accounts or working on his correspondence.

She wished he was there now and was obliged to give herself a little shake. This would not do, she was becoming quite maudlin! Ailsa carefully replaced the inkwell and pen on the standish and as she straightened, she noticed the ball of paper Logan had thrown into the fireplace was still there. It was resting on top of the kindling that had been laid in the fire grate, ready for the master to light when he next used the room.

Ailsa walked to the hearth and carefully lifted out the paper. She would not read Logan's correspondence without permission, but surely there would be no harm in looking at something he had discarded, just to feel a little closer to him? Smoothing out the sheet, she saw it was the beginning of a letter, written with elegant, sloping strokes. Logan's writing, she thought, smiling, and very like the man; bold and decisive. But as her eyes made sense of what she was reading, her smile faded.

My Dear Aunt,
Your letter informing me that Lady Fritchley,
or Lady Mary as I shall always think of her, is
now widowed was news indeed. Also, your as-
sertion that she might now accept an offer from

*me is more encouraging than I had ever dared
to hope after all these years...*

There was no more, but it was enough. What was
it Norry had said? An earl's daughter. Logan's first
love. Ailsa looked at the date in the top corner of the
page. Logan had been writing this when he learned
of her abduction.

'I would not bed a maid and then leave her.'

Ailsa leaned against the wall, feeling slightly sick.
There could be no mistake, his heart still belonged to
this Lady Fritchley. He had broken off from writing
this letter to come to her aid and now, because of what
had happened at the bothy, he felt obliged to marry
her rather than to follow his heart. What other explanation could there be?

The door opened and Shona peeped in.

'Ah, there you are, ma'am! Mistress Noranside sent
me to look for you, so she did. She says I'm to take you
to the dining room, ma'am, if it pleases you.'

'What?' Ailsa stared blankly at the young maid
for a moment, trying to force her raging thoughts into
some sort of order. 'Oh, yes. Yes, I will come immediately.'

She crumpled the letter again and replaced it back
on top of the kindling. Her limbs felt leaden and her
appetite had quite gone, but she must not let it show.
She would save her grief until she was alone in her
room.

Ardvarrick House was a welcome sight in the late
evening sunlight. Logan had only been away one night,
but it felt a lifetime. He had wanted to rush off at dawn,

but Contullach had insisted they hold a meeting to discuss continuing their agreement for a second year. Logan had been obliged to spend precious hours turning his mind to business when he wanted to be riding through the glens back to Ardvarrick. Back to Ailsa.

He hurried indoors and made his way directly to the drawing room, where he found her standing by the window.

'Norry said I should find you here. But why are you in the gloom? We can afford candles, you know. As many as you wish!' He laughed as he pulled her into his arms and kissed her. 'Have you missed me?'

'Of course.'

Her eyes roamed his face anxiously and he shook his head. 'If you are looking for cuts and bruises, there are none. I told you I would not fight Cowie. I left your uncle to deal with the matter.'

'And did he?'

'Aye. Cowie will trouble you no more, Ailsa. I have made it clear that if he sets foot on my land again it will be his corpse I shall be returning to Contullach.' He felt her shudder and drew her close to kiss her again. 'Now, let us put the matter behind us. We must look instead to the future. Do you agree?'

'What? Oh, yes. Yes, certainly, let us not talk of it any longer.'

She would have turned away, but Logan stopped her. He caught her chin and turned her face towards the light.

'But what is this?' he said, frowning. 'You are looking very wan, my dear.'

'I am a little tired,' she said, gently freeing herself from his grasp. 'I did not sleep too well last night.

Norry is waiting for the word to serve dinner, or would you prefer to change first?'

'I cannot sit down with you in all my dirt,' he replied. 'And we can both change our clothes. Your belongings have been packed into two horse panniers which I have had taken up to your room. Come along, I will escort you. You will be able to put on a fresh gown, which I am sure will cheer you.'

Her smile looked a little forced, yet when they reached the door of her chamber and he kissed her, she clung to him and responded eagerly. When at last he broke off and raised his head, he could not prevent a laugh escaping him.

'By heaven, I have only been away one night!' His arms tightened. 'I am sorely tempted to take you to bed now and not wait for the preacher to marry us.'

She blushed adorably, but twisted out of his arms.

'You tempt me, too,' she murmured, 'But we agreed we would wait.' She reached for the door handle. 'And besides, Mrs Noranside will be cross if we are late for dinner!'

Chapter Eleven

Ailsa entered the drawing room a short time later, wearing her best green gown. Logan was waiting for her and, as she came in, he held out his hands.

'That is much better,' he said, guiding her to a chair. 'I have no doubt you are sick of the old one, it has received some very rough wear!'

She smiled at him, determined to be cheerful. 'Yes, indeed. I am glad I can now throw it away.'

'I shall delight in buying you dozens of new gowns, when we are wed.'

She forced herself to look at him. 'Are you—are you sure you wish to do this, Logan, to marry me?'

'But of course, have I not said so?'

'But you have never said that you love me!'

She put her hands to her mouth, aghast that she had given voice to the thought, but Logan showed no signs of anger or irritation. Instead he laughed.

'Is that all? Of course I love you! I am not one to wear my heart on my sleeve, Ailsa. I confess, words do not come easily, but you must trust me on this. There is no one I would rather marry.'

'Not—' She clasped her hands together in her lap and screwed up her courage to say, 'Not Lady Fritchley, now she is a widow?'

Immediately the laughter fled from his face. 'Who told you?'

She quailed before his harsh look. 'I s-saw the letter—'

He paled, his mouth compressed so hard the skin around it turned white. A muscle jerked in his cheek.

'You have been reading my correspondence?'

'No, no!' Her hands writhed together. 'I returned the inkwell and I saw the letter you had started writing to your aunt.'

Almost before she had finished speaking, Logan jumped up and threw himself out of the room. Ailsa waited, dry eyed, her heart thundering in her chest. She had been right to speak, however much it angered him. Pretence was abhorrent to her. It was better that they face the truth now, before they exchanged any binding vows.

Logan came back into the room carrying the crumpled paper in his hand. She closed her eyes and waited for him to speak.

He said heavily, 'I am sorrier than I can say that you found this. I should have burned it. I meant to do so.' She risked looking up and found him watching her, his countenance grave. 'I beg you, Ailsa, forget what you read. Lady Fritchley means nothing to me, do you understand? She rejected me five years ago. She said we should not suit and she was right.' He held the letter to one of the candles burning on the mantelshelf and set it alight, then he dropped it into the hearth. 'When your uncle came to tell me you had been abducted, I could think of nothing else but getting you back safely—' he pulled her up into his arms '—and *keeping* you safe. For ever. As my wife.'

She had not even known she was holding her breath until that moment, but now she let it go and was left feeling weak with relief. She raised her eyes and searched his face.

'Truly, Logan?'

'Yes, *truly.*'

His mouth came down upon hers and he kissed her fiercely. It sent her mind spinning, as if she was tumbling through space. She felt his hands on her body, caressing, exploring and she melted against him while desire unfurled deep inside, heating her blood. He cupped her breast, his thumb circling over the thin material and causing her to whimper against his mouth. She forgot Lady Fritchley, forgot everything except the pleasure of his touch.

'You see?' he murmured, trailing a line of kisses over her neck. 'You see how I cannot resist you?'

'Nor I you.'

She turned her head, her mouth seeking his and joining for another smouldering kiss that left them both hot and breathless. She leaned against him, eyes closed, revelling in the delicious sensations he awoke within her.

Logan hugged her to him, resting his cheek gently on the top of her head.

'I should like to take you to bed this minute, but I suppose we must eat, else Norry will want to know why.'

She gave a sigh. 'I suppose we must.'

A laugh rumbled in his chest. 'You sound as reluctant as I, sweetheart! But it will not be long until our wedding day, and then, I promise you, we shall spend whole days in bed, if we wish it.' He gave her a final kiss, then released her. 'Now, however, we must observe the proprieties.' He held out his arm. 'Shall we go in to dinner?'

They sat together at the table, giggling like children and stealing kisses whenever they were alone in the room. Ailsa could not wholly believe he could prefer her to a beautiful and accomplished English lady, but she vowed she would be a good wife to Logan. She would make him love her.

When they had finished dinner, Logan jumped up from the table and took her hand. 'With all that happened earlier I quite forgot that I have something else for you. Come with me.'

He led her to the morning room, picking up a candelabrum from a hall table as they passed. They entered the room and the flickering candlelight fell upon something in the corner, something shrouded in a linen cover. Holding the candles aloft, Logan pulled away the cloth with a flourish.

'There.' He beamed at her. 'You see, I have brought your harp! Contullach was loath to part with it, but eventually I persuaded him. I even remembered to collect the small stool it rests upon while you play. And in the attics here, I found the chair Grandmama was wont to use when she played. I hope it will suit you.'

Ailsa stared in horror at the *clàrsach*, the silver strings gleaming in the candlelight, and all her hopes for the future crumbled. Could the evening get any worse? She burst into tears.

Logan quickly put down the candles and gathered Ailsa into his arms. 'My love, what is this, what is wrong? I thought it would please you to have your harp here so you could play again.'

'If only I could.' She sobbed against his coat.

He sat down on a sofa and gently pulled her on to his lap, holding her until the spasm of weeping subsided. He pulled his handkerchief from his pocket and mopped her face.

'This is not like you,' he murmured, tucking a silky red lock of hair behind her ear. 'Tell me what has upset you so?'

'I beg your pardon, I did not intend to weep. It is the shock!' She took the proffered kerchief and blew her little nose defiantly. 'It was very, very thoughtful of you to bring the harp for me, Logan, but you see— Oh, I should have told you!'

'Told me what?'

'That I—' she hiccupped '—I can no longer play. It is the curse of the Contullach harpers. Fingal knows it. Did he not tell you? Only virgins can play the *clàrsach*.'

'What? Ailsa, that is nonsense. You cannot believe such a fairy tale.'

'It is not a fairy tale, Logan. My own mother lost her ability to play as soon as she married my father.'

'Why should that be?' he said gently, 'Ailsa, it makes no sense.'

'But it is the truth! Everyone at Contullach knows it. That is why my uncle could not let me marry, why he was so anxious to have me back unharmed.'

Logan frowned. That certainly made sense, the way Contullach had reacted to losing his harper.

'Your uncle may well believe it,' he said slowly, 'but that does not make it so. Most likely it was a legend dreamed up by the Contullach chiefs in order to retain their harpers. It is merely superstition, Ailsa. Heaven knows there is enough of that in this land, with its tales of bogles, kelpies and fairies.'

She extricated herself from his arms and slipped from his lap to the sofa beside him.

'I wish that were so,' she muttered, wiping her eyes, 'but I know it is true.'

She was clearly upset and he refrained from arguing further. Instead he waited for her to continue. Eventually she began, haltingly at first, and all the time dragging the mangled handkerchief back and forth between her fingers.

'My mother was the harper at Contullach, you see. Everyone agrees she was the best in Ross-shire. Then she met my father and married him. After that she never played again.'

'Where is your father now?'

'He died, before I was born.'

Logan put an arm around her shoulders, relieved when she did not shrug him away.

'Could it not be that she was too heartbroken at the loss of her lover to touch the harp again? I can more readily believe that her inability to play was caused by grief than her lost virginity.'

'No, you are wrong. My aunt herself told me that Mother passed the *clàrsach* back to her when she married. It is well known that the harpers of Contullach must remain virgins.'

He said gently, 'You say that, Ailsa, but what proof have you? I say it is a story, a legend. Your talent is part of you. It cannot disappear because you are no longer a maid.' He hugged her closer and whispered, 'Why do you not try to play, Ailsa?'

'Because it would be futile.' She shrank against him. 'Please do not ask it of me.'

Silently, he held her. She was upset, frightened. To insist would only make things worse.

'Very well, my love. It is late. The harp will still be here in the morning. You can try it when you are ready. Now, though, I think it time for sleep. I will escort you to your room.'

Logan left her at the door to her chamber, and Ailsa went in, alone. He had tried to reassure her, but in truth, she felt worse than ever. He was too good, too kind. He deserved better than a wife with nothing to recommend her, not even music.

Ailsa woke early. A good night's sleep and the sun streaming into her room made her feel much more hopeful for the future. She threw on her wrap and stole downstairs to the morning room. The harp was still in the corner and she approached it cautiously. Logan had said there was no reason why she should not be able to play. He said her fears were mere superstition. Perhaps he was right; after all he was an educated man, well-travelled and with far more experience of the world.

She sat down on the chair and touched the strings. The discordant sound did not surprise her. The *clàrsach* had not been played for several weeks and, after its long journey here, it was woefully out of tune. She

picked up her tuning key and set to work, but however much she tweaked the pegs, it was always too
much or too little. She could not achieve the sound
she wanted. She continued doggedly for an hour, but
the sweet notes eluded her and eventually she gave
up. She had lost her touch, her fine ear for the perfect note. With a sob she ran out of the room, her eyes
blinded with tears.

By evening she had decided what must be done and
when she joined Logan in the drawing room before
dinner, she lost no time in suggesting the harp should
be returned to Contullach.

'It was very good of you to bring it, Logan, I am
very grateful, but if I cannot play then it should go
back. My uncle will be wanting another harper and it
is a shame for such a lovely instrument to be wasted.'

But he would not hear of it.

'Let us move it to the little parlour on the north side
of the house. We never use that room, so it will not
in any way be a reproach to you, but it will be there
when you want to try again.' He kissed her. 'Your
nerves have overcome you, Ailsa, I am confident you
will recover and, when you do, I want the *clàrsach* to
be here for you.'

His faith in her brought more tears welling up.

'Logan, I will never play again. My gift is gone.'

'Nonsense. I will not believe that.'

She shook her head, wishing she could make him
understand. He gave a long sigh and put his arms
around her.

'Very well, then. If you do not play, so be it. Our

children shall use it. Our sons, perhaps, but our daughters most assuredly.'

Ailsa knew he was trying to be kind, but his words cut her even more. She wanted to please him, but there was no way around it. The small spinet that had belonged to his mother was beyond her, although Logan could play and he sometimes accompanied her while she sang for him, but her heart ached to be able to play the jigs and reels that he loved so much.

The final weeks until the wedding passed quickly. Màiri wrote to Ailsa to tell her of Kirstin's marriage to Ewan and amid her fulsome descriptions of the celebrations held at Contullach, she could not resist mentioning her father's annoyance that Ailsa had not been there to play for them. However, the successful passage of the drovers through Bealach na Damh with cattle from both Contullach and Ardvarrick went a long way to healing any breach and Fingal accepted Ailsa's invitation for him, his wife and younger daughter to attend the wedding party and stay overnight at Ardvarrick.

There was much to be done and Ailsa was thankful for it. The house had to be prepared for visitors and she threw herself into her household duties, taking pleasure from Logan's praise of her efforts when she put fresh flowers in the hall or the drawing room, or when she rearranged the furniture.

'You will be an admirable Lady Ardvarrick,' he told her one morning, pulling her close and kissing her. 'I am a very lucky man.'

'And I am a very lucky woman,' she replied, laughing. When he released her she stepped back, putting her hands on her hips as she regarded him. 'You are looking particularly fine today.'

Logan grinned, a faint self-conscious blush touching his cheeks. 'You approve of my belted plaid?'

Using the plaid as his cloak when he had ridden to Castle Creag had reminded him what a practical piece of material it was and he had searched the trunks stored in the attics to find a long tunic, thick knitted socks and brogues he might wear with it. Ailsa's look of admiration now made all his efforts worthwhile.

'I do approve,' she told him, her eyes twinkling. 'I noticed you had started to wear it when you were working on the estate. No doubt you decided to take to it after much well-reasoned argument.'

She was teasing him and he responded in kind.

'Of course. One can move far more freely in the kilt than trews. And it does not have to be removed for wading through the ice-cold water that abounds in this land, even in summer!'

He left her then, striding out of the house with an added spring in his step. The encounter with Ailsa had lifted his spirits and it seemed to him that the sun was shining brighter, the birds singing louder. He dragged in a deep breath and let it go again in a sigh of pure satisfaction. On such a day as this there could surely be no better place to be than Ardvarrick.

In fact, he was beginning to realise just how much he had missed his home and how much he was enjoying being back, walking or riding out over his land, watching the seasons change, working hard with Tamhas each day to improve Ardvarrick for himself and his tenants and returning each evening to sit down to a good dinner with Ailsa.

He knew she was working equally hard, for since she had been at Ardvarrick the house was quite transformed. It was no longer a cold empty shell, full of memories of absent family. Now it welcomed him when he returned to it. He would walk in eagerly and, if Ailsa was not in the hall to greet him, he hurried through the rooms until he found her.

He loved the way her countenance lit up when she saw him, the way they could talk for hours about anything or nothing. She was interested in every aspect of Ardvarrick. They discussed plans for improving the land and the tenant farms and he enjoyed telling her of his day, even the problems and setbacks, which always seemed to shrink when he laid them before her. With Ailsa at his side, his responsibilities as Laird no longer daunted him. She had not only transformed his house, she had transformed his life.

His only regret was that she still fretted over her music. She did her best to hide it, but he had walked in upon her one day before she had time to dry her eyes.

'I went to the small parlour,' she said, when he asked her what was the matter. 'The *clàrsach* is so out of tune and I... I c-cannot...'

His heart went out to her and he took her in his arms.

'With so many preparations for the wedding it is no wonder if you are too worked up to play. You must have patience, my love. Your talent is sleeping, that is all.'

'But what if it isn't?' she asked him, her eyes misty with tears. 'I am nothing to you without my music.'

'Oh, my darling, you are wrong! You are so much more to me than a harper!' He smiled down at her, brushing a stray curl from her face. 'It is you I love, Ailsa. Your wit, your grace and beauty. Do you understand? Oh, I do not deny that when I first saw you, sitting beside the loch, your music bewitched me. I had never heard anything so beautiful. I thought at first you were a water sprite, a creature not of this earth.' His arms tightened. 'Now I know you are flesh and blood. I know you to be a brave, intelligent woman and I love you more than ever. Believe me, Ailsa, nothing matters save that I have you in my life.'

He kissed away her tears and she assured him she was better now, but despite her smiles the sadness was still there, at the back of her eyes, and it worried him.

Ailsa was grateful that Logan no longer mentioned her music and she worked hard to please him in other ways. Not that it was a chore because she loved Ardvarrick. She enjoyed keeping house and learning about the land and its people. She also took an interest in Logan's books, borrowing them to read for herself although she liked it best when he would read to her in the evenings, especially the poetry, which they would afterwards discuss.

She might not be the accomplished English lady Logan deserved, but Ailsa began to believe that she really could make him happy. And she wanted to please him so much that it was a physical ache. Her music remained the only cloud on her horizon. She could not forget it. Occasionally she would go into the little parlour and look at the *clàrsach*, but something stopped her from touching it. She could not bring herself to try, only to fail again.

'Not yet,' she told herself, each time she walked away. 'I *will* play again, but not yet.'

Chapter Twelve

The final few days before the wedding became a blur to Ailsa as she kept herself busy with the preparations. Only Tamhas and Mrs Noranside would be in attendance at the wedding ceremony, but Logan insisted upon a dinner and reception afterwards, when he planned to introduce his new bride to his friends and neighbours. A few she knew already, as they were also Contullach's neighbours, but most would be family friends of the Rathmores and people who lived and worked at Ardvarrick.

Logan's English relations would not be making the long journey north from Hampshire, but his aunt had put together and forwarded a selection of gowns for Ailsa as a wedding present, based on the measurements and description of her that Logan had supplied. The gowns needed little alteration and Ailsa chose for her wedding day a yellow satin embroidered with acanthus leaves on the hem and sleeves. When she tried on the gown for the first time, she was surprised at the heady scent that rose up from the sweet-smelling herbs stuffed into the bone-stiffened stomacher.

The matching shoes, too, were something new for Ailsa. They were fashioned in the same yellow brocade as the gown and very elegant, but Ailsa was unused to heels, even though Logan told her they were very modest. She spent the best part of the two days before the wedding walking around the house in the shoes to accustom herself to them.

On the wedding day itself, Ailsa woke early to a golden sunrise. It promised to be a balmy September day and she decided to stroll outside and calm her nerves before Shona dressed her in her finery. The house was looking particularly resplendent in the morning sunshine and, inside, the rooms had been swept and polished until everything glowed. Garlands of pine branches scented the air of the entrance hall and fresh flowers had been collected to decorate the morning room where the private ceremony was to take place. As Ailsa returned to her bedchamber to put on her gown, she made a mental note to thank Norry and the maids for helping her with all the preparations.

The maid had just finished arranging Ailsa's hair when Logan knocked on the door of her bedchamber.

'May I come in?

'Of course.' She shook out her skirts and turned to greet him.

'The minister is here and waiting for us. I have come to escort you downstairs, if you are ready?'

Ailsa stared at him in silence. He looked so handsome that he took her breath away and she was quite unable to respond.

Logan saw her confusion and he gave a self-conscious laugh as he glanced down at himself.

'I hope you approve of my new coat, madam?'

She knew nothing of London fashions, but she thought privately that he looked magnificent. The dove-grey coat was trimmed with silver braid while the wide cuffs were paler and matched the brocaded waistcoat. His unpowdered hair was caught back with a length of silver braid and a diamond sparkled from the lace at his throat.

He went on, 'Perhaps you would prefer me to be dressed in a tartan plaid.'

She smiled at that. 'You would look very fine in it, Logan Rathmore, as you know full well, but your aunt and uncle had that suit made for you and it is only fitting that you wear it.'

'Then it will have to do.' He came closer. 'I have brought you this. Norry had them made up for us. For luck.'

He held out a small bunch of white heather tied with a green ribbon, identical to the one pinned to his own coat.

'Oh, how kind.' Ailsa took the sprig, but her fingers fumbled with the pin and Logan took it from her.

'Here, let me do that.'

She held her breath as he deftly fastened the heather to her gown, trying to conceal how much his proximity affected her, setting her heart thumping and her skin tingling with desire. When his fingers brushed her breast, she thought her face would burst into flames and kept her gaze fixed upon his cravat.

'Thank you,' she whispered, when he had done.

She knew her cheeks were crimson and she was grateful that he made no mention of it.

He said, 'I know we agreed we should not exchange presents, but I thought you might like this.' He reached into his pocket and pulled out a book.

'Oh, Lovelace's poems!' She held the small leather-bound volume reverently between her hands. 'But this is your copy.'

'I know how much you enjoy his poetry and I wanted you to have it.'

'Th-thank you.' She glanced up at him shyly. 'Could we perhaps write both our names in it, and the date, to celebrate our wedding?'

His evident pleasure at the suggestion was all the reward Ailsa needed.

'An excellent notion,' he told her, smiling. 'However, we cannot do that now, I will not risk either of us having inky fingers when we make our vows!' He stepped away a little and proffered his arm. 'Well, ma'am, shall we do this?'

The thought of what was to come sobered her. She stepped up and put her fingers on his velvet sleeve. As they set off down the stairs she was glad of his support, for her eyes were not quite clear and she was obliged to blink several times. How kind he was! And how blessed was she, that such a man would want her for his wife.

In the drawing room, the minister was waiting for them. Norry was there, in her finest gown, and Tamhas, resplendent in new tartan trews and jacket. He was the Laird's groomsman and his only relative, but since only Ailsa's aunt and uncle and Màiri had been invited, she hoped that at the reception to follow, Logan's lack of close family would go unnoticed. The room fell silent as they entered and Ailsa clung to Logan's arm, afraid that if she let go, her shaking limbs would not support her through the coming service.

Even with the windows thrown open the drawing room was warm and airless. Logan wanted to run a finger around his neck. In his haste he must have tied his cravat far too tight. The room seemed much brighter than usual, too, the colourful flowers arranged in pitchers and vases were almost unnaturally vibrant, more reminiscent of high summer than mid-September. He felt light-headed, intoxicated. Only the woman standing beside him kept him steady as the minister began to speak. She was pale but composed, her red curls tamed and caught back from her face in a yellow ribbon. How had he ever thought her anything but beautiful? A cough from the reverend brought him back to the service with a jolt. It was time for him to make his vows.

Ailsa fixed her eyes on the minister's dour countenance and tried to concentrate upon the words of the service, steeling herself to perform her part. She concentrated on taking slow, deep breaths and was thankful that her voice at least was not quivering when she made her vows. It was a solemn occasion, but she wished she felt more joyous, instead of expecting any minute someone would burst in and denounce her as a fraud. Beside her, Logan made his responses in a calm, steady tone and only Ailsa noticed that his hand shook a little when he slipped the gold band on her finger. Strangely, she found his nervousness reassuring.

To Ailsa's overstretched nerves the service seemed to go on for ever but then, in an instant, it was over. Her hand was once again on Logan's arm and he was leading her away to the dining room, where the wedding breakfast had been prepared for them. She was glad to sit down, but she had little appetite and only picked at her food while Logan and the others talked with the minister. Gradually, she began to feel more at ease and eventually she was brave enough to exchange a look with Logan. His smile was reassuring and by the time the meal was over, her nerves had settled and she found she could even look forward with equanimity to the reception that was to follow.

By the time the wedding party left the dining room, the hall and drawing room were overflowing with staff and townsfolk, all enjoying the copious amounts of wine and ale the Laird had ordered to be served. Logan took Ailsa around the room, introducing her to each guest by name.

'Heavens, you have been back in Scotland for barely a year, Logan. I marvel that you should know so much about your neighbours and tenants, their history and their families. I am impressed.'

'Thank you!' He laughed, delighted by her praise. 'I have made it my business to reacquaint myself with every one of them. It is a bad laird who does not know his people and look after them.'

'Very true. I must make efforts to know them, too.' They moved on to speak to another tenant farmer and his family and, after the introductions, Logan was content to stand back and watch Ailsa converse with them. She had a natural friendliness that soon put them at their ease. He listened to her talking of the harvest to the husband and discussing cheesemaking with the wife. She even managed to draw a little conversation from their shy and tongue-tied daughter. Norry was watching from across the room and, catching her eye, Logan gave her a nod and a smile. Ailsa was acquitting herself well—she would make a fine Lady Ardvarrick.

As the conversation continued around him, he was distracted by the yellow ribbon holding her hair in place. His thoughts drifted. He imagined how it would be when all the guests had departed and he could finally take his bride to bed. How easy would it be, he wondered, to free those burnished locks and let them fall over her shoulders? Should he untie the ribbon before or after he had slipped the gown from her shoulders and covered her neck and breasts with kisses?

Ailsa squeezed his arm and he almost jumped. It was time to move on, to speak with more guests, to receive their congratulations and exchange pleasantries when all he really wanted to do was to sweep his bride into his arms and carry her upstairs, where they might enjoy one another's bodies in a comfortable bed for as long as they wished. That was something he had been thinking of almost constantly since they had lain together in the bothy, but it must wait a little longer. Dutifully he summoned up a smile and nodded to the farmer and his wife before leading Ailsa away.

There were so many guests, so many strangers to meet that it was some time before Ailsa was able to speak to her aunt and uncle. She noticed them standing a little apart with Màiri and, since Logan was talking of estate matters with Tamhas, she excused herself and slipped across to join them.

'Well now, Ailsa, you look very grand in your London fashions,' Màiri greeted her, a slightly envious note in her voice.

'Why, I thank you.' Ailsa smiled, determined to remain on good terms with everyone today. 'Ardvarrick's aunt sent this up for me.' She smoothed her hands down over the gown. 'I confess the wide skirts and high heels give rise to no little anxiety. I am very much afraid I shall trip up before the day is out.'

'Nonsense, you move very gracefully, my dear.' Morag leaned forward to kiss her cheek.

Fingal was scowling beside her. He said, 'I hope you think this is worth it, when you realise what you have given up.'

'Do you mean her music?' Màiri gave a shrill little laugh. 'What is that compared to being the Lady of Ardvarrick? She can have anything she wants now.'

'Hold your tongue, child!' snapped her father. 'You know nothing about the gift. When it is lost it eats away at the soul.' He turned his savage glare upon Ailsa. 'It will destroy you, lassie, as it has done others before you.'

His words struck Ailsa like icy water, but she stood her ground, refusing to allow her dismay to show.

Morag laid a hand on her husband's arm and admonished him gently, 'Hush, Fingal, it is her wedding day. Wish your niece well.'

Her uncle glowered for a moment before stooping to buss her cheek.

'May ye be a good wife to your lord,' he muttered. 'And may your house be full of peace and harmony.'

Ailsa dropped a stiff little curtsy. 'Thank you for your kind blessing, Uncle. And as for my music—' her head came up and she stared back at him defiantly '—why would Logan have brought the *clàrsach* here for me, if I cannot play it?'

'Have you tried?' Fingal fixed her with a searching glare that made her blush.

'Not yet, but there has been so much to be done...'

'Hah. I have seen it before,' he told her in a tone of morbid satisfaction. 'Contullach harpers have a rare gift. You chose to throw it away and now you must bear the consequences. You are cursed, girl. Cursed!'

'Fingal!'

'It is the truth, Morag. It destroyed her mother, and 'twill be the same for her, make no mistake about that!'

Ailsa felt her temper rising and she lifted her chin a little higher. 'If I cannot play, then it is God's will and I have no doubt he will bless me in other ways!'

She turned and walked away, desperate to find Logan. Her eyes searched the crowd and she saw him standing on the far side of the room, talking with one of his tenants. She wanted to run to him, to find comfort in his arms, but that would only show Fingal how much his words had affected her. She must play her part, pretend all was well, but although she smiled and chattered with her guests, deep down the little worm of unhappiness gnawed at her. Having married Logan, she had lost the gift that would most have pleased him.

Not that he had said as much. Indeed, when a guest remarked upon the lack of music that evening, he declared it was the custom in English society.

'Is that true?' Ailsa asked him, when they were alone for a moment.

'It is not *untrue*, my love. Many noble families conduct their weddings in private, without even a reception to follow them.'

'I thought you were merely saying it because I can no longer play the *clàrsach*.'

He put his hands on her shoulders and stared down at her.

'You *can* play,' he said. 'I do not believe you have lost your ability. And, given time, you will play again.'

Ailsa was grateful to Logan. He was trying to spare her the embarrassment of having guests invite her to play and everyone appeared to accept his explanation. Only her immediate family came close to guessing the real reason there was no songs or dancing and when Ailsa passed her cousin later in the evening, she felt a twitch of her sleeve.

'Does the Laird dislike music so much,' Màiri hissed, 'or is the lack of it your choice, to cover the fact that you cannot play?'

Ailsa ignored her and would have moved, but Màiri gripped her arm.

'I am sure you would like to hear about Kirstin's wedding.' Her smile was belied by the spiteful gleam in her eyes. 'It was a much livelier affair than this!' She looked up as her mother came up with a group of ladies. 'Mama, I was just telling Ailsa about Kirstin's wedding. You were there too, Mistress MacLeod, did you not think it a splendid day?'

'Aye, it was that!' The matron chuckled and tapped Morag's arm. 'Quite an achievement, Mistress Contullach, to marry off your daughter and your niece in one Season.'

'Indeed, we have been very fortunate,' replied Morag. She would have said more, but her daughter cut across her.

'It was a very different affair from this. My sister's wedding was in the best traditions of Contullach, was it not, Mama? Everyone brought food gifts, as is the custom. Not that we needed them, but Kirstin is so popular we could not refuse to let everyone show their regard.' Another sideways glance at Ailsa. 'And Father found a grey horse to take Kirstin to the Kirk. Greys are very lucky for brides, you know.'

'With such a husband she will need it,' muttered Ailsa, hanging on to her temper with difficulty.

She heard sniggers from the ladies.

'And will ye be observing the old custom of bedding the bride?' one asked slyly.

Ailsa's face flamed at the thought of it; all the guests bustling her into the bedroom and putting her into bed, from where she would have to dispense food and drink to everyone. Before she could frame a reply, she heard a deep voice at her shoulder.

'Alas, no,' Logan drawled, sounding every bit the English gentleman. 'A rather outmoded custom, do you not agree?' He gave an elegant and very visible shudder before continuing. 'Neither will my bride be throwing one of her stockings over her shoulder for the maids to fight over.' He slipped an arm about Ailsa's waist and pulled her closer. 'Apart from my bride, the only person touching those silk stockings will be me!'

Ailsa's face was positively scorching now, but the

older ladies merely laughed and shook their heads at the Laird.

'Oh, how disappointing,' cried Mistress MacLeod. 'Young Màiri here did not win her sister's stocking, did you, my dear? I am sure you would have liked another chance. You will want to be next to marry, eh?'

'No, no,' replied Morag, laughing. 'Màiri is not yet sixteen. Plenty of time for her to be thinking of marriage.'

Màiri, her colour heightened, turned on Logan.

'And I doubt you'll be up for the creelin'?' When he raised his brows, she tittered. 'La, sir, have you been away so long you have forgotten how we go on here in the Highlands?'

'Alas, it would appear so, Mistress Màiri.'

'Dear me, and you the Laird of Ardvarrick.' The pitying look Màiri threw at him enraged Ailsa and it was only Logan's warning squeeze of her waist that prevented her from firing up in his defence.

'Then let me explain it to you,' Màiri continued, with silky insolence. 'The groom has a large basket tied around his neck, which the guests fill with stones. Only his bride is allowed to save him from being throttled by the weight of it.' She sighed. 'Ewan is so very strong that it was no hardship for him. He bore it most manfully and the basket was almost full before Kirstin cut him free.'

'I should have left him to his fate!' declared Ailsa.

A moment of shocked silence followed, then Logan laughed.

'What a bloodthirsty wench you are, my dear, to be sure.' He smiled at the little group gathered around them. 'Perhaps now, ladies and gentlemen, you can see why I am set against these local customs!'

The tension was broken. Everyone laughed and Logan invited them all to make their way to the dining room, where supper had been laid out.

When he would have followed his guests, Ailsa put her hand on his arm and detained him.

'I beg your pardon, Logan,' she whispered, contrite. 'I did not intend to say such a thing, but Màiri made me so angry!'

'I could see that, my dear, but she is not worth your concern.' He pulled her hand on to his arm. 'Lower your hackles, Ailsa, and let us join our guests for supper. We will show them that a civilised couple do not need such violent means to demonstrate their happiness.'

With a final squeeze of her fingers he led her towards the door, but Ailsa was still in a temper.

'Very well,' she muttered, 'but I still wish Kirstin had let the rope strangle him!'

The guests took advantage of the full moon and clear skies to delay their departure, and it was past midnight before Logan took Ailsa's hand and murmured that it was time to go to bed.

He pulled her closer. 'It has been very hard for me to keep away from you for the last few weeks.'

'Has it, truly?' She blushed and wished she had the courage to tell him that she, too, would have liked the comfort and reassurance of sleeping in his arms.

'Damned hard.' He put his fingers under her chin and tilted her face up to place a gentle kiss on her lips.

'But taking you to bed now will be all the sweeter for it.'

Ailsa uttered a half-hearted protest as he swept her up into his arms and carried her up the stairs. She clung to him, her head against his shoulder and a delicious swirl of anticipation gathering inside.

The bedchamber was decorated in rich blues and reds with lavish gilding that glowed in the candlelight. A fire had been kindled in the hearth and Logan set Ailsa on her feet before it.

'I told the servants they would not be needed tonight,' he said, his hands on her shoulders. 'We will be obliged to undress one another.'

There was such a glow in his eyes that her heart began to thud a little quicker. She ran her tongue around her lips and tried to match his seductive tone.

'I am sure we can manage that.'

His jacket was already open and she put her hands on his chest and began to unbutton his waistcoat. She fumbled a little, but he waited patiently until he could slip off the coat and waistcoat in one smooth movement and toss them over a chair. When she tried to unfasten his shirt he stopped her.

'My turn.'

He grasped the ends of the ribbon bows that fastened across the front of her gown. Soon the stomacher joined his coats on the chair and he was busy unlacing the red silk stays beneath the open bodice. It was a delicious torture. Ailsa kept her eyes on his face, watching his rapt concentration as he worked. The faint vibration as each lace was slowly pulled free made Ailsa's skin tingle. She swallowed nervously as he gently removed the bodice and the stays. The satin skirts slipped to the floor with a whisper and billowed around her feet. They were soon followed by the cotton petticoats and her flimsy chemise. Standing naked before Logan, Ailsa felt suddenly shy and she folded her arms across her breasts, eyes downcast.

Logan reached out and gently pulled the ribbon from her hair and the wild curls tumbled down over her shoulders in a fiery cascade. Just as he had imagined.

'By heaven, you are beautiful, Ailsa.'

She gazed up at him, such a look of trust in her violet eyes that the breath caught in his throat. He would remember this moment for ever. She gave him a shy smile.

'Now,' she whispered, 'is it time for me to undress *you* a little more?'

'I think it is.'

He helped her to step over the waves of satin around her feet. He was anticipating the pleasure of removing those fine silk stockings, tied at the knee with yellow ribbons, but first he had to keep still while she removed the froth of lace at his neck and set to work on the buttons of his shirt. As he drew it off over his head he felt her fingers exploring his chest and he closed his eyes, enjoying her touch. He inhaled sharply when he felt her lips on his breast. Desire was pulsing through him, heightened to almost unendurable limits as she unfastened his satin breeches.

'Enough.' His body as well as his voice was trembling as he caught her hands.

'Does it not please you?'

He gave a ragged laugh. 'It does, sweetheart. Too much!' Quickly he removed the remainder of his clothes and lifted her into his arms. 'Time to make ourselves more comfortable, I think.'

Logan carried her to the bed and put her down gently on the covers. She reached for him and he stretched himself beside her, indulging in a long and languorous kiss before turning his attention to removing the final pieces of clothing. He slipped off her shoes and when she reached for the ribbon garters at her knees, he stopped her.

'No. That is my privilege, and one I have been anticipating all evening.'

The promise in his deep voice set Ailsa's body tingling with excitement. She sank back against the soft bank of feather pillows and watched as he pulled away the yellow ribbons that secured her embroidered silk stockings. He had bedded her before and she remembered how the white-hot desire had gripped her, driving all other thoughts from her mind. Even tonight, standing before the fire while they undressed one another, she had felt the heady excitement, but now she was suddenly afraid of giving way to it and succumbing to a passion she could not control.

Logan had eased one stocking down barely an inch when she shivered. Immediately he stopped.

'I go too fast for you.'

She was filled with a new fear, that she would disappoint him.

'I beg your pardon. I did not mean— that is, I—'

'Hush.' He put his fingers to her lips and shifted to lie beside her. 'We have all the time in the world.'

He turned her face to his, kissing her gently. She moved towards him, gradually relaxing as his embraces drove away the uncertainty. Nothing mattered but his touch, the way his hands caressed her body and her sudden, urgent need. He cupped one breast with his hand and her own flew up to trap it there, that he might feel the swift tattoo of her heart. His kiss deepened, turning her bones to water.

Their bodies came together, his was hard, aroused, and she moulded herself to him. She was light-headed, the blood pounded through her and when Logan began to trail kisses over her body she lay back and let the delicious sensations wash over her—the soft feather pillows and silky smoothness of the coverlet at her back, the gentle touch of Logan's hands and mouth on her skin, moving lower, across her belly, her thighs. Inside she was hot, aching, but although she lifted her hips, offering herself, he continued to trail those tingling, butterfly kisses down to her knee.

Gently, with infinite care he began to roll down one embroidered stocking. Ailsa closed her eyes, clutching at the bedding. She wanted to scream out, to drag him on top of her and have him fill her, but the slow glide of the silk from her leg was teasing her senses, enhancing the pleasure already rippling through her. It was almost unbearable and yet she did not want him to stop. First one stocking, then the other, each inch of flesh uncovered rewarded with a kiss, until she was completely naked.

Ailsa moaned and gripped the coverlet, fearing at any moment she might explode. She wondered if she could endure more pleasure. He gently eased her legs apart and kissed the inside of her thigh. It was the gentlest touch, light as a feather, but it sent a yearning excitement coursing through her and she shifted restlessly. Then he was holding her firm, his mouth addressing the hot, aching void between her thighs, kissing her the way he had kissed her mouth. It roused her to a state of frenzy that she could not control.

She cried out, bucking beneath the onslaught. She was drowning in wave after wave of pleasure that left her on the point of fainting. She felt a moment of panic when Logan stopped kissing her, but almost immediately he had covered her with his body and he was easing himself into her. He moved slowly, holding her at fever pitch on the crest of a wave until even his iron control could bear it no longer and he thrust into her, once, then again and she pushed back until with a shout he carried her beyond reason. She was flying, falling, her mind splintering like glass as she lost control.

There were tears on her cheeks. Ailsa clung to Logan, feeling his weight on her, his chest heaving as he, too, recovered from the shattering peak of their union.

'You screamed,' he murmured. 'Did I hurt you?'

'Not at all.' She could not speak above a whisper.

His long sigh of satisfaction warmed her heart. 'I have been wanting to do this with you since the first time. I wanted you to enjoy it, too.'

'I did,' she assured him. 'It was wonderful.'

'Good.' He rolled to one side and pulled her against him. 'Now we are truly man and wife.'

Chapter Thirteen

Man and wife.

The words kept coming back to Ailsa, creeping up to surprise her when she was least expecting it. She was happy, she knew she was. She loved Logan and when she was in his arms, when he was kissing her, nothing else mattered. He loved her, he wanted her, but in recent weeks she had begun to wake up feeling unwell and when he reached for her she was obliged to excuse herself and slip away. During the day, when Logan was away, riding over the estate with Tamhas, her thoughts turned to the *clàrsach* and she would want to play it, but when she went to the small parlour, no matter how hard she tried, her ear would not pick out the nuances in tone required to tune it properly, and the sounds she made were harsh and discordant. They mocked her.

Logan never mentioned her playing, but Ailsa knew he had not forgotten it. She noticed that if he was humming or whistling a tune, he would stop when he saw her. As the weeks went on, frustration began to gnaw at her. She felt constantly tired and headaches made her short-tempered and irritable, prone to burst into tears at the slightest thing. Even worse, the more Logan wanted to help her the more she pushed him away, snapping at him when he tried to comfort her until, inevitably, he lost his temper.

They were in the drawing room after dinner, candles burning and the curtains pulled across the windows to shut out the October night. A cheerful fire blazed in the hearth, but, despite its warmth, the atmosphere between them was distinctly chilly. They had disagreed over some trifling matter at dinner and now Ailsa refused his offer to pour her some wine.

A burgeoning headache was making her tense and the slightest noise was amplified so that just the sound of the glass stopper being replaced in the decanter made her wince and she snapped at Logan, who muttered an oath.

'By heaven, madam, you are turning into a veritable shrew! Is there nothing I can do right for you?'

She wanted to throw herself into his arms, to apologise for her tantrums and tell him just how much he did right for her. How much she loved him. Instead she found herself hunching a shoulder, wanting to hit out, to hurt him.

'You can leave me in peace, Logan Rathmore, that is what you can do for me!'

'Well, you shall have your wish,' he fired back. 'Tomorrow Tamhas and I ride over to Dellbost. We will be away for the night. Nay, maybe two!'

'The longer the better, since we only make each other miserable!'

'Perhaps you regret you ever married me,' he muttered.

'Aye, I do! Just as much as you regret marrying me!' Ailsa was shocked to hear herself giving voice to her fears. It was not at all what she wanted to say to him. She clenched her fists and dug the nails into the palms. 'Oh, Logan, I am sorry. I did not mean—'

But it was too late. He was gone.

Ailsa ran to the door in time to see him disappearing into his study. She wanted to go after him and beg him to forgive her, to try to explain how ill she felt, but the headache was pounding at her temples and making her feel sick. She decided she should go to bed. If she could just lie down the headache would pass quicker. Then she would be able to make her peace with Logan.

After Shona had helped her into her nightshirt, Ailsa dismissed her and climbed into bed. She leaned back against the pillows, thinking how best to beg Logan's pardon for her latest outburst. She must explain to him how ill she felt, but she doubted he would understand, for he was always in the best of health. Indeed, she herself had never suffered a moment's illness until now and she felt very foolish to be brought so low by the veriest trifles. That was why she had done her best to conceal the malady from everyone.

As the hours ticked by, the feelings of guilt increased. She thought of all Logan had done for her and how little she had given him in return. True, she was learning to keep house, but she had none of the accomplishments of a real lady. She could not draw or paint, her sewing was untidy and as for music, the harp had been her only true achievement. She could hold a tune, but her singing voice was too small to be considered fine.

Logan had been so patient and had treated her so kindly since she had been at Ardvarrick, and she was repaying him with nothing but complaints and misery. And now she had as good as told him she was sorry she had married him. It was quite untrue and she must tell him so. Ailsa turned on her side and cradled her cheek on her hand. She loved Logan and she must make him know how much.

Ailsa had no recollection of falling asleep, but when she opened her eyes again it was daylight and some-one was moving quietly about the room.

'Oh, Shona.'

The maid dipped a curtsy. 'Did I wake you, ma'am? I tried so hard to be quiet.'

'What time is it?' She rubbed her eyes. 'Where is the master?'

'Why, 'tis gone eight, madam, and the master left the house these two hours since.'

Ailsa sat up quickly. 'He has left?'

'Why, yes, ma'am. He said I was not to disturb you. That you needed to sleep, which is why I have only just come in.'

The maid chattered on, but Ailsa barely heard her. Logan was gone and she had not told him she loved him.

The sun was rising into the clear blue sky as Logan and Tamhas cantered away from Ardvarrick. It was going to be another clear day, but for once Logan would have preferred torrential rain. Then he would have had an excuse to remain at Ardvarrick and make his peace with Ailsa. He did not like being at odds with her, but they seemed to have been constantly bickering since their wedding day.

Ailsa was increasingly anxious and withdrawn. He had no idea what was ailing her and, with the business of the estate weighing heavily on his mind, he was aware that he, too, had become short tempered. However, until yesterday, their arguments had been over quickly, followed by fervently uttered regrets and kisses in equal measure, but not this time.

This time he had ridden away with the coldness still between them.

Knowing there was nothing he could do about it until he returned, Logan tried to concentrate on the business in hand: preparing his lands to withstand the harsh months ahead. It was just over a year since he had returned to Ardvarrick and he had been pitch-forked into a harsh winter. It had not taken him long to realise how little he knew about his inheritance. Tamhas had guided him through the past year, but this winter he was determined to take more control, to look after his lands and his people as a Laird should.

There was much to be done and time was running out. The weather was turning and the nights growing longer and colder. Logan and Tamhas had spent the past few weeks riding around his lands and discussing what was needed, now that the last of the crops had been gathered in and those cattle not sold to the drovers had been brought down from the hills. A few were to be overwintered, the rest slaughtered to provide food for the lean months ahead. They had now visited all the farms except those that required them to be away overnight, the ones that bordered Contullach lands on the far side of the Bealach na Damh, which was where they were going today.

They were approaching the pass when Logan drew rein and sat for a moment, looking around him in silent contemplation.

Tamhas brought his horse to a stand beside him. 'Is anything amiss, Cousin?'

'On the contrary.' Logan nodded to the loch beside them and looked up towards the bracken-covered slopes beyond. 'The country here reminded me. It is but a year since I first saw Ailsa.'

'She was sitting beside a loch such as this, was she not?' Tamhas laughed. 'I always said she bewitched you with her music.'

'Aye.' Logan set off again, remembering how sweetly she had played, how beautiful he had thought her, even then, before he had fallen so completely under her spell. And it was not just the music, although Ailsa could not be brought to believe she had anything else to offer.

How wrong she was!

It was almost two months since their wedding. Logan had counted every day of it and every night. In many ways Ailsa had blossomed at Ardvarrick. She had told him her education had been rudimentary, but she was quick to learn and Norry, who had never liked figures, had been relieved to hand over the household accounts. Ailsa had insisted Logan should oversee the change, but it needed only short inspection to convince him that Ailsa could cope. Her entries were clear, any notes precise and all written in her neat, firm hand. He recalled how relieved she had been at Norry's approval. And how she had blushed adorably when he had added his praise to that of the housekeeper.

Under Ailsa's rule the house was coming alive again. Rooms long unused were opened up, shutters thrown open, cushions added to hard wooden chairs, flowers and green foliage brought in and fires kindled to make the rooms more welcoming. Logan had spoken to Norry, anxious that his new wife's enthusiasm for homemaking should not upset the old retainers, but he need not have worried.

'Whisht, Master Logan, she has offended no one. She is like a breath of fresh air in the house. If I might say, it hasn't been like this since your sainted mother died, Lord rest her soul.'

She excelled at everything, except the music. Logan was aware of Ailsa's deep sorrow that she could no longer play her harp. He was at pains not to mention it, but it was there, an ever-present sore and, although she tried hard to hide it, he suspected it was making her ill. What else could explain her wan looks, the way she no longer sat down to breakfast with him? The way she had ripped up at him over nothing yesterday.

He was sorry for the heated words that had followed, when she accused him of regretting their marriage. He should have challenged her then. Instead, he had walked away, returning late to bed and rising early this morning. Now he regretted leaving the house without waking Ailsa. Without telling her that of all the things in his life he might regret, marrying her was not, and never would be, one of them.

'Now then, who is this coming down from Bealach na Damh?'

Tamhas's voice interrupted his thoughts and Logan

looked up. Three riders were approaching, their sturdy mounts picking the way down the final slopes to the well-defined track that ran along the valley bottom, beside the river.

'Fingal Contullach,' stated Tamhas, peering at the riders.

'And that is Cowie with him.' Logan's horse pranced a little as his grip tightened on the reins.

Tamhas put out a hand. 'Easy now, Cousin. Fingal has already flogged the man for his crimes. It is forgotten.'

Logan's eyes narrowed. 'Cowie has no more forgotten what he did than I!'

They walked their horses on until they were close enough to speak. Fingal brought his group to a stand and nodded.

'Ardvarrick.'

'Contullach.'

Logan would have moved on, but the man seemed inclined to talk. After a few moments' stilted conversation, Fingal paused.

'I hope you'll see your way to renewing our agreement next year, Ardvarrick. The drovers' price per head of cattle was a fair one and I don't doubt we have both prospered by this summer's peace.'

'We agreed to the terms, Contullach. As long as your people and mine can rub along peaceably—' Logan could not prevent his eyes flicking to Ewan Cowie '—I see no reason why we should not continue with the agreement.'

The old man grunted. 'Five years ago, I'd not have risked coming through Bealach na Damh with less than a dozen armed men.'

'Times change,' said Logan. 'In London they are calling this the Age of Reason. It makes sense to be on good terms with one's neighbours.'

'That's true enough.' Contullach seemed to struggle with himself for a moment, then he nudged his horse closer and put out his hand. 'Then I'll bid ye good day, Ardvarrick. And peace be with you.'

Logan took the proffered hand and gripped it. 'And with you, Fingal. Long may it last.'

'I do believe the old man is mellowing,' remarked Tamhas, when the two parties had moved on and they were well out of earshot.

'I knew he would come around, once he had seen the benefits of the agreement,' Logan replied.

Tamhas rubbed his chin. 'I have my doubts about Cowie, though. I saw the way he looked at you and I think you are right. He has not forgotten what happened between you.'

Logan's lip curled. 'I have beaten him twice. He'll not bother me again, if he knows what's good for him.'

'I am not sure Cowie has the wit to know that,' Tamhas replied. He swung round for one last look at the retreating figures. 'You'd best be on your guard with that one, Cousin. There was murder in his eyes.'

Logan grunted and kicked his horse to a trot. 'Come on. I want to get through the Pass of the Stags before we stop again.'

Ardvarrick seemed very quiet without Logan. Ailsa missed him as soon as she opened her eyes that morning and the knowledge that he had ridden off without saying goodbye was a constant blade in her heart. She kept busy around the house, helping Norry with her chores and collecting herbs and vegetables from the garden, but still the day dragged by.

She decided upon an early dinner, which she would eat with the housekeeper rather than keeping her solitary state in the dining room. Ailsa had been so fatigued recently that she had originally thought she would retire directly after dinner, but tonight she felt awake and restless.

She went to the drawing room, from where she could see the waters of the loch, its ruffled surface glinting gold and silver in the setting sun. She still felt restless, unsettled. It would be the first time she had slept alone since her wedding and she knew she would miss Logan's breath on her neck, his body lying beside hers. Not that he had held her close or curled himself around her last night.

She was beset by a sudden stab of loneliness and dropped her head in her hands.

'Mercy me, now what is all this?'

Ailsa quickly sat up. 'I beg your pardon, Norry, I am being very foolish. I have so much and yet I feel so melancholy.'

'Nay, mistress, there is no need to apologise to me. I thought I'd bring you a tisane of raspberry leaves. It helps, sometimes, you see, for women in your condition.'

'Condition?' Ailsa tried to laugh, but it ended in a sob. 'Oh, Norry, I feel so *wretched*.'

'There, there, my dear.' The housekeeper stroked her head. 'It is quite natural. The late Lady Ardvarrick was just the same, you know, when she was with child.'

Ailsa raised her head and stared at the housekeeper, who regarded her with a sympathetic smile.

'Did ye not know, lass? Did they not tell you how it might be?'

No. No one had told her.

She had heard the maids giggling and had some vague idea of how a child was conceived, but no one had ever explained it to her in any detail. Why should they? She was the Contullach harper, it had never been intended that she should be a mother.

A growing sense of wonder filled her and she looked up at Norry, whose kindly face became wreathed in smiles.

'Bless you, my dear, 'tis the news we have all been waiting for since you wed the master! It is very early days yet, but we all noticed that you cannot eat in the mornings. And other signs, of course.'

Yes, they would, thought Ailsa. The servants, especially Shona and the laundress, would be privy to the most intimate secrets of the bedchamber.

'Can it be?' she whispered, looking up hopefully at the housekeeper. 'Can I be carrying Logan's child?' She put her hands on her stomach. 'What should I do?'

'Do? Why, nothing. Rest when you need to, but otherwise go on as you are. Now—' Mrs Noranside shook out her skirts '—I shall leave you to drink the raspberry tea. I have put it there for you, on the little table at your elbow. You should drink it up and not worry your head about these megrims and crotchets. They will pass and all the sooner now you know what is causing them.'

She bustled out and Ailsa sat back in her chair, her mood completely changed. A baby! Would Logan be pleased? She could not doubt it. She took up the cup and dutifully sipped at the tisane. It was not unpleasant and she drank it all, lost in a pleasant dream of the future. She was suddenly impatient to make everything right with Logan. It would be easier to apologise now she knew the reason for her ill humour. But he would not be back before tomorrow, at the earliest, and what was she to do with herself until then? So many hours to fill!

Ailsa looked out of the window. Perhaps a stroll in the fresh air would help her to sleep. The sun was close to setting now, but the sky was clear and there would be light for a while yet. She ran upstairs to fetch a shawl and made her way to the gardens at the south front of the house. She stopped for a while on the upper terrace, glad of her thick shawl to keep off the chill. She breathed deep, relishing the fresh smell of the sea carried in with the onshore breeze. On the next terrace, the small hedges surrounded only bare earth, the flower beds having been cleared and mulched with seaweed in readiness for spring planting.

Ailsa descended the final steps to the lawn. A few hardy plants still flowered in the borders, soaking in the last, cool rays of autumn sunshine. She remembered how pretty and colourful it had looked in summer. Her hands moved to the still-flat planes of her belly. Perhaps next year she and Logan might bring a rug and sit out here on sunny days, the baby in a crib between them.

A movement caught her eye and she looked up. Someone was standing by the corner of the house, outlined against the sun, and for one exultant moment she thought it was Logan. Her heart leapt. He had come back because he, too, did not wish to spend the night apart! But as the figure moved closer, she realised it was too short and stocky to be her husband.

'Ewan Cowie.' She felt the first stirring of alarm, but she kept her voice calm, unwilling to show her fear. 'What are you doing here?'

'Why, I came to visit you. We are cousins, after all.'

'Only by marriage! You are not welcome here.' She hurried up the steps from the lawn, eager to return to the house, but Ewan was coming down to intercept her.

'How very ungracious of you, Ailsa.'

Nervously, she glanced up. There were no servants' rooms on this side of the house and at this time of day it was unlikely anyone would be looking out from the drawing rooms or bedchambers.

She said, 'Ardvarrick will be furious if he finds you here.'

'But he isn't at home, is he?' Ewan had reached the middle terrace and was close enough for her to see that he was smiling. It made her shiver. 'We have unfinished business, you and I.'

'That is nonsense!'

'Is it? I am Contullach's heir. As his harper, you would have come to me, along with everything else he owned, when he died. I would have taken you then.'

'If you had, Contullach would no longer have a harper.'

'What care I for that?' He was in front of her and blocking her way to the steps. 'But in any case, we know now it is not true. Màiri told me, when she returned from your wedding. You yourself told her that you could still play.'

'What of it?'

He was close enough now to see that his smile had become a leer. 'Only that, if I had known it, I could have taken you years ago and Fingal would have been none the wiser.'

There was another path to her right, between the parterres. Ailsa turned abruptly, picking up her skirts to run, but even as she did so she felt a vice-like grip on her arm.

'Not so fast, my lady.'

'Let me go!'

He laughed as she struggled and swung her around, catching at her wrists.

'You escaped me once, you witch, but this time I *will* take my pleasure. And pleasure it will be,' he said, tightening his hold. 'We will see what your fancy Laird will do when he finds I have enjoyed his lady's charms!'

He was too strong for Ailsa to escape him. She could feel his breath on her face as he pulled her closer and she turned her head away.

'Pray do not do this, Ewan. Think of Kirstin!'

'Kirstin! Why, she'll not let me into her bed above once a se'ennight. What a shrew she has turned out to be.'

His vicious reply shocked Ailsa. 'She is your *wife*, Ewan!'

'And if she'll not give me what I want, then I must take it elsewhere.'

'But not with me!'

'Aye, with you.'

As he tried to take her in his arms, she managed to free one hand and rake her nails down his cheek. The sudden pain of it caused him to release his hold slightly. With a supreme effort she twisted from his grasp and ran. She had hardly gone three yards when he caught her. Ailsa screamed as he tumbled her over the low box hedge and on to the flowerbed. The soft earth cushioned the fall, but she was too shaken to scramble away before Ewan pinned her to the ground with his body.

He held her wrists above her head with one hand while his other tore at her bodice. Ailsa cried out, twisting her head from side to side to avoid his mouth. She was blazing with anger, she wanted to scream, but she was writhing too much to draw a full breath. She struggled valiantly, but with her legs hampered by her skirts and with Ewan holding her wrists, there was little she could do except squirm beneath him. She was tiring, too, but when he pushed her skirts aside and she felt his hand on her skin, she made a last desperate effort. She brought up her knee quick and hard between his legs. He grunted in pain, but did not release her.

'Why, you hag, no more of that or when I have finished with you, I will crush your fingers beneath my boot. Then see how well you can play your damned harp!'

His threat only made Ailsa struggle more, until he dealt her a stinging blow to the face. Her eyes watered and she closed them tightly. She could taste the blood in her mouth, but she would not give in. She must keep struggling. Ewan cursed violently and Ailsa braced herself for another blow, but it never came. Instead, his weight was lifted from her and she heard the smack of a fist against bone.

She opened her eyes and almost fainted with relief when she saw Logan. He was on the gravel path and grappling with Ewan, whose face was covered in blood. Her dizziness was easing and she managed to scramble to her feet, her eyes fixed on the two men. She crossed her arms tightly to stop the convulsive shivering. There was murder in both their faces and she held her breath as she watched Logan drawing back his arm for another blow. Then she saw Ewan's hand reaching into his sleeve.

'Logan, look out. The *sgian-dubh*!'

Her warning was in time for him to jump aside and the deadly blade missed his body, but it slashed across his left arm. Ailsa looked on in horror as a dark stain spread slowly over his sleeve.

'Very well, Cowie.' Logan pulled out his own small dagger. 'If that is how you wish to do this!'

Ailsa put her hands to her mouth, stifling a cry as the two men circled and feinted, each looking for the advantage. Logan's left sleeve was turning black in the fading light. With such a wound he could not last long against Ewan. She should run and get help, but her limbs were paralysed. She could not move, she was rooted to the spot, unable to tear her eyes from the two men.

Logan gritted his teeth. His left arm was almost useless and his strength was failing. He heard a shout from the terrace but he would not allow himself to be distracted. Unlike his adversary. Cowie glanced away and Logan saw his chance. He launched himself at his opponent, dropping his own dagger and grabbing Cowie's right wrist with both hands. He twisted it up behind his back, forcing it higher until the *sgian-dubh* fell from Cowie's fingers and clattered harmlessly on the ground.

'Enough,' screamed Ewan. 'Enough, for God's sake! Ye'll break my arm.'

'Count yourself lucky I don't break your neck!'

Logan wondered what madness it was that had made him drop his own blade rather than thrusting it into his opponent's heart. Then he heard Ailsa cry out.

'Quickly, Tamhas, quickly. Logan is hurt!'

Of course. *She* was his madness. And Cowie was her family, however much a villain he might be.

'And why not kill the rogue?' Tamhas demanded of him as he ran up, sword drawn. 'Or let me do it. I'd be pleased to rid the world of such a cur!'

'No.' Logan shook his head. 'Although God knows he has given me reason enough to put an end to his existence. And I may yet do so,' he growled, giving Cowie's wrist another twist before pushing him away.

Ewan Cowie stood, holding his arm and glaring at Logan, a mixture of hatred and fear in his eyes. Logan's head was spinning now and there was a throbbing pain in his left arm, but he could not think of that just yet. Two of his men had come running up and he turned to address them.

'Take Cowie to the cellars and lock him up. Go with them, Tamhas, make sure he is secure.' He rubbed his temple. It was becoming more and more difficult to concentrate. 'We will decide what to do about him in the morning.'

He watched them march their prisoner away before putting out his hand to Ailsa, who was still standing in the flower bed. There was something he wanted to say to her. Something important, but the pain in his head was growing worse. His eyes hurt, as if he was peering through a tunnel which was becoming longer and longer. Then there was only darkness.

Chapter Fourteen

Logan's hand dropped and Ailsa saw him sway, but before she could reach him he collapsed and she heard the sickening thud as his head crashed on to the base of a stone statue. She screamed for Tamhas who came running back, smothering an oath when he saw Logan stretched lifeless on the ground. Ailsa was already on her knees, gently cradling him, regardless of the sticky blood oozing from his head.

Tamhas stared down at Logan in horror. 'Is he—?'

'No, he lives. He lives.' Ailsa had found Logan's handkerchief in his pocket and was pressing it gently against the head wound. She stared at the blood-soaked sleeve, trying to make her numbed mind think. With a trembling hand she tore off her silk apron and held it out to Tamhas. 'Here, use this on his arm. It will do to staunch the blood until we can get him into the house and undress him.'

'Damn Ewan Cowie for this!' muttered Tamhas as he bound the apron tightly around Logan's sleeve. 'The coward came here knowing we would be out of the way!'

'Yes.' Her mind was as thick as porridge. 'Why did you come back?'

'We met Cowie with Fingal Contullach on the road and Logan suspected he might try something like this.'

'Logan came back to protect me and he might die because of it,' whispered Ailsa. Shock was setting in and she was struggling not to shiver. 'He might die because of me.'

'Stop that, Ailsa!' Tamhas spoke sharply. 'Logan is going to live, do you understand me? Now stay with him while I fetch help to carry him into the house.'

Ailsa nodded and Tamhas ran off. She looked down at Logan and willed herself not to faint. He needed her now. She must not let him down.

The next few hours were an agonising nightmare. It could only have been minutes before Tamhas returned with more men to carry Logan into the house, but it felt like a lifetime to Ailsa. She fought down sickness and a wave of hysteria as she collected her thoughts. With never a tremor in her voice she was able to direct them to carry their precious burden to the bedchamber and to send an open-mouthed kitchen maid scurrying off to find Mrs Noranside. Ailsa would need the housekeeper to help her bind up the wounds.

'If only I had come back sooner,' exclaimed Tamhas as they made their way up the stairs. He wanted to talk, Ailsa thought perhaps he needed to do so and she made no attempt to stop him. 'My horse went lame soon after we turned back and I could not keep up with Logan. Hell and damnation! If I had been here, Cowie could not have stabbed him.'

If Logan had not married me, Cowie would not have stabbed him.

Ailsa pushed the thought aside. There was no time for such indulgence.

'What's done is done,' she said aloud, as much to herself as Tamhas. 'We must try to repair the damage.'

The men laid Logan carefully on the bed and Ailsa looked in dismay at his bloodied body.

'Is there no one we might send for to treat him?' she asked Norry, when the housekeeper bustled in. 'The local midwife, perhaps?'

'Heavens, no. She's a dirty, feckless creature that I wouldn't let near the house!' the housekeeper told her. 'There is Dr Murray, the family's physician, and I have taken the liberty of sending for him already. The worst of it is that he lives in Dingwall, so we shall be fortunate to see him before tomorrow night. In the meantime, we must do what we can, you and I. Come, lassie, it won't be as bad as it first appears. First we must undress him, carefully now. Once we have washed off the blood and bound him up, he will look better, you will see.'

Ailsa nodded silently. There had been broken bones and wounds aplenty at Contullach, but it was the blow to Logan's head and his stillness that worried her. She tried hard to push her worst fears aside. He was alarmingly pale, but there was a faint pulse beating in his neck. He was alive and she would do everything in her power to keep him so.

The women worked quickly, cleaning the blood from his arm and from the cut on his head. By the time the wounds had been tended and bound and Logan had been placed in the bed, Ailsa felt more hopeful. She went off to remove her muddied gown and to wash away the feel of Ewan Cowie's hands upon her body. His attack on her was nothing compared to Logan's injuries and she refused to dwell upon it. She donned a fresh gown and returned to the bedchamber, determined to sit with Logan until he awoke.

When Norry said she would send up her dinner on a tray, Ailsa shook her head.

'I have no appetite for it.'

'Well, that's as may be,' declared the housekeeper, putting her hands on her hips, 'but tell me, if you can, what use you'll be to your man if you starve yourself?'

Ailsa was obliged to acknowledge the wisdom of this and when the food arrived, she managed to eat a little and to drink a glass of wine. Then she settled down to take the first watch of the night-time vigil beside the bed.

At midnight Norry came in to relieve her and Ailsa went away to the yellow guest room to lie down. She was asleep almost immediately but she was up again before dawn and back at Logan's side.

He did not look as if he had stirred at all in her absence. Even against the snow-white bedlinen he looked very pale and her heart turned over. She sat down beside the bed and took his right hand. She felt strangely calm. She was his lady; she must be strong to nurse him and to run his house until he was recovered.

The sun had barely risen when there was a light scratching on the door and Shona came in.

'Tamhas is in the hall, mistress. He is asking for a word with ye.'

The maid looked past Ailsa and stared with frightened eyes at the figure lying in the bed. Ailsa felt equally terrified, but she was Lady Ardvarrick now and must not show it. She rose and shook out her skirts.

'Thank you. Pray watch over the Laird for me while I go downstairs.'

'Me, mistress?' Shona positively squeaked with fright. 'But what if he wakes? What if—?'

'If he wakes, if he even *stirs*, then call for me.' Ailsa gave her maid an encouraging smile. 'I shall hear you from the hall.'

Tamhas was waiting for her at the bottom of the stairs, anxiously feeding the rim of his bonnet round and round between his fingers.

'How is Logan, Mistress Ailsa? How does he go on?'

'He is alive,' she replied briefly, not trusting herself to say more lest her fragile calm should shatter. 'We will know more once Dr Murray has seen him.'

Tamhas nodded, frowning direfully.

After waiting a few moments for him to speak, she said gently, 'You asked to see me, Tamhas?'

'Aye.' He cleared his throat. 'Ewan Cowie is still locked in the cellar, mistress. What would you have us do with him?'

Her control slipped.

'I'd have him stripped, whipped and gelded!' she declared savagely, thinking of Logan lying upstairs in his bed and so near to death. Her ordeal at Ewan Cowie's hands seemed a distant thing now, but it had led to Logan being brought low and that made her blood boil. She could never forgive Ewan for what he had done to her man.

Her man. Her husband. The thought steadied her. She curled her hands into tight fists as she fought down her rage. She must quell her temper, as Logan had done when he threw aside his own dagger and disarmed Ewan.

'But that is not Logan's way,' she went on. 'The Laird of Ardvarrick would demand justice.'

'Some would say what you suggest *is* justice, Lady!' Tamhas was as angry as she. 'We'd be happy to string the villain up for you and be done with him.'

Ailsa was sorely tempted. It would take only one word from her and Tamhas would carry out her orders without hesitation. But Logan had always maintained that an eye for an eye would only lead to more bloodshed. What would Logan do, what would he want, if he could speak? She straightened her spine and breathed in slowly.

'Ewan Cowie must be taken back to Contullach Castle and Fingal must be informed of his villainy. I am too busy nursing my husband to write of it, but you must tell my uncle how Ewan tried to—to force himself upon me. Tell him how he attacked Logan and tried to kill him. His actions have put at risk the fragile peace between Contullach and Ardvarrick. Fingal will not tolerate that.'

'It will put him in a rage, I don't doubt, but Ewan Cowie is his son-in-law. He is unlikely to do more than give the rogue another flogging. By heaven, that's not nearly enough!'

'I agree.' Ailsa's eyes narrowed. 'However, when

Kirstin knows how her husband has behaved, I believe she will exact her own punishment.'

Tamhas looked dissatisfied, but he bowed.

'Very well. If you wish it, he will be taken to Contullach.'

He turned to depart and she called him back. 'He must reach the castle alive, Tamhas, mind me!'

His eyes widened and he put one hand on his breast. 'Of course, Lady, but 'tis a long way to Contullach. It cannot be helped if he should take a tumble or two along the way.'

She watched him stride off, consoling herself with the fact that she could do no more, short of taking Ewan to Contullach herself. Ardvarrick's people would want to avenge the insult to their Laird and, in her heart, she did not blame them. She could only hope they would stop short of murder.

Ailsa ran back up to the bedchamber. Shona was standing where she had left her, eyes fixed anxiously on the bed.

'He's not moved, mistress. Not a hair.'

The girl's distress was evident and Ailsa patted her shoulder.

'He is sleeping, which is the best thing for him at the moment.' It was what Mrs Noranside had said earlier and it seemed to reassure the maid.

Ailsa sent her away and went to stand beside the bed, looking down at Logan. They had decided not to put him in a nightshirt, Mrs Noranside arguing that he would only have to be disturbed again when the doctor came to examine him. Apart from the bandages around his head and his arm they left him naked, with the bedcovers pulled up to his chin. Ailsa gently lifted the sheet until she could see that the pulse was still beating in his neck.

Satisfied, she tucked the covers gently around him once more, smoothing them over his chest and allowing her hands to rest for a moment on his broad shoulders. Impulsively she bent and kissed him gently on the mouth.

'Come back to me, Logan,' she whispered, blinking away her tears. 'I love you, my darling man.'

She straightened, dashing a hand across her eyes and standing for a moment to study his face. Nothing, not even the flicker of an eyelash. If she had been expecting her kiss to work like fairy dust, then it was a failure. She resumed her seat by the bed and settled down to her vigil.

Doctor Murray arrived at dusk and was shown immediately to the bedchamber, where the ladies stood by and waited anxiously while he examined Logan.

'He hit his head and has been unconscious ever since,' Ailsa told him, her hands clutched so tightly the knuckles gleamed white.

The doctor made no reply but continued with his examination.

'Well,' he said at last, 'the cut on his arm is a clean slice and that should heal well. I will leave you a salve to put on it, if it begins to look red and angry, but for now we will see how it goes.'

Ailsa looked at him. 'And his head, sir?'

Dr Murray looked grim. 'As long as he hasn't smashed his brains he will recover, but we won't know what damage has been done there until he wakes up fully. If he ever does.'

The housekeeper nodded silently and Ailsa put her hands to her mouth. She desperately wanted to scream, to give way to her fear and distress, but it was impossible. The servants looked to her and the housekeeper for guidance and she must not add to Norry's burdens by showing such weakness.

A room had been prepared for the doctor and when he had retired, Ailsa and the housekeeper arranged between them to keep a vigil beside Logan's bed for a second night. Norry insisted on taking the evening watch and Ailsa went off to rest.

It was some time after midnight that she took up her bedside candle and made her way back to the sickroom. As she crossed the landing, she saw a light below.

'Tamhas!' she called down to the figure in the shadows. 'You are back already.' She waited for him to come up the stairs.

'Aye. I handed Cowie over to your uncle, told him everything and left the matter in his hands.' Even in the flickering light of a candle she could see he was scowling. 'The rogue is lucky to be alive after what he has done and Contullach knows it. I told him it was Lady Ardvarrick's orders that Cowie was returned to him for punishment.'

Lady Ardvarrick. For an instant Ailsa was at a loss to believe he could mean her. When she thought of her husband lying unconscious in his bed she felt very small and insignificant. Helpless.

Tamhas touched her arm. 'I am sorry if you wanted

me to wait to see what Fingal would do, mistress. I had to come back, to see how Logan goes on. Is there any news?'

'He sleeps.' She tried and failed to give him a reassuring smile, which made Tamhas look even more worried.

'May I see him?'

'Of course. I am going to relieve Mrs Noranside now. You can come with me.'

They went in quietly and Tamhas walked over to the bed. He looked so shaken at the sight of his cousin lying corpse-like between the sheets that Ailsa found her own spirit rising to comfort and reassure him.

'He looks very pale, but the doctor says his wounds are healing well and sleep is what he needs now.'

'Aye, mistress. He is in the best of hands here, I know that.' Tamhas looked back at her and smiled. 'He will soon be up and about again.'

He stayed a few more moments before going off to his bed. Ailsa cast an anxious glance at the housekeeper.

'Have I given him false hope, Norry? Should I have added a note of caution?'

'Not at all, my dear. You said all that you should.' She put a hand on Ailsa's shoulder and squeezed it. 'We shall get through this, I know it.'

In the morning, Ailsa was on watch in the sickroom when Dr Murray returned.

'Has there been any change?' he asked, coming towards the bed.

'He has been restless and, once, while I was here, he moved slightly and cried out in pain, but he has not woken.' She wanted to add that Logan had not known her voice when she tried to calm him, but the very thought of it was painful. 'Mrs Noranside said she managed to get him to drink a little of the saline draught.'

'Well, that is very encouraging. If you can get some nourishment into him, a little broth, ale or even tea, it will do no harm. Now, talking of nourishment, I shall go down and break my fast and then return to see the patient once more before I leave.'

'You'll not stay another night?' Again, she was assailed by fears.

'Nay, madam, I must push on. I've a long journey ahead of me and would prefer to accomplish most of it in daylight. And I've patients to attend in Dingwall. My time is not my own, you know.'

'Yes, yes, I beg your pardon.'

He returned an hour later to make a final, cursory examination.

'He is not feverish,' he informed her, his hand pressed lightly against Logan's brow. 'I do not think we need to bleed him today, my lady, unless you specifically wish for it?'

Ailsa disclaimed, thinking privately that Logan had lost far too much blood already. The doctor finished packing his bag, then turned to take his leave of her.

'Is there anything I should do?' she begged him. 'I feel so useless.'

'Nay, madam, you are not useless at all. Your presence here will make all the difference to the Laird. Some say patients in this state know when loved ones are close and I must be honest with you, there is precious little else that can be done for him now, except to watch and wait. And pray,' he added grimly. 'I shall call again in a se'ennight, unless I hear from you in the meantime. Mrs Noranside is a sensible woman and as good a nurse as any. She will know if you need to send for me.' His rather sombre features softened and he patted her shoulder in a fatherly way. 'Ah, 'tis always hard for a new bride to see her man laid low, but Ardvarrick is strong, mistress. There is no reason why the good Lord should not spare him for you.'

With that he was gone. Ailsa pulled her chair closer to the bed and sat down, reaching out to clasp Logan's hand. It was warm, but otherwise lifeless, and she felt a great welling of fear and grief that she might lose him before she could beg his forgiveness for the cruel things she had said to him.

Wake up, my darling. Please wake up.

Ailsa heard the door open, but she did not look round. She knew by the rustle of skirts that it was the housekeeper.

'You should go and rest, madam.'

'Later.' She kept her eyes fixed on Logan, watching for the slightest change. 'I am not tired and I *want* to sit with him, Norry. You have other duties to attend.'

'Whisht, now, the house will not fall to pieces if I leave the servants to their business for a while.'

She fussed around the bed, smoothing sheets, straightening the covers, clearly loath to leave the room. Ailsa remembered that Norry had been Logan's nursemaid and it struck her that she must love him very much. As did she. Silent tears began to roll down her cheeks. For Logan, for Norry. For herself.

Immediately, the housekeeper hurried around the bed and hugged her.

'There, there, dearie, there's no need for greetin',' she murmured, her own voice breaking. 'The master is sleeping, which is the Lord's way of mending him. You'll see.' She gave Ailsa a final hug, then released her. 'It is the weariness that is making you so low, I'll be bound. You have been here for hours and it is my turn to keep a watch over Master Logan. I know you want to stay, but I shall send for you if he wakes, you have my word on it.'

Still Ailsa hesitated, until the housekeeper gave a little tut.

'Bless you, mistress, do you not trust me to look after your man? Off you go to your rest and be sure to eat something before you return, or I shall have you on my hands as well as the Laird!'

Ailsa knew it was sound advice and she went to her bed, where she managed to sleep for a few hours before going to the kitchen to eat a little food. It was there that Tamhas found her.

'Fingal Contullach has arrived,' he announced. 'He is asking for you, mistress. Do you wish to see him?'

'No, but I think I must.' She pushed her plate away and rose.

'You'll let me come with you.'

His concern was heartening, but she shook her head. 'Thank you, Tamhas, but I will see him alone. However—' her resolution wobbled a little '—perhaps you would be good enough to wait in the hall, in case I have need of you.'

'Aye, I will, gladly.'

They went together to the drawing room and Tamhas opened the door for her. Fingal was pacing the floor when she entered. He stopped and turned his shaggy head to fix her with a fierce stare.

'Ardvarrick?' he barked out the name.

'Alive,' she replied coldly. 'For now.'

'I came to tell ye that I have packed Cowie off to my house in Tain, accompanied by men I can rely upon to keep him there. He knows that if Ardvarrick dies he will stand trial for murder. I will make sure of that, lass, you have my word.'

Ailsa nodded. 'I hope you will not go back on it, Uncle.'

'I will not. Ewan has gone too far this time. If anyone behaved that way with me or mine—' He shot another fierce look at her. 'I must thank ye for sending him back alive.'

'It is what Logan would have done.' She added, 'It was not my choice, believe me.'

'I do believe you. Cowie treated you very ill, did he not? I beg your pardon, Ailsa. It was in part my fault, I admit it. I have been far too easy on him in the past and I am sorry for it.'

'So, too, am I, Uncle.' Ailsa appreciated the effort it took him to say that. Fingal Contullach was not a man to apologise.

'Your aunt wanted you to know, if there is anything we can do, you only have to say.'

'That is very kind, but I have everything I require here.' An awkward silence followed. She said, 'How is Kirstin?'

'She has gone to Tain with her husband.'

'Has she?' Ailsa's brows rose. 'As I recall, you said

the place is well-nigh derelict. Kirstin will not like that.'

He scowled. 'She is determined to stand by Cowie, even though she knows now what sort of man he is.'

Ailsa felt a stab of sympathy for Kirstin, but it quickly faded when she thought of Logan, lying unconscious upstairs.

'If that is all, Uncle, I must go and relieve Mrs Noranside in the sickroom.'

'Of course. I have said what I came to say.'

She glanced towards the window. 'I will not forget my duty to a guest, Uncle. 'Tis growing dark and you are welcome to a bed for the night. If you will wait here, I will tell the servants to look after you.'

'I thank you.' He hesitated. 'You have changed, Ailsa. I thought you were merely a harper.'

'You are so much more to me than that!'

Logan's words came back to Ailsa and she stood a little taller.

'I was never *merely* a harper,' she said coldly. 'If you will excuse me, I must return to my husband's bedside.'

Ailsa moved between the sickroom and her bedchamber and did not see her uncle again before he left the next morning. The day faded slowly into evening. Another night, another dawn and a fourth day with Ailsa dutifully sharing the vigil with Norry. Logan stirred occasionally and when he did, the pain in his arm or his head brought a cry issuing from his lips, but even when he opened his eyes there was no sign of recognition in them. Ailsa's only comfort was when she had managed to feed him a little milk or broth.

'But he shows no signs of knowing me,' she told the housekeeper, when the daylight was fading. 'I sit by his bedside, holding his hand and talking to him. I even told him about our child, but there was no response. He does not know I am here.'

'You cannot be sure of that, my dear.' Norry replied. 'His arm is healing nicely, which is a good sign, but I will summon Dr Murray, if you wish it?'

Ailsa shook her head. 'No, I know in my heart there is little more that can be done. We can only wait and watch.'

'And the good doctor has promised to return, has he not? You must have patience, mistress. Now, off you go to your bed and let Shona share the night watches with me, as we agreed.'

Ailsa nodded. She understood that she must look after her growing baby as well as herself. She also wanted to look after Logan during the day, but as she curled up in her lonely bed, she thought she might find it impossible to sleep more than a few hours after so many broken nights. To her surprise she slept through, waking refreshed and a little more hopeful in the morning as she settled down at Logan's bedside.

The day stretched ahead of her and she decided to fetch the book of poetry that Logan had given her as a wedding gift. She read it aloud, taking comfort from the familiar lines, and when she had finished she went to Logan's study to look through the rest of the books. A few were incomprehensible to her—treatises on government or histories of ancient Rome—but there were the other books of poetry that Logan had read to her. Now she would read them to *him*. She would begin with another of Logan's favourites, Robert Herrick.

At first, she struggled with the print and the unfamiliar phrases but gradually it became easier. Next she picked up Pope's *The Rape of the Lock*. Of all the poems Logan had read to her, she had enjoyed this one the most, although he had explained there was much more to it than the story of a stolen curl.

The poem carried her through until the light began to fade. She stopped at the end of a canto and leaned back in her chair, rubbing her eyes and wondering if her efforts were doing any good at all.

That was when she heard it. A sigh.

Ailsa's eyes flew open. Perhaps she had been mistaken. She stared at Logan. He had not moved but... she put a hand to her throat. Was she dreaming or did he really look more peaceful? Fear gripped her and she made herself look at the point in his neck where she had seen the beat of the pulse. It was still there. Not satisfied with the evidence of her own eyes, she placed her fingers lightly on his skin and held her breath. Yes, it was there. The steady rhythm of his heartbeat.

Ailsa took his hand in hers and began to croon a lullaby. There was movement in his fingers, a slight tightening of his grip. Her heart leapt. She stopped singing and peered at his face. There was no sign of life, no movement. He was motionless again save for the faint, steady pulse in his neck.

Mrs Noranside came in, tutting impatiently in the gloom.

'For heaven's sake, child, why did you not call for light?'

'He gripped my hand, Norry.' Ailsa tried not to sound too eager. 'I felt it, while I was singing to him.'

'That does not surprise me,' replied the housekeeper, carrying a taper to the candles and lamps placed around the bedchamber. 'He always loved his music, did Master Logan. As a child he used to dance around the room while his grandmother played the—' She broke off, flustered, as if realising she had given voice to the unmentionable. When she spoke again her voice was matter of fact. 'Och, well now, I'll sit with the master while you take your dinner. Cook has prepared a fricassee for you and she'll be mighty put out if you refuse it.'

'Thank you, I will go now.'

Ailsa rose and took a bedside candle to light her way to the dining room, but when she reached the hall, she hesitated. Norry's words were rattling around in her head and she moved slowly towards the door of the little parlour. Did she dare to try again, for Logan?

She went in and crossed to where the *clàrsach* stood in one corner, shrouded in its dust sheet. Her hand went out, trembled, then fell again. What was the point? She had tried numerous times to play, but each time it defeated her. She could not even tune the strings. Fingal was right, she was cursed.

Her eyes filled with tears and she dashed them away. This was not a time for weeping, but for action. Logan believed in her; he had been convinced she would play again one day. She pulled the dust sheet off the *clàrsach* and tossed it to one side. Then she picked up the tuning key. Her hand shook a little and she stared at it, trying to steady her breathing. Logan had done so much for her, it was time for her to repay that debt, if she could.

Chapter Fifteen

Ailsa returned to the sickroom less than an hour later to find the housekeeper standing beside the bed and staring down at Logan. Her heart stopped.

'Norry, tell me—is he…?'

The housekeeper looked up, her face pale and drawn.

'No, no. There is no change, mistress. In fact, he has not moved at all since you left and I so hoped that he would. I beg your pardon, Ailsa, I did not mean for you to catch me thus. 'Tis just—' she dragged in a long, shuddering breath '—he is such an *active* man, so very full of life, and it grieves me to see him lying like one dead.' She wiped her eyes with the edge of her apron and turned to look at the servant who had followed Ailsa into the room. 'What in the name of heaven is going on here?'

'I asked William to bring up my *clàrsach*,' said Ailsa, directing him to put the harp down beside the bed. She added, with more conviction than she felt, 'I am going to play for the Laird.'

'But…' Norry paused, her kindly face creased with anxiety. She said gently, 'Mistress, you have not played since you came to Ardvarrick. Oh, I know you have tried, time and again, I have heard you. Do you not think it will distress you, and the Laird, if you cannot…?'

Ailsa positioned her chair and sat down. 'This time I must make sure I *can*.' She had tuned the *clàrsach* in the privacy of the little parlour. That had been a success in itself, but to play here, for Logan, would be the real challenge. Heart beating, she met the housekeeper's eyes defiantly. 'And if I fail, mayhap the cacophony will rouse the Laird!'

Mrs Noranside had been watching her anxiously, but now turned and flapped her hands at William, shooing him out of the door before her.

'Off with you now, we must leave the mistress in peace!'

Ailsa waited until the sounds of their retreating footsteps had died away and silence had settled again. She turned back to the *clàrsach*, so familiar yet so frightening, as if it was some living thing that she must bend to her will. Could she do this? What if she should fail again? What if the tunes would not come? She closed her eyes, hearing Logan's voice in her head.

Nothing matters save that I have you in my life.

And now it was not only her that Logan had in his life. There was the baby, his child. Her heart lifted. Their child.

Suddenly there were no more doubts. She flexed her fingers and placed them on the strings.

Logan was exhausted. As if he had been crawling up from the depths of some deep, dark place for ever. At first there had been much pain and confusion amid the darkness, but more recently he had been aware of gentle hands on his brow and soft voices.

And poetry. Someone reading poetry.

"'Bid me to live, and I will live/Thy protestant to be/ Or bid me love, and I will give/A loving heart to thee.'"

Robert Herrick. He recognised the lines, but who was speaking? The effort of thinking was too much. He was so tired, too fatigued even to make the effort to open his eyes. It was so much easier to give in and allow himself to sink into the blackness, the oblivion.

The darkness was beginning to lift again. This time he heard music. Lilting, angelic sounds. He had gone to heaven and his grandmother was playing for him, waiting to welcome him. Heaven. No more effort. No more pain. But something was nagging at him, worrying at his memory like a terrier with a bone. No longer was he struggling to crawl out of the darkness. Something, someone was pulling him out.

The fog in his head thinned a little more and he recognised the soft, clear, singing notes of the *clàrsach*.

'Ailsa.'

It was the barest whisper, but Ailsa heard it and immediately her hands pressed on the strings, killing the music. She flew across to the bed, her heart leaping when she saw Logan's eyelids flutter.

'I am here, love.' She took his hand. 'I am here, my darling man.'

'Ailsa.'

He was looking at her, blankly at first, then his eyes softened with recognition. His hand fluttered and she caught it in her own, pressing a kiss upon his fingers before emotion overwhelmed her and with a sob she buried her face in his shoulder and wept.

'Do not cry, my love.' His hand stroked her hair.

'I am not c-crying.' She raised her head, smiling through the tears that still coursed down her face. 'I am j-just so happy that you have come back to us.'

His eyes shifted and he looked past her. 'You were playing the *clàrsach*.'

'Aye. I was playing for you.'

'Your gift has returned.'

'It never really left me.' She held his hand against her cheek and smiled lovingly at him. 'You were right all the time, Logan.'

'I was right to take you for my wife.' He touched her cheek. 'My fine Highland lass.'

'Oh, Logan!' She turned her head to press a kiss into his palm. 'I thought I'd lost you.'

'I could never leave you, my love.' His smile faded and she noted the fine crease on his brow. 'I thought… did I dream it, or are you carrying our child? I thought someone said that, but perhaps it was merely something I wished to hear.'

She blushed. 'If you wished it, then I am glad, because it is true, Logan.'

The frown faded, replaced by such a look of joy that her heart soared.

His grip on her hand tightened. He said, 'Oh, my dear, dear love! But how—that is, are you sure, have I been unconscious for so long?'

'No, no, a few days only, but I am sure. At least, all the signs tell me it is so and Norry agrees with me.' She felt the blush stealing into her cheeks. 'It must have happened the night you rescued me from Castle Creag, do you remember?'

'How could I ever forget?' His familiar, roguish twinkle made her blush even more.

'Norry says that is why I have been feeling so sick. And why I have been so out of reason cross these past weeks. I did nothing but pick fault with you, my love. Can you ever forgive me?'

He put his fingers on her lips to silence her. 'That is all forgotten, Ailsa, my dearest love. My lady.'

He sighed, closing his eyes, and immediately she was anxious and contrite.

'I have tired you.'

'No, no, but I am so damned weak.'

'Then sleep, love.'

'I would rather listen to you play. Will you?'

'Aye, if you wish it.'

'I do wish it. With all my heart. What was that piece you were playing when I woke?'

'It is one I wrote after your first visit to Contullach. I call it "Ardvarrick's Air". Do you like it?'

'Very much. Will you play it again for me now, my darling Highland lass?'

She smiled again, and bent to press another kiss on his lips.

'I will indeed, my darling Highland Laird.'

Epilogue

September 1722

Logan left his horse at the stables and made his way to the south front of the house. On such a warm and sunny afternoon as this he was sure that was where he would find Ailsa. He was right. As soon as he rounded the corner, he saw the little group on the lower lawn. They were under the improvised canopy he had fashioned from an old sail, to protect delicate complexions from the sun.

Ailsa was reclining on a daybed with the baby in a basket beside her. Norry was coming out of the long windows from the drawing room, carrying a tray of lemonade. When she saw him she opened her mouth to greet him, but he silenced her with a gesture and, after a whispered exchange, he took the tray from her hands. A glance towards the daybed confirmed that Ailsa had not seen him and he wanted to surprise her.

He had almost reached the canopy when she looked up from the paper in her hand. Her look of delight was everything he could have wished.

'Logan! I did not expect to see you for hours yet.'

'I know.' He put down the tray and bent to kiss her, his lips lingering on her sweet mouth. 'I came back early.'

'You have left Tamhas and the others to gather the harvest?' She teased him lovingly. 'Shame on you!'

'Not at all. We all worked with a will and it is done now.' He straightened, pressing his hands into the small of his back. The ache there was reminding him of the arduous toil under a blazing sun. 'It was hot work and I should go in and change, but I wanted to see you first. To see how you had managed without me.'

'Fie upon you, sir, do you think we need your presence every minute of the day? We managed very well, thank you.'

'And little Grant?' He leaned over the crib.

'He has been an angel.' Ailsa gazed down at the sleeping baby, her face softening with love. 'And since you have brought refreshments, Logan, you should stay and take a glass with us.'

He needed no second bidding. He poured the lemonade into two glasses and after he had handed one to Ailsa, he threw himself down on the grass beside the daybed.

'You are not to wake him,' she admonished, seeing him glance at the basket again. 'He has not long been fed and I want him to sleep now.'

'Are you sure you are happy to feed him?' he asked. 'My mother employed a wet nurse.'

'I want to do it, Logan. It does not tire me, I promise you.'

He heard the anxious note in her voice and he put

down his glass and twisted around to kneel beside her. 'Then of course you must do it,' he said, taking her hand, 'if it makes you happy. And my bonny son is thriving, so it must be good for him.'

He had never admitted it to anyone, but he had been so very afraid that the baby or Ailsa might not survive the birth. Ailsa had refused to agree to his sending for Dr Murray, saying she felt very well and that she preferred to have Norry attend her. In the event, the baby had been born without complications and Ailsa had recovered her own health and strength remarkably quickly, something he gave thanks for every day.

'It does make me happy,' she said now, squeezing his hand. 'As do you.'

The glow in her eyes set his pulses racing and he moved on to the edge of the daybed to pull her into his arms. Her eager response to his kiss inflamed him even more. She wound her arms about him as he gently pushed her back on the couch and deepened the kiss. His heart leapt as she arched towards him, her breasts pushing against his chest and heating his blood with exhilarating desire.

At last he released her and sat up. Ailsa did not move, lying back against the silk cushions, her violet eyes dark and lustrous, inviting him to take her in his arms again, until a faint snuffling from the basket on the floor reminded him that they were not alone. He dragged in a breath.

'We had best stop now, love, while we can. Norry will return any moment.'

'Will she?' Ailsa reached for him, her fingers clasping the open neck of his shirt and pulling him towards her. 'What of it? She knows we are sharing a bed again.'

Logan obliged her with another kiss, then resolutely broke away.

'My darling, at this very moment I am in danger of ripping every stitch from your body and covering you with kisses, and that is *not* something I would want any of the servants to witness, and especially not my old nurse!'

Ailsa giggled and blushed, but she let him go.

'And as well as that,' Logan added, 'our son is awake now.'

Ailsa glanced down to see that the baby was indeed awake and watching them with a steady, unblinking stare. She sighed. Much as she loved her son, the desire for her husband had not diminished. Indeed, it was stronger than ever.

She watched as Logan sat down on the ground beside the basket and reached over to allow the baby to curl his tiny hand around his little finger. She smiled, thinking how comfortable Logan was with his son. How at home he was with his surroundings. She loved to see him as he was now, in the loose shirt and the *fèileadh beag*, the small kilt that he wore when he was working out of doors with his men. It became him so well. He could still be the proud gentleman when he wished or occasion demanded, but he now preferred to dress in the tartan and she had noticed that his speech was returning more and more to the lilting brogue of the Highlands. Which did nothing to lessen his attraction in her eyes...

'What was it you were reading, when I arrived?' asked Logan, breaking into her thoughts.

'It is a letter from my aunt Morag.' She held it out to him. 'Fingal has found a harper to replace me at last. A kinswoman from somewhere in the north and one who brought her own *clàrsach*!'

'Indeed? I am glad he did not ask for yours to be returned to Contullach, I'd have given him short shrift!'

She ignored Logan's truculence, knowing it was mainly bluster. Relations between the two families might not be exactly warm, but they were far more cordial now.

'Oh, and the best news,' she added, smiling. 'Morag writes that Kirstin is with child.'

'Hmm.' He glanced at the letter. 'She is still in Tain with Cowie, then.'

'Yes.' Ailsa sighed. 'She will not return without Ewan, and my uncle insists he cannot come back to Contullach.'

'Fingal is wise to keep him away. And not only because I detest the fellow,' he added quickly. 'We have struck a good bargain again this year with the drovers. Even those of Contullach's tenants who were initially against the agreement are beginning now to appreciate the benefits of working together with neighbours rather than the constant feuding. It is better for everyone and I would not have Cowie coming back and stirring up trouble again before the new way is well established.'

'Nor I,' she murmured. 'I hope, when Grant grows up, that the feud between our families will be nothing but a memory.'

'Aye. That is my wish, too.'

The baby had fallen asleep again and she watched as Logan gently tucked the coverlet around the little body.

'Was that a sigh, Ailsa?' He looked up quickly. 'Is anything amiss?'

'No, no,' She blushed and disclaimed, 'I was merely thinking how blessed I am to have such a fine husband and a beautiful baby.'

'It is no more than you deserve, my love. Although—' he glanced back at his little son, sleeping peacefully in his basket '—our son is sadly lacking in hair, is he not?'

She chuckled. 'Patience, my love! It will grow. I hope he will have fine dark hair, like his father.'

He leaned across to her. 'I would not be displeased if he was red-headed, like his mother.'

'Mmm, I think that might be more suited to our daughters,' she murmured.

'Daughters?' His eyes glinted with mischief. 'And how many do you foresee?'

'Oh, dozens,' she told him, trying not to smile. 'And they shall all learn to play the *clàrsach*. And I hope we shall have more sons, too.'

'Indeed?' He was twirling one of her curls between his fingers. 'It will take a lot of work, to make so many children.'

The warm glow in his eyes roused the familiar lightness deep in her belly. She did not pretend to misunderstand him.

'It will, Husband, but it is our duty to try, is it not?'

A shadow fell across them. Norry was headed in their direction.

'You asked me to tell you when your bath was ready, Master Logan,' she declared. 'And William is with me to carry the little one up to the nursery for you, mistress, now the sun is losing its heat.'

'Thank you,' said Ailsa. She reached out and took Logan's hand. 'If you will look after little Grant, Norry, I will go in with the master.'

'I should like nothing better.' The old lady positively beamed at the prospect. 'Off you go, now, and we shall clear up here.'

Logan helped Ailsa to rise from the daybed.

'Are you tired, love?' he asked as he accompanied her towards the house.

'On the contrary,' she replied airily. 'I thought I might assist you with your bathing.'

She held her breath, waiting for Logan's reply. It did not come until they had ascended the steps and were walking between the parterres.

'It is a pity the hip bath is not big enough for the both of us,' he said slowly.

'Aye, but we cannot have everything. I thought I might wash your back for you. And I might use the water after, if it is still warm.'

'No, you must go first. I am dirty from working in the fields.'

'Very well. I—' She broke off with a little cry as he swept her up into his arms and walked up the next set of steps. 'Logan! What are you about?'

'I am carrying you. To preserve your strength.'

She slipped her arms about his neck. 'I do not require much strength to wash you, Logan.'

He stopped for a moment to steal a kiss.

'True,' he said softly, 'But you will need all your strength for what we will do afterwards!'

His look sent a delicious shiver running through her. She rested her head on his shoulder and gave a sigh of sheer contentment.

'Whatever my Laird commands.'

* * * * *